F
Saracino   Saracino, Mary,
                1954-

                Finding Grace.

F
Saracino   Saracino, Mary,
                1954-

                Finding Grace.

Mynderse Library

Seneca Falls, New York

BAKER & TAYLOR

Also by Mary Saracino

No Matter What
(Published by Spinsters Ink, 1993)

Finding Grace

a novel
by

Mary Saracino

Spinsters Ink
Duluth, Minnesota, USA

First edition published November 1999 by Spinsters Ink
10-9-8-7-6-5-4-3-2-1

Spinsters Ink
32 E. First St., #330
Duluth, MN 55802-2002 USA

Cover design by Sara Sinnard, Sarin Creative

Production:

Charlene Brown	Jean Nygaard
Helen Dooley	Kim Riordan
Joan Drury	Amy Strasheim
Tracy Gilsvik	Emily Soltis
Marian Hunstiger	Liz Tufte
Claire Kirch	Nancy Walker

This is a work of fiction. Any similarity to persons living or dead is a coincidence.

Library of Congress Cataloging-in-Publication Data

Saracino, Mary 1954–
    Finding Grace : a novel / by Mary Saracino. — 1st ed.
      p.   cm.
    ISBN 1-883523-33-8 (alk. paper)
    I. Title.
PS3569.A65F56   1999
813'.54—dc21   99-31974
                                   CIP

Printed in the USA on recycled, acid-free paper

Acknowledgments

My heart is full of gratitude for those named below and those who remain unnamed—friends and family members, acquaintances and strangers, readers and fellow writers—who bless my life and make it richer. My world—and my work—are better because of their generosity of spirit.

I wish to thank . . .

My dear friend—and fellow writer—Jane Hoback, for her careful reading of this manuscript. Her insights, feedback, and support helped me make *Finding Grace* a better novel. Her rack of lamb ain't bad, either.

My brother Steve Saracino for his continual support and ongoing encouragement—not to mention his tongue-in-cheek insistence that *his* editor was impatiently waiting for more chapters. Molto grazie, mio fratello.

My former writing buddies from Minneapolis—Pam Colby, Nancy Kelly, Ilza Mueller, Ann Monson, and Elisa Raffa—for carefully listening to and offering constructive criticism on early drafts.

Norcroft: A Writing Retreat for Women for the precious gift of time and space on Lake Superior's glorious North Shore. The heart-core chapters of *Finding Grace* were conceived and drafted in the sacred quiet of my writing shed there.

Laura Lucas-Silvis for bearing witness and for co-creating a space for healing spirit in my life. And Patricia Schuckert for her unconditional compassion and encouragement during the writing of this novel.

Edvige Guinta for opening doors and bringing me home to a community of Italian American women writers—making dreams come true. Mille grazie, Edi.

My editor, Joan Drury, for waiting patiently for a sequel to *No Matter What* and for offering me the opportunity to publish the rest of Regina's tale. From the beginning, Joan has understood the power inherent in giving voice to a young girl's story. Joan—and her wonderful publishing company, Spinsters Ink—are the publishing equivalent of Grace. They dare to break silences, dare to empower girls and women.

My life-partner, Jane—who makes everything more possible.

My sisters, Teresa and Peg—and the rest of my family and friends—for their love and affirmation.

And always, loving gratitude to my Italian grandmothers—Fiora Vergamini and Immacolata Saracino. Tanti baci, nonne. E mille grazie per tutto.

Dedication

For Jane

Because she embraces grace and knows that spirit heals.

The Road Trip

Oh, how I wished Mama would shut up. She sobbed and sobbed. Tears slipped from her swollen eyes, landing on her red, red lipstick. She was crying for my brothers. Danny and Joey. We left them, and my daddy, back home in Pisa, New York yesterday afternoon. Mama wrote a note, took us girls, and left the house. She had to be with Patrick, she told me over and over again. Only Patrick. Now we were riding in Patrick's big, shiny red car on the way to Wisconsin, just like she said she always wanted. But still, Mama cried and cried, spilling her mistake all over the place.

"Marie, honey. It will be okay," Patrick said. "Give it time. Please, honey, please."

"We've got to call them," she cried. "I've got to tell them I'll send for them."

"In time, Marie. In time," Patrick said. His voice was weary. His face tired. All the driving and Mama carrying on were starting to get to him, too.

"Tonight, Patrick," Mama insisted through her sobs. "Tonight. When we get to the motel. I've got to call them. I've got to."

Finally, Mama blew her nose, took a deep breath. For a second, it was quiet. I let the silence fill me up, stuff itself behind my eyes. Mama was hard to ignore. I grabbed any peace she'd give. Besides Mama's sobbing, my head was full of my dog, Zoomer. If I could have cried, that's who I would have cried for. But there weren't any tears in me. My heart was dried out. Crying would only make things worse. Mama would be more upset, more hurt. And Patrick would get all mad and yell, "Why can't you be quiet, Peanut? I'm trying to drive here."

So, I didn't do anything, except try to be invisible. I watched cows and sky and trees and buildings, waiting for things to calm down. My little sisters, Rosa and Winnie, slept in the backseat. Rosa's head was smashed against the window on the other side of the car. Her eyes were closed real tight. She held her stuffed dog, Binkie, close to her. Every once in a while, Rosa made little sounds, like someone was pinching her. Three-year-old Winnie's head rested on my lap. Her arms were wrapped tightly around her raggedy, yellow blanket.

We rode on and on. We passed a farmhouse one time, and a big black dog chased after our car, barking and barking. I closed my eyes so I wouldn't have to see his white teeth all full of spit. Zoomer was probably going crazy, too, running around our front yard back in Pisa. Barking and barking. I bet our neighbor Mrs. Brown had to stick her head out her front door and yell, "Hush, you dumb dog. Peanut's gone."

It wasn't my fault, I wanted Zoomer to know. Mama wouldn't let me take him. I promised he wouldn't be any trouble. I told Mama he could sleep on the floor in the backseat, near my feet. But she wouldn't listen. "No!" she hollered. Now I won't ever see Zoomer again. I hope he knows I still love him. Sometimes things happen and you can't stop them, 'cuz everyone else is bigger and louder and madder than you are. "Get in the car. No, you can't take your dog." Leaving Zoomer was worse than leaving Danny and Joey. They were just my crummy teenaged brothers. Always yelling and teasing me. What'd I ever do to them?

Next to Zoomer, I missed Daddy. So much I could hardly even pray anymore. Mama hated him because he went to church and said his rosary all the time instead of helping her with us kids. I know she never really loved him. She told me so. I missed him anyway. But I didn't tell Mama. She'd just get mad and pout about it. Instead, I sent my thoughts to the rolled-up picture of the Blessed Virgin Mary that I'd hid in my A&P grocery-bag suitcase way back in the trunk. I tried hard to imagine her listening, imagine the Blessed Mother's kind face, her blue eyes, the golden halo glowing around her head. But my mind could only settle on Daddy. Would he come for us? I wanted him to get mad and tell Patrick to go steal someone else's family. I wanted him to take us home. Even though it surprised me that I missed him so much.

Before we left, before Mama hurried me and my sisters into Patrick's car, I had always sided with Mama, always put my heart with hers. I didn't want to be left behind when she finally decided to leave Daddy. I always knew we would go, someday. I just never thought I'd care so much. But I did. Now Daddy, like home, was gone. We'd left. Just like Mama always said we would. Someday was now. We were heading for some city called Madison. There, a guy named Jack, Patrick's priest buddy from seminary, was gonna meet us and give us a place to stay so we could be a family. That's what Mama had wanted for the longest time. Now she had her wish.

I bumped along in the backseat of the car, sick of the cigarettes stinking up the place. Smoke stuck to the seats, the windshield, our paper-bag suitcases in the trunk, full of stuff we'd brought from Pisa. Patrick lit Lucky Strike after Lucky Strike and rubbed his forehead. When Mama wasn't crying, she lit up Chesterfields. I cracked my window, just a little, to let in some fresh air. I couldn't breathe, but I had to be careful. I didn't want them to yell at me. Any minute Patrick could cuss, "Goddamn it, Peanut! Close that damn window. I can't drive with all that wind blowing on my neck." This time he didn't pay any attention to what I was doing. He crushed his cigarette and reached for Mama.

"Why don't you try to take a nap, honey. I'll wake you when we get to Madison."

Mama rested her head against the window on her side of the car. She closed her eyes. I prayed a quick thank you to the Blessed Virgin Mother for the sudden quiet.

It was weird to feel lonesome in a car full of my family. Mama and my two sisters, I mean. I kept shooting thoughts into Patrick's brain, hoping he would change his mind about going to Wisconsin, turn the car around, and take us back to my daddy. Every once in a while, I'd see him looking in the rearview mirror, checking on us girls. He looked mostly at Winnie, but sometimes, just before he looked away, I'd catch a piece of his eye staring at me. Then he'd turn his attention back to the road, light another Lucky, and keep on driving.

It was creepy. How he stared at me stuck to my insides. Like I'd done something wrong and needed his forgiveness. I'd seen it thousands of times before, back home, when he was our assistant pastor at St. Joan of Arc Church. All the kids from my grade school class would line up outside the confessional and watch Father Patrick stride past in his long, black cassock. He'd eye each one of us with that creepy look before he opened the confessional door and disappeared inside. We'd sweat it out, waiting our turn to confess our deepest sins to him. When my turn came, I hoped he'd go easy on me because he loved my mama. But he never did. He'd slide the confessional screen open, and I'd smell his English Leather cologne. I'd close my eyes tightly, thinking of Friday nights at the coffee shop in Cayuga when that same scent mixed with the smell of greasy French fries and grilled hamburgers. I'd whisper my sins and think of him holding Winnie on his lap, laughing and smiling into her soft curls.

"I hit my brother twelve times," I'd confess. "I talked in church six times. And wanted to disobey my mother five times. But I didn't." Father Patrick would load on extra penance—ten Hail Marys and ten Our Fathers. Just to remind me how important it was to be a good girl. And he'd throw in a lecture on how I should always obey my mother.

Father Patrick's favorite Sunday sermon topic was about family responsibility. He loved to talk about husbands and wives. He called marriage a "holy spiritual union." He said mamas and daddies owed it to God to take care of their children and each other. He said it was the worst sin to break that promise. He said God expected mothers and fathers to be like human guardian angels, watching over their families. His voice would boom from the pulpit. "If you break this sacred promise, you owe a mighty spiritual debt."

I'd sit in the pew next to Mama and listen, worrying about my daddy and my mama. Maybe that's why my daddy visited church so much. He had a lot of praying to do to pay back his spiritual debts. But what about Mama? And Patrick? Didn't they owe something back to God, too? Patrick's sermons never seemed to upset Mama. She'd just sit in the pew, with her hands folded in her lap, listening hard. And she'd smile—a tiny, private smile—as she stared at Patrick up there in the pulpit pointing his fingers at the rest of us sinners in the pews. I didn't know it then, but he was Winnie's daddy. That's why we were in his car, driving a thousand miles away from our home in Pisa. We had to leave my daddy and my brothers, so he could be a daddy to Winnie.

Mama had loved Patrick for years and years before she decided to leave Daddy and the boys. The two of them had planned this whole getaway. They studied books and atlases and encyclopedias to figure out where we should move. "Madison has great schools and good job opportunities," they told me and my sisters one Friday night at Smiley's Coffee Shop in Cayuga. "And a big lake for you girls to swim in." They called it "Happy Town." They told us we'd never be sad again. My sisters and I got all excited. We forgot that we couldn't take Danny and Joey, Daddy or Zoomer. But I didn't realize I would mind that part. Until now.

All those years before Patrick came along, Mama prayed and wished for her life to be better. She looked and looked and looked for someone else to love—somebody who wasn't my daddy. Patrick showed up one day, tall and handsome. An answer to Mama's aching heart. Daddy brought him home to meet us. "Here's the new assistant pastor, Marie," Daddy had said.

"Can you stay for supper?" Mama asked.

Patrick came for supper a lot in the beginning. Every Friday night, he'd eat macaroni with us in our kitchen. And during the week, Mama started volunteering down at the church. Sometime after that, Winnie was born. Then, Patrick got transferred to another parish in a different town. But Mama still visited him.

"He's my friend," she explained to me. "I miss him."

One day, she told me she loved Patrick. I knew that already. I could tell that right from the start by how she looked at him. It was softer than the way she looked at my daddy. Her eyes opened, and stars or sunlight or something else sparkly and alive poured out. The tight edges around her mouth disappeared. After Patrick got transferred, Mama cried a lot. Then one Friday afternoon, she decided to take me and my two sisters and visit him at Smiley's Coffee Shop in Cayuga, a town on the other side of the lake from Pisa, where we lived. I didn't mind at first. It was sort of an adventure. My family never went anywhere, except to church. So going to Smiley's felt almost as good as a ride on the Ferris wheel at the St. Joan of Arc Church carnival. At Smiley's, Patrick wiped Mama's sadness away. He made her smile long after I had forgotten what her front teeth looked like.

On the road to Madison, we sped past farmhouses and small towns. We flew over hills and past long stretches of fields and under cloudy skies. Every once in a while, Zoomer or Daddy would pop into my head, and I'd feel my insides lift out and push through the roof of Patrick's red car. My ghost heart would hover outside. I'd look down at my body, still sitting in the backseat, staring out the window. My ghost self would cry, above the blood-red hood of Patrick's Mercury, and yell at his tight eyes, "Turn this car around right now, or I'll smash your face in." But he couldn't see me or hear my ghost threats. He just drove on. I tried to fly away—go back to Pisa without the rest of them. Then I'd catch a glimpse of Mama out of the corner of my ghost eyes. Her sad face sucked me back into the car. My aching ghost heart hit my body with a thud. I'd make the sign of the cross and whisper, "Hail Mary, full of grace, keep us safe. And make Mama see it's not too late to change her mind. Amen."

※

Rosa was only six years old. She didn't know Winnie was really Patrick's daughter. Neither did Winnie. Just me. I figured it out at the truck stop in Erie yesterday—the day we left Pisa. Something in the way he held her hand as they walked together into the restaurant told me he was her daddy. It was so tender. I'd seen it a million times before, but I never *really* saw it until then. All those times Patrick cuddled with Winnie at the coffee shop in Cayuga. He'd hold her tight, practically lick the baby spit off her slobbery mouth. All the little kisses. All those pictures he took of her. Rolls and rolls of just her. It made me feel like I could disappear, and he'd never care. Sometimes, I wasn't so jealous. I had Mama. When she wasn't lost in Patrick's eyes or when she wasn't too tired or grouchy, she'd smile or sing *My Fair Lady* tunes with me. She'd laugh sometimes, too, if I told her jokes or showed her the latest dance me and my best friend Amelia had just made up. I tucked those times into my heart, pulled them out and remembered them on the all-too-many days when a smile was too much for Mama's mouth to handle.

Rosa didn't get much attention from Mama or Patrick. But she was my favorite. Next to Zoomer, I loved Rosa the best. She was funny, you know. She had a silly side that made me happy. She told corny knock-knock jokes. And she had the weirdest giggle. That was on her good days, before all this stuff with Mama and Patrick started. Sometimes, when things got bad in Pisa, Rosa would hide behind our couch. I'd have to fetch her out. I'd try to make her worries go away, but I wasn't good at it. My own worries got in the way, most days. All I could think of was myself. But when Rosa cried herself to sleep at night, because she was scared

Mama didn't love her, I'd roll over, hold her hand, and say, "It's okay. Mama loves us all, in her own way."

Even if Mama didn't always show her love, it was there. Like the air. You couldn't see it, but you could breathe it in and breathe it out. It helped you live. We'd be dead without air. I told Rosa that, sometimes, when she was real sad. "I love you like the air."

As we drove through Indiana, it started to rain. Heavy drops hit the windshield and bounced off the roof of the car. Thick clouds hid the sun as we passed towns and cities and whole states, going further and further away from Pisa. Mama woke from her nap. She stretched and turned toward the backseat. She gave us girls a wink. I smiled at her then, thinking how beautiful she looked, her sad eyes all fresh from sleep. I loved her then. I almost forgave her for taking us from Daddy and the boys.

"Mama, when we goin' home?" Rosa asked. She didn't realize we weren't just on a vacation. "I wanna see Daddy."

Mama's eyes dropped, and her mouth soured.

"We're going to Happy Town," Patrick answered. "We're going to sleep over in another motel tonight." He tried to sound excited, tried to get my sister to think this whole thing was a great adventure.

"A Best Western," Mama piped in. "They're clean and reasonable."

We had stayed at one last night. After we left Pisa, we didn't stop until we crossed over into Pennsylvania. We ate at the Erie Truck Stop Café; then we piled back into Patrick's car and kept driving until Patrick picked out a Best Western in Cleveland. It was weird. One little room with two double beds. Us girls slept in the double near the bathroom, in case we had to pee in the middle of the night. Mama left the bathroom light on so we wouldn't be scared. Mama and Patrick slept in the other bed near the window. The motel bedspreads were ugly—brown-yellow with big green flowers. The curtains were made of the same material. There was a brown, wooden desk built right into the wall, with a matching wooden chair. Inside the desk drawer, I found a few sheets of paper stamped with the name of the motel— Cleveland Best Western. "Mama, can I have some?" I asked. "I wanna write to Zoomer."

Mama started to cry. I slid the Best Western paper back into the drawer. Later, when Mama went to the bathroom, I sneaked a piece into my A&P grocery-bag suitcase, next to the rolled-up picture of the Blessed Virgin Mother. I figured I could write to Zoomer later, maybe when Mama was napping.

That night—our first on the road—Patrick tried to convince Mama to wait and call my brothers the next morning. Mama didn't like that idea. "I have to make sure my sons don't hate me," she cried.

Patrick said, "No. We're still too close to Pisa. Let's wait until we've made Madison. I don't want Paulie chasing after us."

Mama gave in, but she fell into one of her moods and wouldn't talk to any of us. I thought about what kind of letter I'd write to my dog.

Dear Zoomer,

I hope you aren't still barking like you were when we drove off this afternoon. I don't want your throat to get sore. When we didn't come home, did you go look for me down by the creek? When I wasn't at our secret spot, did you cry? Can dogs cry? Or do they just howl and howl and howl? I miss you. I wish, now, that I would have stayed with you. I don't think Madison is gonna be fun. Even though Mama and Patrick call it "Happy Town." I keep smelling your dog smell everywhere. Up my nose, on my hands, on my pajamas. It makes me want to scream. I miss your cold nose bumping my cheek, trying to wake me up for school. Remember how I'd whisper secrets into your ear as we snuggled together in the back of my bedroom closet? Remember how I'd bring Vanilla Wafers and we'd eat them? If I can figure out how, I'm going to come get you. And if Mama and Patrick won't let me bring you to Wisconsin, I'll stay in Pisa with you. I promise.

The next morning, before we left the Cleveland Best Western, Rosa and I took a bath together. She rinsed soap off her face and whispered, "When are we going home?" I bit my lip and turned away. When I looked back, she was rubbing her face. Tears fell into the bathwater. I grabbed a dry washcloth and wiped her eyes. Later, after we toweled off and put on our underpants and undershirts, I combed her hair, slow and gentle. I put the toilet lid down and set her stuffed dog, Binkie, on top so he'd be nearby. I didn't want her to feel lonesome.

"Everything will be okay, Rosa." I tried to convince her with a smile, but my sister started to cry again.

"Why is Patrick so grumpy all the time?" Rosa asked.

"I don't know, Rosa, but we gotta be brave. Or Mama will get sadder."

"I know," she said. "I'm trying to be a good girl."

"It's better not to cry," I told her. "It only makes things worse."

Rosa and me made a pact that day. We vowed to stuff our sadness in a box and hide it deep inside where no one else could see it. If Mama was ever going to get over this crazy mess she got herself into, we had to play along and help her think it was the best idea ever. I didn't like it, but I knew any other way wouldn't work.

I was having second thoughts about Patrick and this whole Madison thing. When I first met him, I figured he was an okay guy. He made Mama happy. More and more now, I wasn't so sure that would be enough. It was weird being with him all day and all night, instead of just once a week on Friday nights. At Smiley's Coffee Shop in Cayuga, he was usually nice to me because I was Mama's favorite. He wanted to stay on her good side so she'd run away with him. But sometimes, he'd still be mean or tease me. I'd feel left out, like I was warmed-over tuna casserole and Winnie was fresh-baked apple pie. Mama never noticed. But I did. After all, I was ten—he couldn't fool me.

Since we left Pisa, Patrick was grouchier. Whenever I'd ask Mama about where we were going next or when we were going to get to Madison, Patrick would bark, "Leave your mother alone, Peanut. Don't pester us."

He and my mama were planning on getting married, so Mama expected me to treat him like my daddy. But I didn't want to. He had a side to him that my daddy didn't have. If I breathed wrong, Patrick would yell at me. The whole ride out to Madison, I tried not to need anything. I didn't whine, didn't complain, didn't demand anything. I peed only when he decided to stop at a rest stop. I ate only when he decided it was time for lunch. I slept when he told us to take a nap. I did everything he said, just like I was supposed to.

That morning at the Best Western in Cleveland, I watched and waited to see if Mama was gonna call my brothers, like she wanted to.

"I'm hungry," Winnie whined and poked at Mama's shoulder. "In a minute, sweetie," Mama told her. "We'll go get you some breakfast in a minute." Then Mama picked up the phone and dialed.

"Who you calling, Marie?" Patrick's question charged at Mama, startling her and me.

"The boys," Mama said. She tried to sound brave, but her hands shook. She took a deep breath, then burst into tears and hung up. She screamed and ran off to the bathroom. Patrick chased after her. She locked the door. He pounded hard.

"Marie. Let me in, for Christ's sake. Honey, please."

It took a few minutes, but finally Mama unlocked the door. Patrick slipped inside. Me and my sisters waited on the edge of the bed. I stared at my feet and counted to ten over and over again. Little Winnie whined the whole time, "I'm hungry." Rosa did, too.

"As soon as Mama and Patrick come out, we'll eat," I told them.

"I gotta pee," Winnie complained.

"Put your hands between your legs and hold it."

When Mama and Patrick finally came out of the bathroom, Winnie rushed in. I followed to make sure she didn't have an accident. I didn't want to have to clean up the mess before we could go eat breakfast. While I helped Winnie wipe, Mama came back to fuss with her face in the mirror. Her eyes were thick red pillows. She pulled out her compact and patted powder over the bumps, but it didn't help.

"Can't we just grab some coffee and keep driving?" she called out to Patrick. "I don't want people in the restaurant to see me like this."

I swallowed hard, hoping Patrick would agree. I didn't want to sit in the motel coffee shop, either. Looking at Mama's sorry eyes made my stomach hurt. On the way out of town, Patrick bought some donuts at a bakery and some milk for us kids. He and Mama just drank coffee. I grabbed a chocolate donut and took a big bite. I chewed fast. The sweet frosting melted on my sad tongue. I gulped down my milk and grabbed another one as Patrick sped sixty-five miles per hour toward his happy, new life in Madison.

Madison

It was late afternoon of our second day on the road when we got to Madison. Wisconsin was a little bit like upstate New York from where we'd run. Lots of hills and trees. I kept expecting to see Mrs. Scalamassi from down at the beauty parlor, Uncle Tony delivering mail, Daddy heading off to church to pray a quick rosary. But Madison faces were different from Pisa faces. People in Wisconsin had lighter hair and smaller noses, blue eyes and pale skin. Nobody looked Italian.

"You're going to love it here, honey," Patrick said to Mama. "There's plenty to see and do. Four beautiful lakes. Tons of parks. And, look—there's the capitol building."

"It's gorgeous," Mama agreed.

It was pretty, I had to admit. It was the biggest building I had ever seen. It had a shiny white dome with a golden statue of a woman on top. I had to squint from how the sun sparkled off her arms.

"Jack told me there are carved badgers hidden in the cornices over the stairwells," Patrick bragged. "And they have a city zoo and botanical gardens and a place called Picnic Point."

"Sounds wonderful, honey," Mama assured him.

"Over there is the University," Patrick continued, pointing to a big hill with a building on top. "That's Bascom Hall. Just like Jack told us. And, look. There's Lake Mendota."

Patrick slowed the car as we drove past the lake. The water crashed against the rocks. The treetops swayed and waved. The tips of their branches bulged with buds. I thought of the big maple in our side yard, back home. Its leaves were ready to pop soon, too, and I'd miss the chance to climb up high and smell their sweet spring smell.

Lake Mendota was big and pretty, but it wasn't as big or as special as the lakes near Pisa. Mama told me once that the Iroquois Indians—who used to live in upstate New York before the white people pushed them out—had a story that told how God rested his palm on the ground after He made the world. When God picked up His hand, the imprints filled with water, and there they were—the Finger Lakes. God blessed that land with His own skin. I bet He didn't bless Madison like that.

Patrick pulled over, rolled down the window, and gawked. "Look how huge it is, kids. I bet you can't wait to go for a swim here. I've never seen anything so beautiful in my whole life."

Winnie crawled over the backseat into Patrick's lap. She giggled and pointed at the water. "Duck. Duck," she said. Patrick laughed. Mama did, too. Rosa poked her head over Patrick's shoulder to see, then she slid next to me, grabbed my hand, and stared at her grubby old sneakers.

"It's going to be perfect, Marie," Patrick said. "Just wait and see. I can't believe we're finally here."

Mama leaned over and kissed him. "It's great, honey."
She called to me and Rosa in the backseat. "Isn't it wonderful?"

Rosa squeezed my fingers. I tried to smile, but I could only manage a quick nod.

"It's gonna be great," Patrick said again. His eyes danced all over Mama's face. He kissed Winnie's forehead over and over.

"It's a beautiful city, honey," Mama assured him. "I wouldn't want to be anywhere else."

I knew it was a lie. Her mouth twisted down, a tiny bit, at the corners. She swallowed hard. She still had Danny and Joey on her mind. I dreaded the phone call that was coming later when we found a motel room in Madison for the night.

"It's getting late, Patrick," Mama urged. "And we've still got to get to Jack's house and then check in at the motel."

"Yeah, okay." Patrick scooted Winnie over the back of the seat. "Sit tight, sweetie. We'll be home soon." He stole one last look at the lake and turned the car around.

It took a while to find Jack's house. He had sent a Madison map and handwritten directions, but it wasn't enough. Patrick handed the map to Mama. "He said to take State Street."

Mama grabbed a red pen from the glove compartment and tried to match Jack's directions to what she saw on the map. "This city is so big, it's hard to figure it out."

"For Christ's sake, Marie," Patrick scowled. He grabbed the map back. "The last thing we need is to keep Jack waiting."

"I'm sure he'll understand," Mama insisted.

Jack had been Patrick's roommate in the seminary, his best friend, Mama had told me. I couldn't imagine Patrick having any friends. Was this Jack guy smart like Patrick? Did he look like Mickey Mantle? Or was he small and round like Uncle Tony? Did he like baseball and football like Daddy and the boys? Or did he read books like Patrick? All I knew about him was that he promised to help us find a place of our own in Madison. And for that, I was grateful. I was sick of riding in the car.

"Mama, I'm hungry," Rosa whined.

"Honey, not now," Mama stalled her. "We'll get you something to eat after we meet with Jack."

I pulled half a donut left over from breakfast out of my pocket and nudged Rosa. "Here," I whispered. "Don't get them all riled up." She took my bribe and ate it in two bites. Winnie grabbed for some crumbs. Rosa swatted her fingers. Winnie cried.

"For Christ's sake, what's the matter now?" Patrick lit into me. "Peanut, can't you keep your sisters occupied so we can think up here?"

Every time Rosa or Winnie got crabby or picked on each other or whined, it was my fault. I felt like the guard of the backseat dungeon. I wanted to yell, "It ain't easy keeping two cooped-up kids from killing each other."

But I didn't. Not out loud anyway. I screamed it plenty of times in my head. My invisible mouth opened wide and shouted until Patrick's eardrums burst. I wanted him to die. Slump over the steering wheel and wheeze his last breath. Then Mama would have to drive us back to Pisa, and we could all live with Daddy and Danny and Joey again. And Zoomer. My wishing never worked, so I gave up and tried to comfort Winnie. "Let me braid your hair, sweetie." My fake tone was good enough to fool Patrick, but not my sisters.

Rosa snorted, "Oh brother, Peanut."

Winnie complained, "No, Peanut, no." She pinched my arm as I turned her head to comb her hair.

"How about a story, then?" I was still trying to get my way.

"We don't got any books in the car," Rosa snapped. "You forgot to bring 'em, remember?"

"I don't need books," I boasted. "My head's fulla stories—about fairies and castles and evil kings and beautiful princesses. And ugly sisters." I shot mean eyes at Rosa.

"Shut up, you twerp," Rosa hissed. "Mama, Peanut's being mean."

"Peanut!" Mama hollered. She turned her tight face to me. "Be nice to your sisters. We'll be at Jack's in just a little bit."

"But Mama, they're not listening to me."

"Hold on just a little longer," she urged. "Soon we'll all be able to get out of this car and get some air." To my sisters she added, "Girls, let Peanut tell you a story."

Rosa and Winnie obeyed, but neither of them would sit next to me. They held hands and huddled close together on the opposite side of the car.

"I wanna hear a story about a little sister who grows up to be bigger than her bratty big sister," Rosa demanded.

"Me too," Winnie agreed.

I gave them what they'd asked for. I told them a story I usually saved for myself, for the times I was mad at Danny and Joey. My brothers could be such creeps. "Little P was very, very tiny, and all the boys and all the girls laughed when she went outside. So Little P stayed inside, all the time, except when she had to go out to go to school or church. One day, on her way to school, the boys were really mean to her. Little P cried as she walked, and her teeny-tiny tears hit her teeny-tiny feet. Halfway down the block, her teeny-tiny feet weren't teeny-tiny anymore. They were BIG— HUGE AS A GIANT'S. And so was the rest of her. The mean kids all ran screaming because Little P was so GIGANTIC they were scared of her."

My sisters' sour faces began to soften. I continued, "Big P was bigger than all the people in town and prettier, too. She was the biggest, prettiest girl in the whole universe. The town built a special house and a special classroom just for Big P. They even made a statue of her. She became famous. None of the kids picked on her anymore. Amen."

I always ended my stories with "Amen." Stories were kind of like prayers to me. I wanted God and His Holy Mother to notice.

After I said "Amen," my sisters slid over to my side of the car. We were friends again.

"We're here, girls."

I'd heard Mama say those words millions of times back in New York when we'd roll into Smiley's parking lot in Cayuga on Friday nights to visit Patrick. But this time, her voice was jittery.

"Wait here," Patrick ordered. "I'll see if he's home."

He bolted out of the car and rushed to Jack's front door, taking the steps two at a time. He rang the doorbell, pulled a comb from his pocket, and fixed his hair. He leaned against the railing, waiting.

Back in the car, Rosa complained. "My legs are achy. I wanna stretch."

"Me too," Winnie mimicked.

Rosa opened the car door before I could stop her. She and Winnie hopped out. Rosa stretched and leaned against the side of the car. Winnie took off, heading straight toward Patrick. "Peanut!" Mama growled. She chased after my baby sister. Rosa stuck her tongue out at me. I reached out the car window and slapped her arm. She tore off after Mama, too. I followed them. We were halfway up the driveway when a man with dark black hair and a long, thin face opened the door.

"Paddy!" The man smiled and opened his arms.

"Jack, how the hell are ya?"

"Great. How about you?"

Winnie had reached Patrick by then, waving her hands to be picked up. He scooped her into his arms.

"I'm a little tired, Jack. But not too worse for the wear." Patrick must have seen our odd parade rushing toward him. He stepped in front of his friend to block his view.

"Come on in," Jack said. "We've made some sandwiches. And we've got milk, too, for Winnie. That's the baby's name, isn't it?" He jiggled Winnie's foot. "She's about three, isn't she? Same age as our Timmy."

"Yes," Patrick said. "On both counts." He let out a nervous laugh. That's when Jack noticed me and Mama and Rosa. He frowned and looked at Patrick. "You didn't mention there'd be three children." His eyes narrowed as we neared the steps.

"Marie's girls are with us, too," Patrick confessed.

"Well . . . it doesn't matter, now, does it?" Jack muttered. "We'll figure out what to do."

I saw his fake smile. I heard him plain as day. Mama did, too. She stopped dead on the sidewalk, just short of Jack's front steps. Rosa and me piled up behind her. Mama let out a long, slow burn of hot air. I added Patrick's latest lie to my growing list of reasons why I hated him. Mama counted to ten under her breath before she took me and Rosa by the hand. Patrick shifted from leg to leg. Jack cleared his throat.

"This is Marie," Patrick said. "And her daughters. Rosa's six, and Regina's almost eleven. Her nickname's . . . Peanut." His voice trailed off.

Patrick studied Mama's face, searching for clues about how sore she was. Mama stayed calm.

Mama said, "It's nice to meet you." She shook Jack's hand. "Patrick has told me so much about you." She wore her fakey voice, the one she pulled out to hide her real feelings.

Jack smiled back. "Let's go inside. My wife has a pot of coffee ready, and we've made sandwiches."

"How thoughtful," Mama said.

Jack stepped aside. Me and Rosa followed Mama into the house. Patrick and Winnie were right behind us.

Jack's wife met us in the hallway. "Welcome, I'm Annie," she said. She hugged Mama and Patrick. "Pleased to meet you," Mama said. Annie smiled and shook Rosa's hand and mine. I smiled back, remembering my manners even though I was really mad at Patrick. Jack was finished smiling. His mouth was a dark line across his face.

"Let's visit in the living room, shall we?" Annie said.

I didn't know if that was a question or an invitation, but I followed Mama and sat next to her on the big gray couch.

"Where's your son?" Mama asked.

"He's at the sitter's," Annie replied. She didn't look at Mama when she talked.

"That's too bad," Mama said. "I hoped we could meet him. I thought he and our Winnie might become friends."

Annie tried to hide a frown. She left the room quickly. When she came back, she carried a tray with sandwiches, milk, coffee, sugar, and cream. She set it on a low table in front of us. Beside the tray she set a stack of small square things with pads of spongy stuff in the middle.

"They're coasters, Peanut," Mama said, reading my mind. She directed me with her eyes and a nod of her head. "Take one, and rest your milk glass in the center part."

Annie had made tuna fish and pickle sandwiches, which

I hated. Mama put a few on a plate and set them in front of us girls. "Eat now," she ordered. I took a little bite and chewed it a long time, thinking about how to spit it into my napkin without getting caught. The grown-ups talked about places to live and jobs and other things that bored me. Once in a while, Annie or Mama would glance at us girls, so I had to swallow the tuna and pickle sandwich and offer it up as penance. To keep from misbehaving, I let my eyes explore the room. There were a couple of pictures of a little boy. Maybe he was their son, Timmy. But there weren't any pictures of dogs. That was a big disappointment. I did notice a crucifix and a picture of the Blessed Virgin Mother. There were other pictures, too—one of Jack standing in a boat holding a big fish and one of Annie and Jack smiling under a big tree with a baby between them.

Their house had lacy drapes, and their windows were clear and sparkly. No smears, no dust, no dirt. I wondered how that kid, Timmy, would ever be able to play in a place like this? What if he spilled his grape juice on the couch? Or colored on the wall? I bet he'd get it for sure then.

Their wooden floor was as shiny as silverware; they had a fancy rug with red and black and dark purple swirls. With long fringes on both ends. I thought they must be pretty rich. I understood better why Mama insisted that I eat my sandwich and use that wooden cork thing. She didn't want me to embarrass her in front of fancy people.

A big, nervous laugh brought me back to the grown-ups' conversation.

"That's kids for ya," Patrick snorted.

"We taught her how to say Patrick, real fast," Mama added in her cheery-fake voice she saved for company. She'd been talking that way since we got there.

She and Patrick must have been telling the story about the time Winnie first tried to say Father Patrick and it came out sounding like the "f" word Mama always yells at Danny for using.

The grown-ups laughed again. Then Patrick checked his watch. "We'd better get going. We've got to get to our motel."

Jack shifted in his chair. Annie glanced out her clean windows. Mama picked at her fingernails.

"You're welcome to stay here," Jack offered, politely. "Until you find a place of your own."

Annie's eyes tightened, just a bit, at her husband's invitation. But she caught herself and added, "You and Marie could stay in Timmy's room. We have a foldout couch for guests up there. Timmy could sleep in our room for a while. And your girls could stay down here, on the couch."

"That's very kind of you," Patrick said, "But you've already done too much."

"Thank you, but no. Really," Mama added. She'd noticed Annie's stingy eyes, too. "You've given us good leads on apartments and even some great job prospects. We couldn't ask for more."

"It's the least I could do for my old buddy," Jack said.

"Thanks, Jack," Patrick said. "We'll keep in touch. We'll have you over for dinner as soon as we settle in."

He stood, and so did Mama. I sprang to my feet. Rosa followed. Winnie grabbed Patrick's hand.

"Thanks so much for all you've done," Mama said, again. She was itching to get out of there, and so was I.

"It's nothing," Jack insisted. "Others helped us when we were starting out."

I could tell Mama didn't like Annie and Jack. Maybe it was Patrick lying about me and Rosa that set Mama off. I don't know, but I didn't think Mama and Patrick would end up being friends with them. And I didn't think Annie would mind that at all.

Jack and Annie walked us to the door and stood on the

steps until we settled back into Patrick's car. They waved as we drove away. Half a block from their house, Mama lit a Chesterfield and took a long drag. She blew the smoke out in one huge swoosh.

"So, how come you didn't tell him about Peanut and Rosa?"

"Look, Marie, don't start on me," Patrick said. "I didn't want Jack to try to talk me out of leaving. I thought if he knew there were five of us, he'd say it was too complicated and caution me to think about it a while longer."

Mama bit her lip. Patrick clenched the steering wheel. He stared straight ahead at the road.

"Marie, you know I want Rosa and Peanut here as much as you do. Honest, honey. We can talk about it later. After we get to the motel."

Mama seethed. "And what about the boys? I suppose you never had any intention of sending for them." Her eyes were cold and hard.

"Not now, Marie." Patrick cautioned. "We'll discuss the boys later."

Mama took another drag off her Chesterfield, turned, and hung her arm over the backseat. "I love you girls." She hugged us with her eyes, reached for us with her fingertips. "Winnie, you too, sweetie," I touched Mama's fingers for a second and tossed her a small smile. It was the best I could muster. Mama winked at me. I still had the magic. Not even Patrick could take that away. She turned back toward the front of the car, and we drove on.

Nobody said anything for the longest time; then Mama broke the silence.

"Jack and Annie are real nice." It was Mama's turn to lie.

"Yeah, Jack's like a brother to me," Patrick said.

"I could tell," Mama said, pretending everything was rosy.

The Best Western

After we left Jack's house, we checked into another Best Western Motel—just off Highway 94. Mama told us, "This is home until we find an apartment." We set our A&P paper-bag suitcases on the carpet and took a tour. It was short. The motel room reminded me of a teeny-tiny house with everything shoved into it. There were two double beds, a table, two chairs, a dresser, and a desk with another chair. No stove. No refrigerator. No upstairs. No safe places to hide. Although it was smaller and more crowded than our Pisa house, it was fancier. Especially the bathroom. It had a big bathtub and a shower, a brand-new toilet, and a light in the ceiling that warmed you up after you got out of the bath-tub. I loved that. I flipped it on and dreamed about me and Rosa staying all toasty under that big bulging red eye, after we took a bath. "Turn that damn light off," Patrick hollered. "It's too hot in here."

It didn't take us long to unpack our A&P suitcase bags.

We girls didn't have much stuff. We had to leave Pisa too fast. I only had time to toss in a few pairs of underpants, a couple of shirts, two pairs of slacks. And a sweater. Mama hadn't brought much, either. Patrick had a real suitcase with a lock and a clear plastic patch where he wrote his name. I noticed he'd scratched off the "Reverend" part, though. He unpacked five shirts, four pairs of pants, tons of socks and underwear, a couple pairs of shoes, and a jacket. He had a special, smaller black zippered bag for his toothbrush, toothpaste, deodorant, and shaver. He set that on the counter in the bathroom before he put his other stuff in the dresser. Afterward, he stuffed the papers Jack had given him into the desk drawer.

"I'm beat," he sighed.

"It's been a long day," Mama agreed.

Patrick tugged off his shoes, unbuttoned his shirt collar, lay back on one of the two big beds, and rubbed his face. He yawned. I prayed he was ready for a nap. I liked Patrick best when he was sleeping. When he closed his eyes, the hard lines in his face relaxed. He seemed smaller then, even though his legs nearly hung off the edge of the mattress. When he was asleep, I got a break from his bossiness. He even looked handsome and soft when he snored, more like the friendly man my mama had fallen in love with, years before.

"Marie, do you think you could keep the girls quiet for a little bit while I rested?" he asked.

"Sure, honey. Come on, girls, let's go snoop around the gift shop."

Mama ran a comb through her hair and checked her face in the mirror. She must have liked what she saw 'cuz she smiled.

I couldn't wait to get out of that room. I was worried that I wasn't gonna be able to keep the girls quiet if we stayed while Patrick rested. Mama took Winnie's hand. I grabbed Rosa's.

"Don't spend a lot of money," Patrick called as the door closed behind us.

In the motel gift shop, Mama was as silly as a little kid. She oohed and aahed at the twenty kinds of saltwater taffy and the rows of key rings in the shape of Wisconsin. There were tons of cows, everywhere—on coffee mugs, T-shirts, bumper stickers, baseball caps, even playing cards. Winnie poked her nose into each one and said, "Moo." Rosa tried on a pair of black and white cow sunglasses. "Can I get these, Mama? Pleeaase," she pleaded. Mama checked the price tag and told her, "Absolutely not." Rosa pouted until Mama explained that she'd come back and buy them after we got settled and Patrick found a job. That suited Rosa. She put the sunglasses back where she'd found them and explored the candy section.

"Look at this, girls," Mama laughed.

She flashed a postcard of a cow in a red flannel shirt. I laughed, too, but not because of the cow. I thought that was stupid. I was just relieved that Mama wasn't crying or shouting about something.

"Can I have this, Mama?" Rosa waved a Reese's peanut butter cup.

Mama thought for a second. "Can't be any harm in getting a little treat," she said. "Winnie? Peanut? What do you want?"

Winnie grabbed a Tootsie Roll POP, and I got a Milky Way. Mama picked a Butterfinger. We ate our treats in the motel lounge and watched the color TV hanging on the wall. Winnie snuggled into Mama's lap. Rosa and me shared a big blue chair, like the one back in our motel room. "Jeopardy!" was on. Art Fleming read the answers, and the contestants rang their buzzers to give him the right questions.

I liked "Jeopardy!" Mama, me, Danny, and Joey played every afternoon during the summer. We'd compete to see who'd be champion. Mama'd keep score, writing down when one of us got 100 or 200 or 1,000 points. I never won. Danny said it was because I had a pea brain, just the right size for a dumb girl named Peanut. Mama said it was because the game was made for big people, not kids, and I'd win a lot when I grew up because I was very smart. She told me not to pay any attention to Danny.

Under the category *World Architecture,* Art read, "This Tuscan city on the Arno is famous for its leaning tower."

"What is Pisa?" Mama said to Art's TV face. Then she burst into tears. She scared Winnie, who started bawling, too. Rosa and I leapt up from our chair.

"Don't cry, Mama." I held her hand so she could feel me real and alive right next to her. "Don't cry, Winnie," Rosa said. "It's okay. It's okay."

I dug into my pocket for a Kleenex. Mama snatched it from me and handed over Winnie. I scooped my baby sister into my arms and held her close as Mama wiped her eyes and blew her nose. "We've got to go back to the room," she said real fast. She stood in a hurry and rushed down the hall. We girls scrambled after, running to keep up. Rosa stayed right behind Mama, but having to carry Winnie slowed me. Halfway down the hall, I set my sister down, grabbed her hand, and raced back to our room. By the time we closed the door behind us, Mama was having a fit.

"I don't care what you think, Patrick," Mama shouted. "You may be able to pretend to Jack that my daughters and sons don't exist, but I've got to send for those boys. I can't go on like this. We should have waited for them to come home from school. Or pulled them out early. Why didn't we take them?"

Mama flew all over the place. I held my sisters back, so

we wouldn't get caught in her crazy windmill. Patrick tried to reel Mama in. He grabbed one of Mama's arms, but she spun out of his reach and stormed off. He followed her and tried to calm her down again, but her temper was too slippery. She escaped his grip again, and their struggle started all over.

Mama was blowing like a human tornado. Her mouth was twisting and turning, and her eyes were flashing something so ugly I didn't recognize her. I herded Rosa and Winnie into the bathroom so they wouldn't have to see Mama so crazy. We played with the heat lamp, turning it on and off. The red light covered everything in a warm glow, but it didn't help. We got bored with the lamp, so I sang a couple of *My Fair Lady* tunes, but still we could hear Mama ranting. To drown her out, we covered our ears, closed our eyes, and sat on the cold tile floor, waiting.

Finally, things got quieter. I figured it was safe to check if everything was okay. "Girls, stay put 'til I come get you," I ordered, before I slipped out.

Mama was slouched in a chair by the window. She cradled her face in her hands. She cried softly as Patrick wrapped his arm around her shoulder. His face was close to hers.

"Marie, honey. Marie," he said. "It'll be all right, honey. I'm here. I'm here."

Winnie wiggled past me and headed straight toward Mama's chair. I grabbed the edge of her shirt and held her back.

"Wait a second," I whispered. "Mama needs a few minutes."

I hoped I was right. I had a funny feeling about Mama. It isn't true that people wait until the end of their life to die. Some people, like my mama and me, die in little bits and pieces all the time. Not just at the end when they're ninety-nine and old and gray and wrinkled. Some people leave little chunks of their heart in places they don't remember, when they're six or ten or twenty or thirty. They don't know why. Parts just get too heavy, and they have to set them down, like dirty rocks.

"Mama," Winnie called.

Mama lifted her face and motioned us to her. "My sweeties," she cooed. "Where would I be without you?"

All three of us girls rushed to her side. Winnie buried her face in Mama's lap. Rosa snuggled into Mama's shoulder. I stood an inch away, just watching. She touched my hand. My stomach relaxed.

"I'm just having a hard day, girls, but I'm all right now. There's nothing to worry about."

I wanted to believe Mama, but I'd seen it happen too often. She might be able to convince Rosa and Winnie, but not me. I met her eyes. There was worry inside them and a sort of plea for me to love her. She looked so little, so alone. I gave her everything. I wiped the hurt and the worry from my own face and gave her only happy eyes. Eyes that told her I believed everything she said, that I would love her forever and never hate her for how she left me all the time. Eyes that told her I knew about the hard places, and I didn't care. Eyes that forgave her for being unhappy and selfish and cruel.

"Why don't we grab some hamburgers in the coffee shop?" Patrick suggested. "You hungry, girls? Marie?"

Mama turned her sweetness on him now, sharing the calm place she'd gotten herself to. "That sounds good, honey."

Now, everybody was standing up with dry eyes, hungry for something. Hamburgers might do. French fries would help. A chocolate malt might take all the sadness away. Mama washed her face and combed her hair. We girls huddled around her, afraid to let her out of our sight. Patrick grabbed his wallet, and we headed to the restaurant. Rosa and Winnie skipped down the hall. Mama and Patrick strolled hand in hand. I walked behind them, pretending I was going to the creek with Zoomer to tell him all that had happened. I needed his advice.

The Phone Call

The next morning, the alarm clock woke me early. Mama switched it off right away and tiptoed past our bed on her way to the bathroom. I lay quietly, so she wouldn't see I was awake. The bathroom door shut softly. I listened to the water running and Mama humming, sweet and low. It made my heart hurt. She sounded so different from the tornado Mama of last night. I wanted her to hold me and make it all better. But I knew that was only a dream, a fairy-tale version of my mother—one that would never be mine again.

Later, when Mama stepped out of the steamy room, she smelled of wet hair and Ivory soap. My sisters were wide awake by then, and so was I. Mama blew us kisses as she walked past. I caught one and held it to my heart. She sat on the edge of her bed and tightened the belt of her bathrobe. She leaned over and kissed Patrick. "Morning, honey," she said. She pulled away and announced, "I'm gonna call now." Her fingers brushed Patrick's chin.

"Are you sure you're ready?" Patrick propped himself

up, still half asleep. He reached for her. She squeezed his hand.

"As ready as I'll ever be."

Her face held a glimpse of the playful mama she used to be when I was a little girl, the silly, happy woman she tucked away like a secret. Patrick rubbed his eyes awake and sat beside Mama on the bed.

"Besides," Mama added. "It's been two days since we left. I don't want my boys to think I've forgotten about them."

I held my breath, expecting her eyes to sink like they usually did when she talked about deserting my brothers. That morning, there was no trace of her familiar, faraway look. She dialed and settled in as if she were getting ready for a friendly chat with her sister, Stella. Then, without warning, Mama sprang up fast as if her bathrobe had caught fire. She slammed the phone back into its cradle.

"What if they won't talk to me? What if they hate me?"

"You're their mother," Patrick comforted. "They love you."

She dialed again. "I don't know, I don't know . . . ," she muttered and started to hang up once more. A thin "hello" escaped from the other end of the line, and Mama quickly pressed her ear to the phone.

"Joey, honey, is that you? It's Mama." Her voice rushed to hug him.

"Yes, yes, I'm okay. We're safe. We're all safe. How are you? How's Danny?"

She raced on, afraid to stop, afraid to take a breath, scared that my brothers would hang up on her. If I were Joey and Danny, I'd hear her lonesome voice and burst into pieces. My neck would get hot, and I'd kick the phone across the floor. I'd scream and shout, "Why didn't you take me?"

The longer Mama talked, the more her face changed.

Her smile faded. Her mouth grew round and small. I expected her to whimper, "I didn't mean to be a bad girl, honest . . ." My stomach heaved. I rushed to the bathroom, bent over the toilet, ready to lose the hamburger and French fries I'd eaten for supper the night before. Nothing came except gagging sounds and gross spit. I brushed my teeth to take away the sour taste, but the Crest didn't help. Rosa sneaked up and tapped me on the shoulder.

"Do you think Daddy's gonna come get us when he finds out where we are?" she whispered. Her eyes were wide, hopeful.

"I don't think Mama's talking to Daddy." I shut the door so Mama and Patrick wouldn't hear us. "But here's the deal," I cautioned. "We still got to pretend we're happy. We can't let them know that we miss Danny and Joey and Daddy. And Zoomer. Remember how crazy Mama was last night? You don't want that to happen again, do ya?"

Rosa shook her head. "I'll be good, I promise."

I hugged my sister and kissed her forehead. "Want me to brush your hair?"

Rosa nodded. Her dark hair was chocolate-brown like Joey's. I picked a couple of pillow feathers out of her tangles and remembered how my brothers used to hate it when Rosa and I played beauty queen. We'd sit at the kitchen table fussing, using Mama's favorite brush and her red lipstick because she was finally in one of her rare good moods and had said "okay."

"Girls are weird," Danny had teased. "Ain't you got better things to do than smear all that junk on your faces?"

"Like what?" I sassed.

"Like watch TV. Or play baseball. Or convince Mama to stop seeing that jerk priest, Patrick," he complained.

I stuck out my tongue. He slapped my arm. "You're such a mama's girl, Peanut. You make me sick."

A sharp knock on the bathroom door made Rosa jump. I dropped the brush. "Come out here, girls." It was Patrick. "Your brothers want to say hello."

"I gotta pee, first," Rosa said, trying to stall.

It didn't work. Patrick opened the door. "March yourselves over to the phone right now," he commanded.

We found Mama perched on the side of the bed, crying, trying to sound braver than she looked. "Here they are," she sobbed. She pushed the phone into my hand and nodded for me to talk.

"Peanut?"

It was Joey. He sounded far away. I didn't know what to say.

"Hi . . . Joey." I found my voice, even though I sounded more little than I wanted to. "What ya doin'?"

"Nothin'," he answered. He sounded funny—sad and tired, but something else, too, something I couldn't describe. It scared me.

I wanted to tell him a million things. Like, I was sorry about the time I hid his baseball mitt in the garbage can, and it smelled like spaghetti and meatballs for a month. And how I forgave him for being rough on me that time I sneaked up on him and his buddy Stevie Androzzi. They were peeking through Mrs. Brown's bathroom window when she was taking a bath. I told him I was gonna tell Mama, but he twisted my arm and pushed me in the dirt and swore he'd hurt me worse if he ever found out I ratted. Most of all, I wanted to tell him that it was weird to not be home in Pisa with him and Danny and Daddy. Even though I hated Joey sometimes, I still missed him a whole lot.

But I couldn't say any of that. Not with Mama staring at me with round cow eyes, counting every word that came out of my mouth, hearing between the lines like I was holding secrets from her. Which I was. There was no way I was going to admit it. Then I'd have to tell her the truth, and Mama didn't want to know the truth. How could I tell her that I would have given just about anything if we'd never left for Madison with Patrick?

"Hurry up," Patrick urged. He stood behind me, all antsy. "This is costing a lot of money."

"Tell him you love him," Mama insisted. "Then let Rosa talk."

"See ya, Joey," I said.

I shoved the phone at Rosa's chest. I couldn't say "I love you." It felt like a lie. Even though I did love him, I'd never told him before. And I couldn't say it in that motel room with Mama's crazy eyes pushing those words on me and Patrick's itchy breathing stirring things up. I don't know what Rosa said. I couldn't hear anything but the buzzing in my head. I didn't even remember to ask him about Zoomer. Or Daddy. Or Danny. My heart beat so fast I could hardly swallow. I sat on the edge of the bed, closed my eyes, and disappeared. I didn't come back to the room until Mama touched my forehead.

"You okay, Peanut? You look a little flushed." She checked my forehead but decided I wasn't sick. She got me a glass of water. "Here, honey, drink this."

I took a few sips and opened my eyes. I was still in that Best Western in Madison, Wisconsin. I hadn't been zapped back to Pisa like I'd wished. When Mama saw I was all right, she left me sitting with the cup of water in my hand and started telling Patrick everything my brothers had said.

"Paulie wasn't there." She leaned into Patrick like she was sharing a secret. "Just the boys. Paulie let them skip school. Goddamn him. Their grades better not slide. That S.O.B. never did care if his sons got a good education. I always had to push. 'Get good grades,' I told them. 'Go to college. You don't want to end up like your dad.'"

Mama was huffy now. She thought Daddy never did anything right. Not even helping her raise us kids.

"Joey said, 'Send for us right away, Ma. Please.'" A tear slipped down Mama's cheek. "He sounded so little—just like a little boy. Like when he was three and I left him with a sitter. I had to go to the beauty parlor, get my hair cut. 'I wanna come with you, Mama,' he pleaded. Such a sweet baby, that Joey. Such a sweet child."

Patrick's face showed nothing. I couldn't tell if he was mad or bored or just listening.

"Danny said he'd come, too, if Joey does," Mama said, excitedly. "I told them we'd send plane tickets as soon as you got a job. Which should be within a week, don't you think, honey?"

Patrick's mouth tightened. I plugged my ears, expecting a big holler to burst out of him, but nothing did. Instead, he stood up, walked to the window, pulled back the drapes, and looked out at the parking lot, as if he were checking to see if his car was still there. He rubbed the back of his neck. "You shouldn't have promised them that, Marie. What if I don't get a job for a while? We have to be careful. We only have two thousand dollars. When it's gone, it's gone. I can't ask my parents for help. Not this time. And there's no way I would impose on Jack."

"I didn't mean to . . . ," Mama apologized. "It's just . . . hearing their voices . . . They weren't mad at me . . . They said they'd come . . ."

She reached for Patrick, but he turned away.

"You don't want them here, do you?" Mama accused. She crossed her arms, shoving her fists under her armpits.

"Of course, I want them to come," Patrick said. His back tightened, and he kept staring out the window. "I just don't want you to promise something I can't deliver. I told you a thousand times, we can't send for the boys until I can afford to support them. We have three kids to take care of now, Marie. For Christ's sake, how are we going to feed and clothe five?"

I'd heard that story my whole life. Daddy complaining about making ends meet and Mama yelling, "Quit being so cheap." It made me want to give back the candy bar Mama'd bought me last night at the gift shop. I didn't want to be a burden to anyone, especially not to Patrick. I had the feeling he'd never let me forget it.

"I can get a job, too," Mama insisted.

She unlocked her arms and moved closer, trying hard to make it better, like I do with her when I'm afraid I've been too bad and she won't love me anymore.

"After you get a job and we find a house, I can get something part-time. We can find a sitter for Winnie. Maybe that person who watches Jack and Annie's son, Timmy."

Patrick faced her. He didn't look angry anymore, just tired. "No," he said. "I want you home with Winnie. She's too little. We'll figure it out, somehow."

He opened his arms, and Mama stepped in. I helped my sisters put on their shoes. I was relieved that they had stopped fighting, but I worried about how this stuff with the boys was gonna turn out. Since we'd left Pisa, I prayed before I fell asleep that Daddy would make Mama come back and bring us girls with her. That would be the end of it all, I decided. Patrick would have to give us up, wouldn't he? We belonged to our daddy, not him. Except Winnie. But maybe Daddy didn't know about Winnie. Maybe he'd fight for her, too.

Mama and Patrick kissed and hugged. After they made up, we all went to the motel coffee shop for breakfast. We ate pancakes and scrambled eggs. Nobody said another word about Danny or Joey or Pisa. Mama smiled and sipped her coffee. Winnie sat on Patrick's lap when she was done eating. Rosa and I swapped secret glances, promising with our eyes to stick together. Mama smoked a lot of Chesterfields. Patrick paid the bill.

Back in our motel room, Patrick brushed his teeth and combed his hair. He had to meet his buddy Jack about a job over at the University and at some other school called Edgewood College of the Sacred Heart. He kissed Mama good-bye and whistled down the hallway. Mama and us girls headed for the indoor swimming pool. We had forgotten to pack bathing suits in our A&P paper-bag suitcases, so we couldn't go swimming. Instead, Rosa and I dangled our feet in the water and pretended we were mermaids on a deserted island waiting for a handsome fisherman to fall in love with us and take us home.

The Note

We stayed at the Best Western for ten days while Patrick looked for work. After he got a job at Edgewood College of the Sacred Heart, he and Mama started checking out places for us to live.

They went apartment hunting every evening after supper. My sisters and I stayed back at the motel. Mama told us we couldn't go to the pool or to the gift shop and by no means could we go back to the restaurant. We had to stay put in the room and watch TV or play cards. One night when Mama and Patrick were out, I unrolled the picture of the Blessed Virgin Mary that I had packed away in my paper-bag suitcase. I laid it on the motel dresser. I set the Best Western Bible and the Madison phone book on top to flatten her Holy face. I wanted Her to be ready so I could hang Her next to my bed when we finally left the motel and got a Madison home.

That night, Mama and Patrick came back to the motel

and had a big fight because the only place they could afford just had two bedrooms, one for them and one for us girls.

"Where are the boys gonna sleep?" Mama complained.

"On the porch," Patrick argued. "It's a three-season. We could put a couple of cots out there and a space heater during the winter."

Mama stewed a few hours about that. Eventually, Patrick convinced her it was the right thing to do. "We've been looking for days, Marie," he insisted. "It's the best thing we've seen for the price. Plus it's furnished. I think we should take it. We'll fit the boys in somehow."

We moved into our Madison apartment on a gray Saturday morning in early April. It was really the top half of a duplex. The Andersons, who owned the whole place, lived downstairs. Mama said we'd get a real house, all to ourselves, after Patrick got his Ph.D. "Then he can become a professor and not just a teacher," she told me. "And maybe land a job at the University." At Edgewood, he taught something she called religious studies. "Is that like catechism?" I asked. "Sort of," Mama said. I figured it fit in real well, with Patrick being a priest. Anyway, Mama said Patrick had a master's degree, so he was smarter than other people and could get a better job. She said if Patrick hadn't had that, he would have had to try to get work in something she called the civil service. I don't know why he just didn't get a job at Sears.

For all Mama's complaining beforehand, the apartment wasn't too bad. Except, I wished we could have had our own furniture.

"Who left their crummy stuff here?"

"Nobody," Mama told me. "This furniture comes with the place."

The couch sagged, and the beds were soft and squeaky. The chairs in the living room were okay. Their arms were scratched, but the cushions weren't too mushy. The floor slanted a little, so the dining room table wobbled if you leaned on it.

"Nothing a little folded newspaper can't cure," Patrick assured.

The bathroom was tiny, and there wasn't any heat lamp. It made me miss the Best Western a whole lot. Every room had pale yellow walls.

"Kind of dingy," Mama said. "But maybe the Andersons will let us put on a fresh coat of paint."

There were lots of windows in the apartment, and that helped make things brighter. I taped the picture of the Blessed Virgin above my bed and said a short prayer: *Holy Mother, please tell Daddy to come get us, quick.*

That three-season porch Mama and Patrick had fought over was the best thing about the place. It was high in the trees, kind of like a fort, only you didn't have to go outside to get to it. And on clear days I could see Lake Mendota off in the distance. Right away I made plans to use it as my own hideout, my own special escape place when Rosa and Winnie were bugging me or when Mama was in one of her moods. I sure didn't want to give it up for Joey and Danny.

After we got settled, Patrick and Mama took us down to meet our landlords, Mr. and Mrs. Anderson.

"You remember my wife, Marie," Patrick said.

I didn't like him calling Mama his wife. My cheeks felt hot.

"This is Winnie," Patrick continued. "And this is Rosa. And here's Regina. But we call her Peanut. Their last name is Giovanni. Marie is divorced. But I hope to adopt these girls someday."

I couldn't believe the lies he was telling. Mama wasn't divorced from my daddy, unless getting in a car and driving to Madison can make you divorced. And that talk about adopting us girls made me feel like the run-down furniture in our apartment.

Mrs. Anderson smiled. "How nice. You girls are lucky to have such a wonderful stepfather."

Rosa pinched my arm, but I didn't wince. I looked at her out of the corner of my eye, knowing she was as disgusted as I was. Inside I yelled, "He ain't a wonderful stepfather. He's grouchy, and he's a liar! I'm not ever gonna let him adopt me and Rosa!"

"These are our children." Mrs. Anderson gestured to the living room, where a boy about my brother Joey's age and a girl a little older than me were watching TV. "Mikey, Suzie, come say hello to our new neighbors."

Suzie obeyed, but Mikey didn't. He acted stupid like my brother Danny. He wasn't interested in a bunch of little girls. I could tell he lumped me in the same pile as Rosa and Winnie. He hardly looked away from the TV set when his mama introduced us. Dumb little farts, his face said, and he went back to watching his show.

"Oh, dear," Mrs. Anderson worried. "You'll have to forgive my son. He's fifteen, you know, and not very social."

Mama nodded. "My Joey's fifteen, too."

"Oh, you have a son . . ." Mrs. Anderson's voice trailed off.

"Yes . . . ," Mama muttered. "Actually, two sons. They live with their father."

"Oh, I see . . ." Mrs. Anderson reached for her daughter's hand. "This is our Suzie. She just turned thirteen."

Suzie had bright yellow hair and small blue eyes that looked like tiny, cold lakes in her pale face. Her perky nose turned up at the end, and her teeth were as white as marshmallows. Mikey's hair was darker, but he had the same blue eyes. Just like their daddy's.

"Hi." Suzie smiled and shook Mama's hand, then Patrick's. "Pleased to meet you."

She nodded a hello to Rosa and me before she bent and hugged Winnie. "What a darling daughter you have, Mrs. Shaughnessy," she cooed. My stomach ached when she called Mama by Patrick's last name.

Suzie petted Winnie's curly hair. My baby sister grabbed Mama's leg, trying to avoid Suzie's pawing. Winnie didn't have to try too hard. After a minute or so, Suzie got bored and left her alone. Then she disappeared into her bedroom. I prayed I wasn't going to her school.

"Kids," Mr. Anderson said, shrugging his shoulders, apologizing for how rude his daughter had just been.

Mrs. Anderson's eyes caught Mama's, then looked away, quickly. "Teenagers," she said to the floor. "Well, would you care for some coffee?" She rebounded with a polite smile.

"Can I help?" Mama asked.

"No, please, just make yourselves comfortable." Mrs. Anderson nodded toward the dining room before she rushed off to the kitchen.

We followed Mr. Anderson and sat at their round, wooden table. Patrick held Winnie in his lap. I sat next to Rosa, who sat next to Mama. Mr. Anderson laid his folded hands on the table. He smiled at Mama and Patrick without saying a word. Then he looked at Winnie, then at Rosa, then at me.

"What grade are you in, Red?" Mr. Anderson asked me.

My mouth opened, but no words came out. He had used the nickname my daddy called me sometimes, because I had red hair like him.

"Peanut," Mama nudged me with her voice. "Mr. Anderson asked you a question."

"Fifth grade," I said to his thin lips. I couldn't look at his kind eyes. "I'm almost eleven."

"You are not," Rosa insisted. "Your birthday ain't 'til July."

I shot her a mean look, and Patrick noticed.

"The apartment's great," he said, jumping in to make sure me and Rosa didn't start a fight. "It's got everything we need."

"Just perfect," Mama agreed.

Mrs. Anderson came back carrying a tray with a silver coffeepot and four cups with matching saucers for the grown-ups. She brought pop for us kids and a plate of Oreos.

"Where is it you said you were from?" Mrs. Anderson asked. She handed coffee to Mama and Patrick.

"Pisa, New York," Mama told her. "It's a small town, not too far from Buffalo."

"Lots of snow in Buffalo," Mr. Anderson said. He sipped his coffee, winked at me, and smiled. I blushed and grabbed a cookie.

Patrick laughed. "We were hoping for a saner winter here."

"Oh, it gets plenty cold in Wisconsin," Mr. Anderson said. "If you were looking to escape winter, you should have picked California."

"We chose Madison because it has great schools and good job opportunities," Patrick said. "Wisconsin is a beautiful state. I know we're going to love it here. A little cold won't scare us off."

Mama nodded, agreeing with everything Patrick said. She didn't talk much. She just smiled like a Barbie doll.

Mrs. Anderson didn't say much, either. She sipped her coffee and checked the supply of Oreos. One time, she did mention to Mama how to get to the Montgomery Wards, so we could buy school clothes. And she also told Mama which grocery stores had the best prices and where to take us kids for ice-cream cones. "Memorial Union, over at the University, is the best place in town," she insisted. "If you want to buy quarts and gallons, go to Babcock Hall."

Mr. Anderson tried to chat with Patrick about the Green Bay Packers football team, but Patrick told him he wasn't much interested in sports. They talked about the weather instead and where to get good deals on cars. "You're lucky to be over at Edgewood," he told Patrick. "Been some trouble brewing at the University. What with all the draft card burning and the sit-ins. Kids are going crazy over that Vietnam War."

"The idiots don't know how good they have it here," Patrick asserted.

"Can't say I blame 'em," Mr. Anderson interrupted. "We never should have gotten messed up in that in the first place."

Every once in a while, I'd feel Mr. Anderson's eyes on my face, and I'd glance over to see him smiling. He seemed like a nice man, and I wanted to ask him if he could help us get back to our daddy, but I knew I better not get myself in trouble.

Later, when we went back up to our apartment, Mama warned us about Mrs. Anderson. "She's a Nervous Nellie. Be careful not to run around too much. And keep your voices down. We don't want to upset her and end up on the street or back at that Best Western."

At breakfast the next morning, Mama announced that we were going to Wards to buy school clothes.

"We wouldn't have that expense if Peanut would have packed her uniform in her bag." Patrick scowled at me.

I took a big gulp of orange juice and looked to Mama for help.

"It doesn't really matter, now, does it?" Mama soothed, meeting my worried eyes. "Their new school isn't Catholic. They won't be wearing uniforms."

"Well, why can't she wear the clothes she already has, then?"

"Patrick, she can't go to school in stretch pants and T-shirts. Don't worry so much. I'll get a part-time job if things get tight."

"Mama, it's Sunday. Won't Wards be closed today?" I asked.

"Oh, you're probably right."

"Good," Patrick butted in. "Then we can take a drive around town and do some sight-seeing."

"Is that what you want to do today, honey?" Mama asked Patrick. She walked over, slid her arm around his shoulder, and kissed the top of his head.

"Aren't we going to Mass first?" We hadn't been to church since we'd left Pisa, and I was starting to worry about my immortal soul.

"No, Peanut. Not today." Mama's voice was edgy, now—not soft like before, when she'd rescued me from Patrick's outburst about my school clothes.

"How come?" I pushed for an answer, even though I knew she might get mad. I didn't want God to hate me for missing church.

"After we get settled in and find a parish. Then we'll go." Mama sighed, tired of my questions. "Finish your toast, now, and hush up."

I wasn't sure if God would let Patrick visit him anymore, since he ran away from being a priest. And he lied about me and Rosa. And Mama's last name. I sure hoped none of that rubbed off on me. I made a quick prayer to be safe. *Dear God, I can't help it if he left. I still believe in you.*

After breakfast, I helped with the dishes. When we were

done, Mama announced, "Now we can go on our little outing!"

We grabbed our coats, headed downstairs, and climbed into Patrick's car. The Andersons and their kids pulled into the driveway right beside us. Their car door swung open, and Suzie hopped out—wearing a pink dress, white gloves, and white patent leather shoes. Mikey scooted out the other side; he had on a blue suit and a striped tie. He was carrying a box of donuts like a football in the crook of his arm. His mother tapped his shoulder, signalling for him to hold them properly.

She noticed us watching and called, "Good morning!" She waved, too, looking a little embarrassed.

"Morning." Mama waved back. To us she whispered, "She sure is a nervous woman."

"Mama, I want a donut," Rosa said. She'd been eying Mikey's box the whole time.

"You just ate breakfast," Patrick insisted.

Rosa pleaded. "Can't we get some later, after we go for a drive? Just for a treat?"

"You've got to learn you can't have everything you want," Patrick scolded.

"Honey, she's only six," Mama said. "What's wrong with a little treat every now and then?"

"We still have to buy school clothes," Patrick harped. "You know money doesn't grow like weeds."

Winnie started crying. "I wanna donut."

"Oh, for heaven's sake," Patrick complained. He turned and looked at Winnie. "Okay, I'll buy you one."

"Me, too?" Rosa asked.

"Of course, honey," Mama answered.

I didn't care about any stupid donuts. It was Sunday, and we weren't going to Mass. That was the worst mortal sin. I promised to pray a rosary when we got back to the apartment. I didn't want to get the Blessed Virgin Mother mad. I had to start school soon, and I needed all the help I could get. I had a lot on my mind. I hoped my class wasn't going to be full of girls like Suzie Anderson—a whole room of blond-haired, blue-eyed snots in pink Sunday dresses. I hadn't been to school since we'd left Pisa. It had been almost two weeks. I wasn't sure I'd be able to catch up with the rest of my Madison class. My grades hadn't been so hot back at St. Joan of Arc's. I had a hard time concentrating. Mama was still mad about that.

Patrick drove to Lake Mendota. We sat on a picnic table near the shore for a while. Rosa and Winnie wandered off to see the ducks, and I sat under a tree, wishing I could close my eyes and will myself back to Daddy and the boys. I always thought I'd want to be with Mama. But I was wrong. Things hadn't turned out the way she and Patrick said they would. Madison wasn't Happy Town. Not with Patrick's crabbing about money and picking on me for the stupidest things. I didn't know what I was gonna do, but I knew if things didn't get better soon, I'd burst.

I watched Mama and Patrick laughing and talking, sitting close to one another on the picnic table, and I felt selfish. They looked happy. Maybe things weren't as bad as I was thinking. Maybe I just had to give it more time. Sure, Madison wasn't Pisa. But it had its pretty parts. Patrick was right about this lake being beautiful. I just missed Zoomer so much I could hardly think about being happy. I even missed my brothers and Aunt Stella and Uncle Tony. And Daddy. I wondered if he was in church right now, praying a rosary, asking God to help him get his daughters back. Did he miss me, too?

Before we went back to the apartment, Patrick took a spin around Edgewood College so we could see where he worked. We found a small bakery near the University that was still open. Patrick bought a donut for each of us.

"Welcome to Happy Town," he said as he tossed the waxy white bag into the backseat. "Don't mess up my car now, you hear?"

"Stop it," Mama teased him. "You sound like an old biddy."

On Monday, Mama took Rosa and me to Wards. She bought us each two skirts, three blouses, a couple pairs of socks, and a pair of school shoes. She slipped in a bag of chocolate-covered peanuts for us girls.

"Here you go," Mama said. She put a few pieces into Rosa's palm and plopped one in Winnie's mouth. "Chew it slow, now."

"I don't want any," I told her. I still needed pens and pencils and notebooks and red rubbers for my feet when it rained. And a raincoat. Where would we find the money? As hard as I tried, I couldn't stop feeling like a burden.

Patrick didn't find out about the chocolate peanuts. Mama never said anything, and he didn't check the receipts in the bags we brought home. She just gave him back his change and gave him a big kiss. She made spaghetti for supper, and we watched TV until it was time to go to bed.

"Tomorrow's a school day, Peanut. You need a good night's sleep."

Mama came with me on my first day in fifth grade at Madison Elementary School. I sat outside the principal's office while she talked to him. His door was open, and I heard her say, "Regina's a good student. Her grades suffered during the divorce. But she's smart. She'll catch on real fast here."

I chewed my lip and made a vow to work hard to get at

least B's on my next report card. I sealed it with a prayer to the Holy Mother. There was only a little time left before summer vacation anyway. I could do it if She helped me.

When Mama and the principal were done talking, my new teacher, Mrs. Benson, came to take me to class. "Hello, Regina."

Mrs. Benson smiled like Betty, my favorite waitress at Smiley's Coffee Shop in Cayuga near Pisa, back home. Her face was wide and roomy. I blushed and stared at her black heels until I got brave enough to look into her eyes. They were green and calm and made me think of my secret meetings down by the creek with Zoomer. I hugged Mama goodbye. Then my new teacher took my hand and walked me to her classroom.

"We have a newcomer joining us today," Mrs. Benson announced to her students. "Her name is Regina Giovanni, and I want each of you to be especially nice to her. Regina and her family just moved here from Pisa, New York. Can you all join me in greeting her?"

"Hi, Regina." Their voices roared at me. Tall kids and skinny kids, short kids and fat kids, girls with long hair pulled into ponytails and boys with braces and freckles. They all stared at me, and I stared back, my head full of questions. Which ones had a sad mama? Which ones had a daddy who tucked them in at night? Were there any Amelias out there? I missed my best friend back home. I hoped one of those girls with the ponytails and bright smiles might take her place. And I hoped none of them would pick on me at recess.

"Regina, take the spot behind Julie Farley," Mrs. Benson coaxed me toward the empty desk right behind a girl with short brown hair and bangs. She didn't have a ponytail or wear any barrettes, and she had shiny brown eyes. She watched me walk the whole way down the row. Before I turned to sit behind her, she tossed a tiny smile at me. I liked her right off the bat.

At recess, Julie Farley took my hand, and we headed for a grassy spot near the swings.

"Regina Giovanni. What kind of a name is that anyway?" She wasn't snotty or mean like Suzie Anderson, just curious.

"I don't know. It's just my name."

"I've never heard of anybody with a name like that before," she continued. "Is it true that you come from New York?"

"Yep."

"Have you ever seen trees before?"

I squinted at her, trying to understand.

"New York City is way bigger than Madison," she said. "Nothing but concrete and tall buildings. Will you take me there someday?"

"I've never even been to New York City," I explained. "We lived in Pisa. It's a small town, smaller than Madison, and a long way from New York City. It's got plenty of trees and not any tall buildings. But it's got lakes that look like monster fingers, way bigger than Lake Mendota."

"Oh," she said.

Julie watched the other kids on the playground for a while. I think I disappointed her. Just when I was starting to worry that my first friend was gonna be my last, she cocked her head and said, "It don't matter. I like you anyway."

I took a deep breath. I'd passed the first test. I had a friend, and she wasn't anything like Suzie Anderson. Before I got on the bus to go home that afternoon, Julie tucked a piece of paper in my hand.

"See ya tomorrow."

I scrambled for a seat and opened the note. She'd written her phone number and her address. I folded it like it was a hundred-dollar bill and tucked it safely into my pocket. I'd have to write her a note with my address and number and give it to her tomorrow.

The bus let me off at the corner, and I hopped off and raced down the block to our duplex. I flew up the stairs in a hurry to tell Rosa about Julie. I rushed through the door. I knew Rosa would be home. She only went to kindergarten in the morning. Mama picked her up before lunch. In Pisa, it used to make me jealous that she'd be home with Mama while I had to stay in school all afternoon. But here, I didn't mind as much. Patrick ate lunch at home, now that he worked so close. It made Mama happy, but I'd rather be at school.

"I'm home," I yelled.

Nobody answered. Maybe they were at the grocery store or out for a walk. But then I heard Rosa's and Winnie's voices in our bedroom. I tossed my books on the kitchen table and skipped off to join them. My sisters were on the floor playing with their Barbie dolls.

"What's up, guys?" I hopped onto my squeaky twin bed and bounced around like a wild thing, still excited about Julie and her note. "I made a new friend today," I bragged.

My sisters ignored me. Winnie rolled her Barbie in her favorite yellow blanket. She wrapped and unwrapped it over and over again. Rosa tore the dress off of her Barbie and threw it in the corner. Then she tossed the naked doll at me. Barbie's pointed plastic breasts knocked me on the forehead.

"You brat!" I shouted. "What'd ya do that for?"

"Mama talked to Daddy this afternoon." It wasn't good news. I could tell by the wrinkles on Rosa's forehead, the tiny pout on her rosy mouth. "He ain't gonna let Joey and Danny come live with us."

Rosa reached for her stuffed dog, Binkie, and held him tight. This news meant Patrick would be glad that the boys weren't coming, but he'd still be all riled up because Mama would be a pain to live with.

"Where's Mama now?" I asked, afraid of what Rosa might tell me.

"In her room. She's been in there since she got off the phone. She swore a lot and hollered at Daddy. She said 'They're my sons, you can't have them,' then she slammed down the phone and marched off to her room and slammed the door. She yelled at the walls for a while, then she cried, then everything got real quiet. She hasn't even left her room to pee."

I wanted to erase everything my sister had just told me and go back to this morning when I'd first met Julie Farley. I wanted to climb into my new friend's happy brown eyes and never come out. My legs got shaky, and I knew I better not try to walk over to Mama's room just yet. I could understand Daddy feeling lonesome and not wanting the boys to go away, but why didn't he tell Mama she had to come back and bring us with her? Maybe he did. Maybe that's why Mama shut herself up in her room. Maybe she was trying to figure out a way to tell Patrick that leaving Pisa was a mistake, and now it's time she took us girls home. I'd miss out on not knowing my new friend, but I still had Amelia. We hadn't been gone that long. She probably hadn't replaced me, yet.

When my legs stopped shaking, I slowly headed for Mama's bedroom. I stood outside for a second, trying to figure out what to say. Then I knocked once, turned the knob, and let myself in. The shades were pulled down tight, and in the center of the room, Mama lay on her bed with a washcloth folded over her eyes.

I whispered, "Mama, are you all right?"

"Peanut? Is that you?"

She turned on her side. The cloth fell from her eyes. She reached for me, and I took her hand. She pulled me close.

"The boys," she sobbed. "He won't let them come. He's such a selfish bastard."

She cried hard then. My head rode against her chest as she breathed in her anger and pushed out her sadness. Her pounding heart filled my ears, and I felt trapped in a dark cave. Every time I pulled back, she pulled me closer, until my face pressed into the buttons on her blouse. When finally I said, "I'll get you some Kleenex," her hungry arms let me go.

I set the tissue box on the edge of the bed right beside her and sat further away, down by her feet.

"Come here, honey. Closer."

I inched my butt down the bedspread a bit. That seemed to satisfy her. I was itching to ask her what was really on my mind, but I wasn't sure if she was ready. After she'd finished blowing her nose and wiping her eyes and her breathing sounded regular again, I brought it up.

"If Danny and Joey can't come to Madison, does that mean we're gonna go back to Pisa?"

I must have sounded too anxious, because Mama barked, "No, Peanut. We are never going back there."

I wasn't ever gonna see Daddy again. I couldn't stand the burning behind my eyes, the empty, achy way my stomach felt when the truth of it sunk in.

"So, are you just gonna give up?" I asked, more to myself than to her.

"Hell, no. I'm gonna fight for those boys."

Mama sat all the way up now, full of her fury. She was pissed at Daddy. I could plainly see that, but she was wagging her fist at something else that was in the room, too. Something I couldn't see, but I could feel it, cold and hard and mean, like it could peel the skin off your bones and not feel sorry about it. I shivered and stood up quickly.

"I got homework to do, Mama," I announced, glad to have thought up a reason to escape.

I hurried out of her room. I was gonna hit something if I didn't find another purpose for my hands. I wanted to strangle Patrick and Mama and anybody else who tried to stop me from getting back to my daddy. I shoved my fingers into my pockets and stumbled into Julie's note. I thought about calling her, but what would I say? How could I tell her about the mess I was in? It would scare her away. A scream burst inside of me. Without a sound, it shook from my toes through my head. I loosened my fists, pulled the folded piece of paper out of my pocket, tore it into a million pieces, and threw it in the wastebasket.

Uncivil Wars

Things were pretty tender around our apartment after Daddy told Mama he was gonna keep the boys.

Mama complained, "That son-of-a-bitch never thinks about anybody but himself. He ain't gonna steal my sons. I'm gonna take them away from him if it's the last thing I do."

She cussed at the air, at the stove, at the refrigerator, the walls, the bathroom mirror. She slammed cupboards and shoved pans. Her temper boiled hotter than spaghetti water. I tried to stay out of her way, but she kept calling me into the kitchen. "Fetch the macaroni. Grab the Parmesan. Stir the sauce. Add the meatballs. Chop some garlic. Wash the lettuce." She had me hopping like crazy. Rosa wandered in for some grape juice, and Mama added that chore to my list, too. I didn't know which way was worse—Mama all sad and lonely or Mama bursting with fire. Both scared me.

After a few hours, she wore herself out. She swapped the yelling and stomping for moping and crying. It didn't feel much better to me. When Patrick came home from work that night, Mama was holed up in their bedroom with all the shades pulled. Patrick marched to the bedroom door and charged in. I followed him, staying back a bit so I wouldn't get in trouble.

"What's the matter?"

"Patrick," Mama sobbed.

He wrapped his arm around her shoulder.

"It's Paulie," she bawled. "That no-good S.O.B. said, 'You took my daughters. You're not gonna get my sons. You made your decision, Marie. Now live with it.'"

Patrick kissed Mama's cheek. "He's angry, Marie. Did you really think he'd give up without a fight?"

Mama pulled away. "Why you taking his side?"

"I'm not taking anybody's side." Patrick reached for Mama's hand. She turned away.

"You don't want the boys here. Why don't you just admit it?"

Mama bolted up from the bed, leaving Patrick alone, his empty hands open at his sides. She stood by the window and rubbed her palms over the worn sill. Small chips of paint flicked to the floor, falling on her shoes.

"Marie, I'm too damn tired to do this tonight," Patrick said. "You're reading all kinds of nonsense into my remarks. Let's talk later when you've had a chance to calm down. Then we can figure out what to do, like two rational adults."

"Don't you leave this room until we finish!" Mama threatened. She faced him. Her whole body shook.

Patrick walked away, brushing my shoulder as he passed. "Don't you have anything better to do?" he boomed.

"Peanut," Mama whined, "come here."

My feet froze. *I can't,* I wanted to say, but her weepy eyes made me weaken. On wobbly legs, I went to her. I knew exactly what she needed, and it wasn't an angry jerk stomping out of the room. Mama needed someone to tell her she wasn't bad for leaving the boys. Someone to pretend with her that she could fix the mistake she'd made. Someone who could scoop up her sadness and carry it around, so she could have a little rest. Part of me didn't want to be that someone anymore, but I bargained with the Blessed Virgin Mother. If I make it easier for Mama this time, even just a tiny bit, I prayed, maybe Mama would love me more than Patrick. I wanted Daddy to win this fight with Mama. Then we'd all get to go home. I wanted my family back, all of us together again—Mama and Daddy, me, my sisters, and the boys. No Patrick. No Happy Town. No Lake Mendota.

I hugged Mama. "It's okay," I comforted. "We'll get Joey and Danny here, somehow."

She touched my hair, softly, and I knew the Blessed Mother had heard my prayer. "You still got me and Rosa and Winnie," I reminded her.

"You girls are my Rock of Gibraltar."

It's what I wanted to hear. But this time, her words weren't comforting. I was too tired to carry Mama's bones around any longer, even with the Blessed Virgin's help.

"I got homework to do, Mama," I said, pushing away.

"In a minute." She pulled me back, held my head between her hands. She kissed my forehead. "I'm so glad you're my girl, Peanut."

All the love she had for me spilled from her eyes, and I felt guilty for feeling suffocated. I wanted to love her back that way, pour all the secrets in my heart into her lap so she could read them, but I couldn't. A door slammed inside me. Suddenly, Mama's room felt cold. I shivered.

"Go do your homework," she told me.

She looked calmer now. Her eyes were red from crying, but her mouth had relaxed. It was a good sign. Maybe she wouldn't fret about Daddy all night long. Maybe she'd talk to

Patrick without yelling. Maybe they could figure out what to do. I gave her one last hug before I left her alone in her stuffy room.

After supper, Mama and Patrick sipped coffee at the kitchen table and talked about my brothers.

"I've been thinking," Patrick began. He took a swig from his mug and leaned back in his chair. He loosened the top button of his shirt and folded his hands behind his head. "In most divorce cases, the mother gets custody. I'd say our chances are pretty good. I'll call Jack tomorrow and ask him if he knows of a good lawyer. I don't think Paulie has a legal leg to stand on. You were the one who raised those kids. He was always too busy—off praying in church. I'm sure you could get plenty of people to testify on your behalf."

Mama's eyes danced. She flew over to Patrick's end of the table. She kissed him over and over again. "I knew you'd know what to do."

"We'll fight that ignorant bastard," Patrick stated. "Even if we have to take him all the way to the Supreme Court."

I didn't like Patrick calling my daddy names. But I was relieved that he had made Mama happy again.

A week later, Mama and Patrick met with a lawyer. I knew the news was bad when Mama slammed the car door and stomped up our apartment steps.

"That Jack gave us a lousy lawyer," Mama hissed.

"It's not the lawyer, Marie," Patrick argued. He closed the door quickly so the Andersons wouldn't hear.

"I can't believe that son-of-a-bitch is suing for custody!" Mama seethed. She yanked off her sweater and threw it on the floor. "Your father says I'm living in sin," she ranted at me and Rosa. "Says I'm a bad influence on you girls. Says he won't let me ruin his sons, too."

Mama marched from one end of the apartment to the other, spitting her anger all over the place.

"I didn't desert my family!" she hollered. Her face got redder and redder. "That no-good bum. Where the hell has he been for the past seventeen years? Kneeling in a church pew. Who taught the boys to hit a baseball? Who taught Peanut to ride a two-wheeler? Who took Rosa to the emergency room when she needed stitches? Me. That's who. Who wiped their asses and dried their tears? Who made breakfast and lunch and dinner every damn day, three hundred sixty-five days a year? Me. That's who. Me. I'm their mother. Nobody loves them more than me. *Nobody.*"

The last "nobody" fell out of her with a sorrowful cry. It echoed in my head for the rest of the night. I tried to think of other things. I read *The Cat in the Hat* to Winnie three times and helped Rosa draw a picture of purple tulips for her kindergarten bulletin board, but Mama's shouting wouldn't leave me. Long after the ranting stopped, her eyes still howled, ready to devour anything that got in her way.

Patrick and Mama talked long into the night, past when we girls went to bed. I listened to their low voices across the hall as I tried to fall asleep. Once in a while, Mama's voice got loud, and I'd hear, "They're MY sons" or "That son-of-a-bitch."

One time, Patrick said, "They'd be better off in Madison than with that religious zealot."

I didn't know what a zealot was, but from how he said it, I guessed it wasn't a good thing to be. I wanted to punch his face in. I imagined Joey and Danny helping me. They'd go for his eyes, and I'd knock out his teeth. I knew they hated him. I was beginning to understand why. If my brothers had any sense, they'd forget about coming to Madison. "Stay in Pisa," I wanted to warn them. Maybe Mama was wrong. Maybe Daddy could be a good father. Maybe the boys could love him just as much as they loved Mama. After how she'd left them, maybe they could love him even more.

Battle Scars

I won't ever forget May 5, 1967. Winter was finally over. The sun bragged all over the cloudless blue sky that morning. Birds chirped like crazy. Buds swelled on the tips of trees. Mama opened the kitchen window and inhaled.

"I just love the sweet smell of lilacs," she said. "Makes a person hopeful."

I wasn't feeling as hopeful, myself. I liked the birds and the sun and the lilacs, but I was too worried about the English homework I never got around to doing the night before. Something more important always got in the way. Mama needed help with supper. Rosa needed a bath. Winnie needed a story. What I might be wishing for or needing never seemed to matter. I'd finally gotten an A on an English test, and that made Mama happy, but I wasn't sure I'd be able to pull it off again. There wasn't too much room in my brain for studying. It was crammed full with worrying about whether Mama was gonna stop fighting with Daddy and let him just keep the boys. On top of all that, I missed Zoomer worse than ever.

Rosa slurped Cocoa Puffs in the chair beside me, and Winnie banged her spoon against the table until it gave us all a headache—even Patrick. He gave Mama a look, and she told Winnie to quit it three times before she got up and finally took the spoon away. Patrick read the newspaper. In between bites of toast, he complained about draft resisters and sissy students who didn't have the guts to go to war.

"They think they can just run away. Go to Canada. Neglect their responsibilities."

Every morning at breakfast, Patrick read the paper and got all riled up. Every evening, he scowled at the TV screen, cussing at the young hippies with long hair and protest signs. Just weeks before, one hundred thousand people had protested in New York City, twenty thousand in San Francisco. Peaceniks, the TV guy called them.

"Bunch of goddamn idiots," Patrick complained.

Mama always said, "They're just kids. Why should they go get killed in an unjust war?"

"Because it's their duty," Patrick always griped.

She poured Patrick more coffee and shook her head, but she didn't say anything about the protesters or war or boys being killed in the jungles far away from their mamas. When the phone rang, she jumped. We didn't get many calls. We didn't know many people in Madison. I think Patrick expected they'd be friends with Jack and Annie, but it never happened. Mama was still mad at Jack for that lawyer he got them, and she always found some excuse when Patrick urged her to call Annie and meet for coffee. I worried the phone might be my teacher, Mrs. Benson, calling to rat on me. The day before, I had hit Timmy Johnson during recess. He spit a big wad of gross gunk at Julie Farley after she wouldn't let him play kickball. Even though we never became best friends, Julie still let me play with her and the other girls. So I wanted to stick up for her when Timmy was being mean.

Or maybe it was Mrs. Anderson reminding Mama that our rent was late again. My stomach settled a bit when Mama said, "Hi, Stella."

It was my aunt. Mama's sister. Those two hadn't talked since we left Pisa back in March, two months before. They used to be close until Mama fell in love with Patrick. That ticked Aunt Stella off. Mama said Stella just didn't understand what true love was all about.

"What's up?" Mama asked in her fake, cheery voice.

"Bad news? What? What's wrong, Stella?" From how Mama's voice rose, I knew Stella wasn't sharing beauty parlor gossip—making fun of Mrs. Scalamassi's bad perm or Mrs. Parma's no-good brother-in-law.

Patrick noticed, too. He set down his newspaper and walked over to Mama. "Oh, my god, Stella. No! No, no, no!!!" She threw the phone at Patrick, but it slipped from his hands and clanged to the kitchen floor. Mama screamed. My skin prickled. It was the saddest, eeriest sound I have ever heard.

"Marie, what is it?" Patrick held Mama to his chest. "Calm down, Marie. Calm down."

Mama pushed herself free and shrieked again. Her screams turned into sobs as she slammed her fists against her chest, her face, her head, shouting, "My god, my god! My son, my son!"

The more Mama yelled and pounded her chest, the more I shivered. Rosa's face was a tangle of worries. She hugged her stuffed dog, Binkie, like there wasn't ever gonna be any space between them again. Winnie climbed out of her chair, still sucking her yellow blanket. She rushed to Mama, reaching for her. Mama pushed her away. Mama raced around the living room like her legs were on fire.

Winnie cried, "Mama. Mama."

Patrick hollered, "For god's sake, Peanut, take care of your sister."

I couldn't move. Mama was gonna burst; I could feel it in my stomach. Rosa knew it, too. She and Binkie hid behind the couch. That's what she used to do back home when things got real bad. Too many times, I'd see the bottoms of Rosa's sneakers poking out from behind our brown sofa.

Winnie threw herself on the couch and bawled. Snot dripped out of her nose and down her pouting lips. I knew I should wipe her face, but I was gonna wet my pants if I moved.

"For Christ's sake, Peanut, you're useless," Patrick yelled before he picked up the phone.

"Stella, what the hell's going on?" He tried to sound cool, but he paced the kitchen, rubbing the back of his neck the whole time. Aunt Stella must have told him what she'd already told Mama 'cuz his knees caved in. He slouched into a kitchen chair. His mouth flung open. I stared at the bumpy edges of his back teeth.

"Goddamn," he moaned. "Goddamnit."

Mama wailed, pushing something ugly from the bottom of her heart. I shoved my hands between my legs to keep my pee from leaking out. Mama exploded. Sobs and moans landed like ashes all over us.

Patrick covered his face. I could have sworn he was crying. He wiped something from his eyes as he stared at the kitchen floor, talking softly to Aunt Stella. When he hung up, Patrick wagged a finger in my face and seethed, "I'll deal with you later." He hurried to comfort Mama, but it didn't help. She was howling herself sick.

I wanted to shout *What happened? Who got hurt?* but

the words stuck in my throat. My eyes jumped back and forth between Mama and Patrick. When would they tell us what was going on? I had to pee something terrible by then, but my legs wouldn't let me leave the room. Patrick didn't give up. Mama turned away from him. He grabbed her shoulders, trying to bring her back to him. Finally, finally, she gave in and let him hold her.

"Marie, you can't blame yourself. Paulie wouldn't let them come. You know that. We'll get through this, honey, we will."

She wailed over and over again, "Joey, Joey, Joey. Ohmigod, what have I done?"

A shiver hit me hard. That's why Stella had called. Was Joey hurt? Or sick? Was it an accident?

Mama sobbed, "My baby's gone. My baby's gone."

My knees buckled. I hit the floor. Splinters of me flew all over. Pieces of my eyes and hair and mouth hit the ceiling; chunks of teeth, skin, and bones skidded across the floor. Whole chunks of my heart splattered against the worn-out furniture. I tried to scoop up my mess, but it was too slippery. My pants were soaked with pee.

"Regina!" Patrick ordered. "Get your butt off the floor, and take care of Winnie."

This time his yelling worked. I looked at Winnie still sobbing on the couch, and I don't know how, but I managed to walk over and pick her up. She arched her back and kicked me, but I held her tight. Finally, Winnie gave in. She slumped into my lap. She didn't even care that my pants were wet and smelly. I hoisted Winnie into my arms and stood up. I tapped the soles of Rosa's sneakers with my foot. She was still behind the couch, her shoes poking out, betraying her hiding place.

"Come on, let's go," I whispered.

Rosa wiggled her way out. Her eyes were puffy and red.

Binkie's face was sopping wet. "Where are we going?" she asked. "Back to Daddy?"

"Naw," I said, trying to steady my voice. "Just to our bedroom. Let's go play cards."

"Don't we got to go to school?" Rosa demanded. "I got kindergarten. Mrs. Forrest will be real mad if I skip."

"Your teacher will understand," I assured her. "Patrick or Mama will write you a note. And if they don't, I'll forge one. Don't worry."

In our room, I tucked both my sisters into Rosa's bed. I peeled off my peed-on clothes, climbed into my own bed, and pulled the covers over my head. Joey's empty eyes stared back at me. I kicked off my sheets and crawled into Rosa's bed. "Peanut," Rosa complained, "you're squishing me!" I shivered, and she moved closer to Winnie, making room for all three of us. I reached my arm across the covers and held tight to my sisters' skinny arms. "I wanna go home," Rosa cried. I kissed her forehead. Winnie whimpered and laid her head on Rosa's shoulder. Mama's wild sorrow had gotten to all of us. We stuck our fingers in our ears to drown out Mama's pleading, "God, give me back my Joey. I'll do anything. Anything! Give me back my Joey."

I didn't want to believe that my brother was dead. I bargained all sorts of horrible things with the Blessed Virgin. *Please make him just be in the hospital,* I prayed. *Just chop his leg off. Or let him lose an eye or a finger.* He'd never be able to play baseball again, but at least he'd be alive. *Kill Patrick instead.* Anything to make it not be true.

I hated myself for all the times I had wished Joey dead. He could be such a sassy smart aleck, teasing me for no good reason, getting on my case about me being Mama's favorite. He'd pull my braid or pinch my arm. Sometimes, he'd steal my Barbie doll and drop her out of his second-story bedroom window, yelling "Bombs away!" as she plopped head first into the dirt and stones below. Once, he even buried her in the side yard, under the maple tree. He made a fake tombstone out of cardboard and printed Peanut Giovanni R.I.P. on it. He was just plain jealous, and I knew it. But that's what made him maddest of all. I had something over him, something that could hurt him. So he always tried to get me first. It was a kind of stinging that never went away.

"Peanut, what happened to Joey?" Rosa asked.

"I don't know."

"Tell me!" Rosa demanded. "Is he in the hospital? Did he get hit by a car? Did Danny do something to him? Or Daddy?"

Rosa was smarter than I thought. All those times she looked like she wasn't paying attention, she was storing up everything she heard. Even from behind the couch, she saw it all, with a second set of eyes that didn't have anything to do with her real eyes. But I wasn't gonna budge on this one.

"Rosa, remember when we used to drive home from Cayuga after saying good-bye to Patrick, and Mama would get all sad and quiet? She'd stay like that for a couple of days. It was like living with a zombie. Remember how she'd never pay attention to things, never even answer questions, even if you asked a million times?"

"Yeah," Rosa said. "I hated that."

"Well, I'm trying to tell ya that something's happened to Joey. I don't know for sure what, but I do know that Mama's gonna be a zombie for a long while. I'm just telling you so you can get ready. Patrick's gonna have his hands full making Mama happy again."

Rosa nodded slowly. "Will Patrick get grouchy, too?" she asked.

"Probably."

"Maybe Daddy will let us come back home now," Rosa

said. "Maybe just until Mama feels better. That couldn't hurt Mama, could it?"

"She ain't gonna let us go anywhere," I said. "We're stuck here for good."

"Why?" Rosa whined. "Why can't we go home, just until Mama gets better? I wanna see Daddy. I wanna see Joey and Danny. And Zoomer."

Her fussing made me itchy inside. I lit into her, "Rosa, we just can't, that's all. Quit asking so many questions."

Rosa slapped my arm. She grabbed Binkie and snuggled closer to Winnie. My head ached. I hadn't meant to hurt her feelings. I blurted out the first thing I could think of, to make it all better.

"Maybe we can have pizza tonight." It was Rosa's favorite. She sniffed back tears and wiped her nose against Binkie's fuzzy head.

"I don't want pizza," she insisted. "I want Daddy."

"Okay," I said. "But you got to be patient. This stuff takes time."

The Funeral

The next morning, Mama sat us girls down to tell us what had happened to Joey.

"There's been an accident," she said, before her voice stuck in her throat and she couldn't talk anymore. She raced out of the room.

Patrick watched her go and shook his head. He took a deep breath and let it out slow and long. "Your brother Joey isn't going to live with us in Madison."

"How come?" Rosa asked.

Patrick swallowed hard. He reached for Winnie. "Come here, honey." My baby sister crawled into his lap, and he hugged her. "Girls," he started up again. "There's no good way to tell you this . . . Joey's dead."

Rosa buried her face in Binkie's chest and sobbed. A weird chill shivered up my back.

"How'd he die?"

Patrick ignored my question. "Your Mama is going back

for his funeral. She'll be gone for a few days. You girls will stay here with me."

I tugged at his sleeve. "How did Joey die?"

"He's gone, Peanut. That's all you need to know."

"I wanna go to his funeral, too."

"No."

"Why not? He's my brother."

"We can't afford to fly everybody back. I'm sorry. We just don't have the money right now."

He wasn't mean about it. I wanted to offer him my entire savings—the five dollars and spare change I had hid away for a rainy day—but I knew it wasn't near enough for a plane ticket.

"Your mother is very upset," Patrick continued. "It'll be tough around here for a while. But if we all stick together, we'll be all right. I want you to watch your sisters, Peanut. Go play. Your mama and I have to call Stella to arrange things."

I did what he asked, but my sisters and I stayed in the living room, close enough to hear what they were saying to my aunt. From the sour look on Mama's face, I could tell she didn't like what she was hearing. She said, "I don't give a good goddamn what those small-minded bigots think, Stella. He's my son."

She hung up and ran off to the bathroom. Patrick followed. I did, too.

"What did Stella say?" Patrick asked.

"My face isn't welcome in Pisa," Mama sobbed. "I took off . . . left the boys. People are mad. Even madder now that Joey . . ." Mama caught a glimpse of me out of the corner of her eye and cried harder.

"For Christ's sake, Peanut," Patrick hissed. "Can't you leave us alone?" He slammed the bathroom door in my face. I leaned against the wall, listening to Mama's shaky voice leak through the plaster. "They can't blame you for what happened, Marie."

"Stella doesn't. It's just those bastards." Mama's voice rose. "They got nothing better to do than tear me to shreds."

"Who, Marie?"

"Scalamassi and Parma. Shooting their mouths off. Stella ran into them at the grocery store. 'She's got a lot of gall even thinking about showing up,' they said. 'She's a rotten mother. Should be ashamed of herself.'"

"So, didn't Stella defend you?" Patrick raised his voice.

"She lit into them. But they were just saying what every other busybody in town is thinking. Stella's right. They'll crucify me if I go back now."

"Maybe it *would* be better to stay here."

It was quiet for a second; then Mama opened the bathroom door. "I can't believe you'd take her side," she screeched. I hurried into the living room before she could catch me eavesdropping.

That night at supper, Mama loaded our plates with spaghetti and announced, "I'm going. Joey's my baby. I'm not gonna let anybody keep me away." There was fire in her eyes, and I liked how brave she looked. She wasn't scared of those busybody ladies or Stella or Patrick. By the time I swallowed my last bite of macaroni, things had changed. Mama shook her head at some imaginary face on the wall and cried, "I can't go back there! They'll eat me alive."

She waffled back and forth like that the rest of the night. She made us all tired. Patrick got grumpier and bossier. I wanted to shout, *Mama, pick one way—go or stay.*

"Why don't you come with me?" Mama reached for Patrick's hand. "That would help a lot."

"Have you lost your mind?" Patrick asked. "They'd probably lock both of us up. Or stone us to death. The more I think about the whole idea, the more I think you should stay home."

"I could take Peanut with me."

Patrick's lips tightened. "No."

"Why?"

"It's ludicrous, Marie. You traipsing off to Pisa with her in tow. I can see the two of you now, draped in black in the front pew. Evil-eyed neighbors stabbing you in the back through the whole funeral Mass."

"Why should I give in to those bastards . . ."

"It's not safe for you to go. Besides, how'd I manage here if Peanut went, too?"

"I'll go alone, then."

"No, Marie. I said no, and I mean it."

"But, Patrick . . ."

"My decision is final. You'll just stir up trouble going back there, and you'll be worse off than before."

"He's my Joey . . . I can't . . ." Mama started to cry.

"There's nothing you can do to save him now, Marie. He's gone. Going to his funeral won't bring him back." Mama looked at Patrick as if she didn't believe those words were pouring from his mouth. She started to protest again, insisting that she had a right as Joey's mother to be at his funeral, but Patrick stopped her. "I've decided, Marie. Your place is here with the living."

On the day of the funeral, Mama didn't get out of bed.

I made a pot of coffee for Patrick and some toast for me and my sisters. Patrick scowled, "Peanut, if I catch either you or Rosa bothering your mother today, there's going to be hell to pay."

He stayed home from work that day. He corrected papers at the dining room table. He called our principal and told him there was a family emergency. We wouldn't be at school for a few days. I would have given up chocolate cake for a whole month to go to school. Anything would have been better than hearing Mama wailing all morning.

Rosa and I hung out on the front porch. We played Go Fish and Candy Land while Winnie played with her Barbie. In the afternoon, when Winnie took a nap, Rosa and I asked if we could go outside. Patrick grumbled, "Don't go too far. I need you to watch Winnie when she wakes up."

We sat on the curb, and Rosa told me she and Binkie were sick and tired of this whole mess.

"Patrick scares me, and Mama's too sad. I'm gonna get back to Daddy if it's the last thing I do," she insisted.

It wasn't make-believe. She said she thought about it before she fell asleep every night and first thing every morning. The night before, she'd dreamed she and Binkie could fly. They soared over the top of our apartment, over the trees, past the golden arms of the lady on the capitol statue, further past Lake Mendota and the outskirts of Madison. They flew past hills and towns and states all the way back to Danny and Daddy.

"You can't just flap your arms and get there," I told her. "You've got to take a plane or a bus or a car or a train."

"I know," she sassed. "I'm not dumb. I know it's far. But maybe I could walk."

"It would take you forever." I said it real bossy, so she'd get that idea out of her head. "Besides, Mama and Patrick would come find you right away. Or they'd send the cops."

It was my duty to tell her the truth. There was no way she'd be able to get back to Pisa on her own. That's the trouble with being a kid. Grown-ups have made it so that there's just some stuff you really need them for. I made her promise me she wouldn't do anything stupid.

She stared at her sneakers and spit at the ground. "I hate being little."

Mama was still holed up in her bedroom when we came back inside. We played with Winnie until suppertime. Patrick made a frozen pizza for dinner. We ate it in the living room with the TV set blaring. More news about the war in Vietnam. Pictures of children with burned faces, whole villages torched by soldiers, people crying, college kids waving angry fists, cops with narrowed eyes. I couldn't sleep at all that night.

The next day, Mama joined us for breakfast. Her face was pale; her hair a mess of brown snarls. She sipped her coffee and stared at her hands. When the phone rang, she jumped. Patrick answered it.

"Hi, Stella," he said. "How'd it go?"

Mama lit a cigarette and waited. Patrick talked to Stella for a while, then asked Mama if she wanted to say anything to her sister. Mama shook her head. Patrick said good-bye to my aunt, hung up the phone, and joined us at the table.

"A lot of people showed up," he told us. "All the kids from Joey's baseball team were there. And his coach. Kids from his ninth grade class. Lots of neighbors. Mr. and Mrs. Brown. Mrs. Marco."

"Was Uncle Tony there?" I asked.

"Yes."

"How about Daddy?" Rosa added.

"Yep. And Danny. Stella said Danny's holding up well."

Mama muttered something under her breath and walked into the kitchen. She slammed a cupboard door and called back to Patrick. "I should have been there. Oh, my poor Danny."

"Marie, he's fine." Patrick went to Mama. He reached for her, but she turned away.

"Paulie's a wreck, though."

"I don't care about that son-of-a-bitch," Mama sulked.

"Okay, honey." Patrick offered his arms again. Mama accepted. "Stella said you would have been proud of Danny. He helped a lot. It was his idea to dress Joey in his baseball uniform. He put Joey's favorite bat and mitt beside the coffin. And set a Mickey Mantle baseball card in Joey's hand."

Mama broke down and started to sob. I slipped outside to forget about that stupid card resting between my brother's cold, white fingers.

For days and days, Mama barely came out of her bedroom. She refused to talk to Aunt Stella when she called to check on her. Every night when Patrick came home from work, he'd kiss Winnie hello, check on Mama, then grab a bottle of wine. He'd plant himself in front of the TV and not move for hours. He'd swear at the news or at some stupid show and drink until the wine was gone. Then he'd get up and open another bottle. He'd call to Winnie, tell her to come sit on his lap. He'd kiss her forehead and say, "I love you. You're the most important thing in the world to me."

Sometimes, he remembered to put a pizza in for supper, and sometimes, he remembered to pull it out before it burned. Plenty of times he'd forget. Smoke would seep out of the oven. Then he'd swear, "Goddamn son-of-a-bitch. Peanut, why can't you keep an eye on that?" Lots of times, we girls ate cereal or toast, so he wouldn't yell so much.

Being mad was one thing. But being mean was worse. He'd pick on Rosa for leaving her Barbie doll clothes all over the couch. It was Winnie's fault, too. They always played together, but Winnie never got blamed. He yelled at me for leaving my sneakers in the hallway and for leaving dirty dishes in the sink. He even yelled at me for dusting *after* I vacuumed. "Any fool knows you dust first," he scolded.

I'd wait 'til he turned his back, then I'd shoot him a hateful glance, careful so he wouldn't see me. He had a lot on his mind, with Mama being weird and sad, but I hated how he took it out on me and Rosa. He even picked on Binkie. He wouldn't let Rosa bring him to the table.

"Get that dirty thing out of here."

"Mama lets Binkie eat with me," Rosa resisted.

"Well, I'm not your mama," he glared at my sister. "I don't want it at the table. So out it goes."

Everybody had sad eyes those days. Patrick and Rosa, Binkie and me, Mama and Winnie. National Guardsmen and protesting students. Dying marines and TV reporters. Danny's eye were sad, too, probably, if I could have seen his face. Nobody could see Joey's eyes anymore. Or Daddy's. Aunt Stella told Patrick that Daddy had asked permission to stay at the Franciscan monastery in Cayuga. She didn't know when, or if, he'd be back. Daddy was praying that the archbishop would let him become a monk, even though he was married and had kids.

"Your father's a stupid fool," Patrick scoffed.

Danny moved in with Aunt Stella and Uncle Tony. I guessed that Mama would want Danny to come live with us, once she got over being sad about Joey. Especially if the monks let Daddy stay with them forever.

That part worried me a lot. If Daddy really did become a Franciscan, Rosa and me would never be able to live with him. The monks didn't let girls into the monastery. Even if they were someone's daughters. All Rosa's dreams about flying, all her wishing for a plane or a bus ride back home to Pisa would be wasted. More and more each day, I wished I could talk to Zoomer. Crazy things were piling up inside me, and I didn't have anybody to tell them to. Sometimes I'd imagine Joey lying in his coffin, all white and waxy. He wore a sweet smile, like he was relieved that it was over and he wouldn't ever have to hear the fighting again. He wouldn't ever have to wish he could kiss Mama even though her cheek was a thousand miles away from his lips. Mama and Aunt Stella cried because they were sad that Joey died. I cried because I was jealous. He was safe now. Nobody could hurt him anymore.

I promised myself that I would go to the school library. I wanted to look up New York State in the atlas. I had to figure a way to get me and Rosa back home. We could take a Greyhound bus. There had to be one that went to Pisa. I just wasn't sure who I could ask. Or how much it would cost. And I hadn't figured out how to get the money yet. I could sell something, if I had anything worth selling. I could steal it, if I had a gun. I could save my allowance, but that might take forever. I only got fifty cents a week. With the way things were going, I'd have to figure something out. Soon.

When I got home from school the next day, Mama was sitting at the dining room table eating a tuna fish sandwich and reading a letter. Seeing her up surprised me. Her hair was combed, and she smelled good, like lily of the valley bubble bath. She even smiled at me.

"Hi, Peanut."

The Ghost Mother had vanished. A calmer Mama was

swallowing bites of sandwich and wiping mayo from the corners of her mouth. I kissed her cheek and stayed close a second longer, taking a big whiff of her tuna-fishy breath. She wrapped her arm around my waist and gave me a little hug. Her skin felt warm. Oh, how I'd missed her. I kissed her cheek again and sneaked a peak at the letter in her hand. It was from Danny. I recognized his handwriting.

I wiggled away and went to the kitchen to grab a glass of milk and a couple of Vanilla Wafers. Mama slapped the letter down, stood up, and swore. "Goddamnit, Daniel." She pushed her chair back and huffed off to her bedroom, slamming the door behind her.

Rosa poked her head in from the other room. "Is Mama okay?" My sister's eyes were wide with worry.

I didn't answer. My attention wandered to Danny's letter. I knew I shouldn't, but I picked it up. He'd addressed it to Mrs. Marie Giovanni. I was surprised the mailman had delivered it. Nobody here knew Mama by that name. In Madison, people called her Mrs. Shaughnessy, even though Patrick and her weren't really married. I knew it was wrong, but I waved the letter at Rosa. She came to the table, and I read it to her out loud, keeping my voice low so Mama wouldn't hear.

Dear Ma,

I've decided I can't come to Madison. It just wouldn't be right. Joey really wanted to live with you, and I would have gone with him. But that's not gonna happen now. If I came anyway, it would be like rubbing it in his face. It's too hard, Ma. Every day I miss you, and every day I miss Joey. Aunt Stella and Uncle Tony have been real good to me, but they just remind me of Joey and that makes it all worse. I decided to go live with my friend Mrs. Marco. She has a spare room in her house, and she said I could stay with her as long as I needed. Maybe someday I'll feel different about it all. But for now that's the way it is. I'll be all right there. And at least I can go visit Joey at the cemetery.

Take good care of the girls. Oh, yeah, tell Peanut that Mrs. Marco is letting Zoomer stay at her house, too. He's doing okay. She doesn't have to worry about him.

Love,

Danny

I tossed the letter on the table. "Oooh," Rosa sighed.

I was bursting mad. And jealous. My head hurt trying to figure out how Danny got to have MY dog. I put the letter back, just the way Mama had left it.

"Is Danny mad at us, too? Is that why he doesn't want to come live with us?" Rosa asked.

"Naw. He's just sore at Mama. And he misses Joey."

"I miss him, too." Rosa started to cry. "Why'd he have to die?"

"I don't know, Rosa." Tears slipped out of my eyes, but I wiped them away fast. I couldn't cry for Joey. Not now. I didn't want to believe that I'd never see him again.

"Peanut, what are we gonna do now?"

"What do you mean?"

"About getting back to Daddy?"

"I think we got to forget about that, Rosa."

"No, Peanut! You got to call Daddy, tell him to come get us before it's too late."

"We can't, Rosa. Daddy's with those monks."

"Then call Aunt Stella. Maybe she'll help us. Maybe we can live with her."

"That ain't gonna work, either, Rosa. Mama won't let her

sister have her girls. Use your head. We're stuck here. Get used to it."

"No! I hate it here. I hate Patrick. I hate Mama. I hate you for being so stupid, Peanut."

She hurried off, all huffy. I thought about chasing after her, trying to calm her down, but I was too tired. She'd have her fit and get over it. Rosa never stayed mad at me for long. This time, I wanted to help, but it was complicated. I just couldn't see a way out. I still only had five dollars and some change that I'd saved for our getaway bus tickets. We needed a whole lot more than that, I was pretty sure. There was one thing I knew, though. If we did finally get back to Pisa, my first stop was gonna be Mrs. Marco's house. It had been almost three months since I'd hugged Zoomer.

I took a swig of milk and popped another Vanilla Wafer in my mouth. I sucked it and closed my eyes, remembering the closet in my bedroom back home where I used to hide with my dog. For a second, I thought I smelled him. Tears rolled down my face, and I brushed them away. I grabbed a couple more cookies and headed for the front porch.

Crime and Punishment

After Mama got Danny's letter, she and Patrick fought a lot more. It felt like I was back in Pisa with Mama and Daddy chewing each other's heads off.

"You never did want my sons with us," Mama accused.

"That's not true," Patrick hollered. "I just wanted us to settle in first, make sure I found a job, so I could support everybody. It's not easy, you know."

"It ain't easy for me, either," Mama yelled back. "Joey's gone, and Danny won't live with us. You don't know what it's like to be shunned by your own flesh and blood."

"Marie, don't get hysterical. You agreed the boys would come later. I didn't decide that alone. I won't be your scapegoat."

"You son-of-a-bitch!" Mama screamed. "Think you know everything just because you got a big, fancy college education. You don't know shit. You don't have the guts to admit it's your fault Joey's dead."

I thought Patrick was gonna hit Mama. His jaw tightened, and his fists swept past her chin and slammed against the kitchen table instead. "Go to hell, Marie!" he shouted. "If anybody killed Joey, it was you and Paulie. I didn't fuck up your marriage. It was dead long before I ever set foot in Pisa."

Patrick grabbed his keys and left in a huff. His car tires screeched as he peeled away. The house fell quiet with his leaving. Mama muttered under her breath as she shoved pots and pans around in the kitchen. Rosa grabbed Binkie and hid behind the couch for an hour until I fetched her out. I bargained with the Blessed Virgin. *Dear Holy Mother, let Mama give up her silly dreams about making a family with Patrick.* I crossed my fingers and prayed hard. *Please make her ready to go home. We could live with Aunt Stella and Uncle Tony. Just until we found a place of our own. We could even move back into our old house, now that Daddy is at that monastery. Maybe you could even talk Danny into coming home, too. Or at least make him give me back Zoomer. Amen.* My heart beat fast.

Hours went by, and still Patrick hadn't come back. Rosa felt calmer with him gone, too. She and I shared private smiles. Mama had traded in slamming things in the kitchen for pacing around. She smoked Chesterfield after Chesterfield. From time to time, she'd plop down on the couch and flip through a *Family Circle* magazine, but she never rested long. Before supper, she called Patrick's friend Jack. "No, there's nothing wrong," she lied. "I just thought he might have stopped by for a visit. I need him to pick up a box of zitis for supper, that's all. If you see him, Jack, tell him for me, okay?"

We girls ate Cap'n Crunch cereal and toast for supper that night. Mama ate nothing. She watched TV and drank Chianti. Every time she swallowed, I prayed a silent prayer that Patrick would die in a car crash or drown in Lake

Mendota. When she'd swigged the last of the bottle, Mama called Aunt Stella.

"How the hell should I know where he is? No, he didn't leave me any money. Get off my back, Stella. I told you we had a fight. He left all pissed off."

My sisters and I went to bed early. Mama stayed up for a long time, waiting. Voices from the late-night TV movie lulled me to sleep. The next morning, I found Mama curled up on the couch, fast asleep, hugging her empty Chianti bottle. I checked the driveway, and Patrick's car was still gone. I hurried back to my bedroom to tell Rosa.

"He didn't come home, he didn't come home," I whispered, nudging her awake. She cracked open one eye.

"Are you sure?"

"Yep."

Rosa jumped out of bed and danced around the bedroom. "He's gone, he's gone."

She woke up Winnie. "You silly," Winnie giggled. She crawled out of bed and twirled around Rosa. I felt like celebrating, too. I spun and kicked, pretending I was back in Pisa with my best friend, Amelia, playing June Taylor Dancers on her patio. I smiled, remembering how Amelia's curly hair used to bounce around her sparkling eyes.

Without warning, Mama yelled from the doorway. "What in hell are you three doing in here? Trying to wake the dead?"

She crossed her arms over her chest. Her cold face froze our smiles. Binkie slipped from Rosa's arms and tumbled to the floor. Rosa joined him. Winnie hurried back to bed and buried her face in the covers.

"Sorry, Mama, we were just playing."

I didn't want her to know that Rosa and I were having a going-away party for Patrick.

"Well, pipe down," she snipped. "I've got a huge head-ache."

"Okay," I apologized.

"Sorry," Rosa said.

Mama walked away.

"We better get dressed and pick stuff up in here," I said to Rosa.

We got changed in a hurry. Then Rosa helped me dress Winnie. I handed our little sister her ratty yellow blanket. "Wait for us before you go watch cartoons."

"Hurry," she pouted.

"Let's make the bed—quick, Rosa." We snapped the sheets tight and pulled the blankets over them, tucking the corners in as fast as we could. "Not too bad," I said, looking at the job we'd done. On a good day, it wouldn't pass Mama's inspection, but she wouldn't be checking too closely with her sour-puss mood. I let the messy edges be.

"Let's go have some Cap'n Crunch."

"We ate that for supper last night, Peanut," Rosa complained. "I want somethin' else."

"How 'bout Cocoa Puffs?" I offered.

Rosa pouted.

"I'd make you waffles," I insisted. "But I don't know how."

"Okay, okay," Rosa gave in.

"Don't be a crab," I scolded.

"Quit fightin'," Winnie whined. She clapped her hands over her ears.

We found Mama sitting at the kitchen table, sipping coffee, and smoking a cigarette. I grabbed three cereal bowls and a box of Cocoa Puffs and set them on the table.

Rosa stared at Mama, then looked at me. "I wanna eat in the other room."

"Me, too," Winnie mimicked.

"Is that okay, Mama?" I asked.

She nodded as she crushed what was left of one Chesterfield and lit up another. "Pour me another cup of coffee first."

I filled her cup and then put Winnie's breakfast on the coffee table. "Sit here," I whispered. "Be careful. Don't make a big mess."

We girls watched "Bugs Bunny" and "Tom and Jerry" cartoons as we ate. Rosa laughed so hard she spit milk on the floor. Winnie giggled. I grabbed Rosa's cereal bowl so she wouldn't spill the whole thing.

Mama didn't even notice. She stayed at the kitchen table, smoking and drinking her coffee, wearing her zombie face. She stared straight ahead at nothing. Before "Tom and Jerry" was over, I heard the apartment door open. Patrick stepped inside. I held my breath. His hair was all messy, and his shirt was wrinkled. Mama didn't look at him, but her mouth relaxed, and she closed her eyes.

Patrick sat next to her. She sucked a long drag off her Chesterfield and blew smoke at the ceiling. "I went to Lake Mendota," he said. "I stared at the water until it got dark. I thought about taking off, heading to Minnesota or the Dakotas, but the thought of never seeing Winnie or you again was worse than all the fighting. I slept in the car. When I woke up, I came home." Mama sized him up out of the corner of her eye. After a long minute, she squeezed his hand. "I love you, Marie."

She led him to the couch, held him in her arms. They both cried. I couldn't look at Rosa. If I saw the disappointment in her eyes, I'd start crying. She and I were back where we started. The Cocoa Puffs soured in my stomach.

"These last few weeks have been so damn hard," Patrick said. He pulled back from Mama's hug and searched her face. "I don't know how to reach you anymore, Marie. When you go away like that, you shut the door and I can't get to you. I don't know whether to scream or kick the walls in. Don't push me away. We're in this together. It doesn't make any sense, otherwise."

"I can't handle this alone," Mama said. "Losing Joey was the hardest thing ever. It's like somebody cut off my arm. A part of me is missing, and it won't ever grow back."

She cried harder then, and he held her until she got quiet. She blew her nose and called, "Come here, girls." An invisible cord pulled me to her. The part of me that wanted to run to the other end of the apartment lost out. Her tugging was too strong.

Winnie ran to Patrick. Rosa stared at me and Mama a second before joining us. Mama put her arms around us both and squeezed tight. The five of us huddled on the couch. "We're a family now," Mama said. "We stick together through thick and thin."

"That's right," Patrick agreed. He kissed Winnie and smiled at me and Rosa. It wasn't his best effort, but I grinned back to make Mama happy. Rosa didn't. She rested her head on Mama's shoulder and asked when we were gonna eat lunch.

"Didn't you just eat breakfast?" Mama asked.

"Yeah."

"So what?" Patrick interrupted. "I haven't eaten since yesterday. I'm hungry. Let's go to McDonald's." He beamed at us girls.

Winnie clapped her hands. "French fries!"

"That's a great idea," Mama said. "Peanut, Rosa, don't you think so?"

"Yep," I lied. Normally a trip to McDonald's *was* a real treat. I just didn't want to go with Patrick.

Rosa said nothing, but Mama and Patrick were so overjoyed at their reunion, they didn't notice my sister's pout or my sad eyes.

"Give me a second," Patrick said. "I want to wash up and put on some clean clothes."

"Peanut, get your sisters ready," Mama told me before she dashed off. "I've got to brush my teeth and comb my hair."

"Put your sneakers on, Rosa."

"I don't wanna go," she whined.

"It won't be so bad. You like McDonald's."

"I hate McDonald's, and I hate you, too." She ran to our bedroom.

"Rosa, listen!" I slipped in behind her and closed the door so Mama and Patrick wouldn't hear.

"We'll figure something out. You gotta trust me. I'm trying to save money to buy us some bus tickets to get back to Daddy. But I only got a little over five dollars so it's gonna take a while. You gotta be patient. And quit being so crabby. I don't like Patrick being back any more than you do, but I don't take it out on you, do I?"

She scowled. "I'm sorry. But I wanna go home. I can't wait forever."

"I can't, either. Just play along for a while. Make believe you're happy here. Then maybe Mama and Patrick won't be so wigged out all the time. Okay?"

"Only if Patrick stops picking on Binkie."

I nodded, knowing nothing made her madder than somebody being mean to her puppy.

We ate burgers, French fries, and chocolate malts at McDonald's. Then Mama and Patrick took us to the park. They took turns pushing Winnie on the swings. Rosa and I watched from a bench nearby.

"Maybe you could swipe some money from Patrick's wallet when he goes to sleep tonight," Rosa whispered to me.

"What for?"

"The bus tickets."

"Stealing's not right, Rosa. I ain't gonna do it. The Blessed Mother would get real pissed, and we'd end up in hell if the bus got in an accident and we died."

"He's got a bunch of money," Rosa urged. "I saw it when he paid for lunch. He won't miss it."

"No deal, Rosa." I was tempted, but it was a bigger sin than I'd ever committed. I'd lied, and I'd talked in church plenty of times, but I'd never killed nobody, and I'd never stolen anything. Those were mortal sins. Only really bad kids did that stuff. The other stuff the priest could forgive you with just a few Hail Marys and maybe an Our Father. For mortal sins, you had to say novenas and junk like that, and I wasn't gonna risk getting on God's bad side.

"You're such a chicken, Peanut. Is that how come you got such a stupid nickname?"

"Shut up, brat." I slapped Rosa's arm and joined Mama and Patrick.

Rosa stayed put, kicking her feet against the park bench. She was hatching a plan, and I worried what kind of ideas she was getting into her head. But I was sore at her for being mean about my name, so I tried not to care. All the way home in the car, she wouldn't look at me. I tried to make up five times, but she was set on being mad. I gave up and stared out the window. I figured she'd get over it when she was ready.

Later that evening, after Winnie had gone to bed, the rest of us watched the "Jackie Gleason Show." Mama and

Patrick were both in a good mood for a change. During a commercial, Patrick went to the bathroom, and I got up to get some pop. Rosa got up, too. I thought she was gonna follow me to the kitchen, but she didn't. I poured her a glass anyway. Then I heard her scream.

"OUCH! You're hurting my arm!"

"That's not all I'll hurt if I ever catch you doing something like this again!"

I heard a loud thwack. Mama jumped. So did I.

"What's going on?" Mama called out.

Patrick dragged Rosa by the arm and hauled her and Binkie into the living room. Her dog's soft legs nearly scraped the floor.

"I caught her red-handed," Patrick told Mama. He waved his wallet at us.

"Rosa!" Mama was shocked.

Rosa's face was filled with panic, but there was no way to rescue her. She'd gone and done it. Now she was in for a wicked punishment. I could see it in Patrick's eyes. She'd given him the ammunition he'd been waiting for. He went crazy. He spanked her butt. But that didn't satisfy him. He slapped her legs and her arms and the back of her head, too. His palm came down against the edge of her cheek and slipped across her eye, catching the curve of her nose. "You little thief," he shouted as he hit her, over and over.

"Make him stop, Mama!" I hollered. "Make him stop!"

Rosa screamed and cried. She tried to cover her face with Binkie, but Patrick ripped him away and tossed him far from Rosa's reach. She scrambled to escape, but he held tight to her shirt and pinned her to the floor. "You're gonna learn to respect me," Patrick barked. "I'm not a weak-kneed wimp like your father." He smacked her hard. Red welts rose on her skin.

Mama didn't move. She stared at Patrick with stone eyes, mouth open as if she meant to shout but wasn't able to.

I nudged her, trying to loosen whatever glued her in place, but she wouldn't budge. "Mama!" I felt frantic. "Mama!"

"Patrick!" Mama finally screamed.

Winnie cried from the bedroom.

"Peanut, go see about your baby sister," Mama ordered. But I couldn't. I had to stay, to help Rosa.

Patrick didn't let up. He spilled his anger onto Rosa's skinny body, slapping and hitting, boxing her legs and arms. I rushed at him, kicking his legs, trying to get him off my sister, but he pushed me away. "Stay out of this Peanut, or you'll be next."

Mama rushed at me, hollering, "I told you to check on Winnie!"

"Help Rosa!" I demanded.

"Winnie!" Mama yelled at me, pointing at the bedroom. My eyes filled with Mama's fear. I stared back at her, but I didn't move. She swallowed hard, bit her lip, and finally pushed herself between Patrick and Rosa. "Patrick, stop. Stop. She's just a child."

I don't know if she reached some part of him that had sense left or if he was just too tired to keep going, but his arms fell limp at his sides, and he stopped. He turned away and sat down by the window. Rosa lay on the floor, curled in on herself, her creamy legs all pink and purple and full of bumps. I grabbed Binkie and hurried to her. Red trickled from her nose.

"Mama!" I screamed, pointing at the blood.

"Dear God."

Mama was shaking real bad now, but Rosa was shaking worse. I shot ugly glances at Patrick. I was afraid he'd come after me, too, but I hated him so much right then, I didn't care if he killed me. All Rosa had wanted was a few bucks to get back to her daddy. Patrick didn't have to beat her up. My sister crawled into Mama's arms, still crying. Blood dripped from her nose. I grabbed a washcloth and some ice and made a detour into the bedroom to check on Winnie. "Everything's okay, sweetie," I lied. "Just go back to sleep." I tucked her ragged blanket under her arm and pulled the covers tight, kissing her forehead. I heard her whimper as I left the bedroom.

In the living room, Mama was checking Rosa's face and arms and legs.

"Take her to the doctor," I pleaded.

"No," Mama whispered. "Nothing's broken. She just needs some tenderness."

Patrick stood by. A dazed, empty look washed over his face. He stared at his swollen hands. Most of his blows had landed on Rosa's backside, but the red slap marks and bruises on her legs and her face were bad. She was gonna be sore for a long while. I wished so hard it had been me who'd taken the money. I could have fought back better. I was almost eleven, taller and stronger than Rosa. She was only six years old.

Mama carried Rosa to the couch. She watched Patrick from the corner of her eye as she passed.

A knock on our apartment door made all of us jump. "Go answer it, Peanut," Mama ordered. I opened it to find Mr. Anderson's big blue eyes staring down at me.

"Is everything all right, Red?" He searched my face for an explanation.

"Yeah," I lied. "My sister just fell down. Everything's okay. Good night."

I closed the door, and Mama said, "Good girl." Patrick smiled, and I felt sick.

"I'm sorry, Marie," Patrick said. His voice slipped out of a deep place, all soft and sorrowful. "I don't know what came over me."

Patrick crouched down next to Mama and Rosa. "I didn't mean it," he said. "I just went crazy. I'm sorry. It will never happen again. I promise." He bent closer to kiss Rosa, but she cried out and buried her face in Mama's chest.

"Hush, honey," Mama tried to calm her. "I'm gonna clean Rosa's face and then put her to bed."

I followed her. I didn't want to be alone with Patrick. I never wanted to be alone with him again. I believed he was sorry, but I knew he'd do it again, if something ticked him off in just the right way. Something me or Rosa did. We'd have to be extra, extra careful now.

"Peanut, check on Winnie," Mama told me.

"I already did."

"Do it again. I need you to help out here. Stay in the bedroom with your baby sister."

I obeyed. Winnie lay shivering and crying under her bedcovers. I crawled in next to her and held her. "Shussh, honey. Everything's all right."

I snuggled with Winnie until Mama tucked Rosa in. "Leave the light on," Rosa pleaded.

"Sure, honey," Mama agreed before she kissed us all good night. "Get some rest."

When she closed our bedroom door, I crawled out of Winnie's bunk bed and knelt beside Rosa.

"Are you okay?" I whispered.

She didn't say a word, just cried soft and low.

"I'm real sorry," I told her. "I tried to get Mama to help. I kicked him, too, trying to make him stop. I won't let it happen again, I promise. I'll kill him first. I swear, I will."

She grabbed my hand and squeezed it. "Take me home to Daddy, Peanut." Her voice was as swollen as the shiner under her right eye.

Search & Rescue

When I woke up the next morning, Rosa's bed was empty. Her pajamas lay in a heap on the floor, and Binkie was nowhere to be found. I hoped my sister was out in the kitchen, eating Cap'n Crunch. But I knew it wasn't true. I got up and checked. She wasn't at the table. I looked behind the couch, but no luck. I checked the bathroom and the front porch. She wasn't in any of those places, either.

Rosa had done it. She had run away. Patrick slapping her last night just made it happen a whole lot sooner than she or I had figured on. I didn't blame her. I would have taken off, too, if he had hit me like that. I hated the thought of my sister out there, in the big city, all alone. And I hated the thought of Mama going berserk when she found out Rosa had ditched.

Mama wouldn't like it if I ditched, too. But there were some things she didn't understand. Like how it was for Rosa and me living in Madison with Mama and Patrick. I felt bad for thinking it, but I was mad that Mama hadn't stopped

Patrick, sooner, last night. My mind couldn't shake the picture of Rosa's swollen eye. Half of my heart kept yelling Mama's name, and the other half kept tugging at me to remember my sister. This time Rosa won. I had to find her. I'd promised to help her get back to Pisa. Now that she'd gone and left without me, I figured I'd better hop to it if I was going to make good on my word. I couldn't stay in Madison without Rosa. I'd go crazy. I'd die, just like Joey.

I had to think fast to get out of the apartment before Mama or Patrick woke up. I rushed back to my room and ripped off my pajamas, quickly but quietly. I didn't want to wake Winnie. I didn't need her getting in my way. I pulled on a T-shirt and some pants and grabbed my sweater from the floor where I'd tossed it the night before. I tiptoed back to the kitchen, to make me and Rosa some sandwiches. I was too late. Mama was at the counter, still in her bathrobe, making coffee.

"Is Rosa up yet?" she asked through a yawn.

I panicked. I didn't want to rat on my sister, but Mama would find out sooner or later. I eyed the door, wishing I had the guts to just tear off down the stairs. I was three steps from freedom, but I couldn't move.

"Peanut?" Mama asked. "Is something wrong?"

I swallowed hard. "Rosa's gone, Mama."

"What do you mean?"

"She ran away." I took a deep breath and waited for her to fall apart.

"Ran away? She's just a little girl. How could she run away?"

Mama stared at me with a curious look on her face, as if she couldn't understand what I had just said. Slowly, her eyes cleared. She set the coffeepot on the counter, pushed past me, and rushed to our bedroom. She flung back the covers on Rosa's bed, searching for a sign of my sister's skinny legs, her bruised arms. She opened the closet, rummaging through our clothes, shoving boxes around. She hurried to the living room and tore up the couch cushions, throwing pillows all over, looking for Rosa in places she was way too big to hide. In a panic, she raced to her bedroom and shook Patrick awake.

"She's gone!" Mama shouted.

"Who?" Patrick wiped the sleep from his eyes and propped himself up in bed. "Who's gone? What do you mean?"

"Rosa. She ran away," Mama burst into tears.

Patrick jumped out of bed, fetched his wallet, and rifled through it, counting his money. "It's all here. She can't be far."

"We've got to call the cops," Mama cried.

"No, Marie. We should try to find her first."

"We don't know when she took off, or where to look," Mama insisted.

"Peanut—where'd she go?" Patrick grilled me.

I shrugged my shoulders. He glared at me, trying to force me to tell, but I kept quiet, and he turned his attention back to Mama.

I smelled a fight brewing. It would be a while before they'd calm down enough to even start to figure out how to find Rosa. While they were quarreling, I sneaked back into my room and broke open my Snow White bank. All my clanging and Mama and Patrick's arguing woke up Winnie.

"Peanut," she complained.

"It's too early to get up," I whispered. "Go back to sleep."

"I don't wanna," she sassed. She crawled out of bed and left the room.

I slipped my life savings—five one-dollar bills and sixty-three cents—into my pocket and rushed back to the kitchen to make peanut butter and jelly sandwiches for me and

Rosa. I slapped Peter Pan crunchy on four slices of Wonder bread, slopped on some grape jelly, and shoved the stuff into a paper bag.

"I want some, too," Winnie insisted.

I snatched one out of the bag and handed it to her. "Go watch TV, now."

I slapped another sandwich together and slipped it into the paper sack. I grabbed my jacket and Rosa's from the hall closet. It was only May. It'd be cold by dark. I just hoped I could find my sister by then. I had a hunch about where she might be, and I'd already made up my mind that if Mama and Patrick caught me before I got out the door, I wouldn't tell them if they asked. I wanted Rosa to get away.

I tucked our coats under my arm and ran down the steps, through the backyard, past the woods behind our apartment, past the creek, and into the next bunch of woods. I ran hard and fast until I hit the school yard. When I got to the edge of the playground, I scrambled down the hill to the river. I was almost at Rosa's secret place. I knew about it because she took me there one day when I was missing Zoomer. She'd said the trees would help. She was right. Rosa's special spot was set in the middle of a grove of birches. Nearby were two speckled rocks she liked to sit on. She'd go to those trees sometimes after Mama and Patrick had a fight. She'd spend the whole afternoon there.

I searched and searched until I spied the rocks, a ways off, next to the birches. I tore off over the field. I ran fast again. The sack of peanut butter and jelly sandwiches flapped against my arm. When I got to the spot, Rosa was nowhere in sight. I sat down to catch my breath. Where else could she be? I stared at the ground, thinking, then I noticed some Oreo crumbs next to a leaf. And an orange peel. Rosa's favorite snack. The peel was fresh. My heart raced. I stood up and called her name, softly, so only she could hear.

"Rosa. Rosa. It's me, Peanut. It's okay. I'm alone."

I waited for the wind to carry my message. In a few minutes, Rosa poked her head out from behind a tall birch tree. Her eye was still swollen, and her hair was messy with leaves and twigs. She clutched Binkie. Other than the bruises from last night, she looked all right.

"Peanut," she cried. "Don't let them take me back to Mama and Patrick."

"I won't, Rosa. I've come to run away with you. We're gonna go back to Zoomer and Daddy and Danny."

"Promise? You said you didn't have enough money."

"I know. But I'll get us there somehow."

My teacher, Mrs. Benson, had just finished reading *The Adventures of Huckleberry Finn* to my class. If that Huck boy could float a raft down the Mississippi, I knew I could get me and Rosa back to Pisa.

"Come on," I said. "We gotta hurry before Mama sends Patrick or the cops to find us."

She took my hand, and we were off. We hiked for a long time, until the woods ended. We found ourselves in a part of Madison I'd never been to before. There were lots of small shops and houses on tight, busy streets. People were rushing all over the place. A man with a newspaper tucked under his arm nearly knocked us over to get to the bus stop. A woman in a navy blue raincoat smiled at us, then quickly looked away. Two dogs followed us past the bakery, sniffing at our bag of sandwiches.

"Get out of here," I ordered. My legs were sore from all the walking, so I led Rosa to a small park across the street from a gas station. I'd noticed a telephone booth in the parking lot, near the gas pumps. I had it in my mind to call Daddy and tell him to come get us. But I didn't know the phone number at the monastery. I was trying to remember how to call long distance for information. I needed more time to think. "Let's sit by the fountain and eat our sandwiches," I told Rosa.

"Good, I'm real hungry," she said.

Rosa bit into the soft bread. Grape jelly squirted down her chin. She wiped her face clean, then looked at me with a kind of hope. Even her puffy, purple eyes believed I could get us home. I had to try. I ate my sandwich and thought for a bit. "Stay put until I get back," I said to my sister. "And if you see any cops, hide behind a tree or something." Rosa nodded.

I crossed the street to the gas station. The tiny bell jingled as I opened the glass door. The guy behind the counter glanced up at me. He was a little bit older than Danny, so I knew he wouldn't ask too many questions. His face had grease smears on it, and the place smelled like old tires and gasoline. A radio on the shelf behind him blared Beatles songs.

"Excuse me, sir. Can you loan me a couple of dollars? My sister and I are too tired to walk home, and we need some bus fare. My daddy's a doctor, and he has plenty of money. I'll pay you back tomorrow. Honest."

The gas station guy looked me over before reaching into his pocket to hand me a couple of quarters.

"Here," he said. "Go on now. We're due for a storm. Just heard it on the radio. Better get home."

"Thanks." I pocketed the gift and headed back to Rosa. I watched the sky as I crossed to the park. Thunderclouds were piling up. I had to get us somewhere fast. I found my sister where I'd left her, by the fountain. "No cops," she said with a brave smile.

So far, so good. But we still needed more money. I figured I could use the same story at some other gas station or maybe even a candy store or two. Eventually, we'd have enough cash for two Greyhound tickets, if I added it to the cash I already had. I took Rosa's hand. "I got us city bus money," I assured her.

"That's not gonna get us to Pisa," she worried.

"I know," I insisted. "But it's a start. We've got to get someplace quick. It's gonna rain."

We waited at the corner stop and took the first bus that came along. I didn't know where it was going, but we rode it as far as it went. It was raining steady by then. Before the bus driver opened the door to let us off, he glanced at Rosa's black eye. "Are you two all right?"

"Yes, Mister," I told him. "Our daddy's gonna be picking us up in a few minutes."

He nodded. "Stay inside that bus shelter 'til he gets here." The door opened, and we stepped off onto the sidewalk. I held Rosa's hand so I'd feel braver. The driver waved as he drove off. The sky darkened. The wind blew dirt in our faces. We hurried for cover under the bus shelter roof.

Through the rain I tried to make out where we might be. I saw lots of trees but not many houses. The oak woods behind us scared me. I had to keep telling myself we'd be okay. The bus shelter was open on two sides, so we stood on the bench and huddled close to one of the walls. Soon, the wind whipped the rain at us, and our legs and our sweaters got soaked. "Here, put this on." I handed Rosa the coat I'd brought for her. She stuffed Binkie inside to keep him dry. I zipped her up and did up my own jacket, too.

"It's too cold here, Rosa. Let's try to find a better place."

She nodded, took my hand, and we walked a few blocks, looking for a church or some other safe place to wait out the storm. We didn't have any luck. Nothing but tall tree trunks and dark, bent branches. The oak forest looked like soldiers on the TV war news. My stomach twisted. The wind blew harder, and the rain fell steady and heavy. I prayed that the trees were really trees and not marines. I prayed that nobody would jump out from behind the forest with bombs and burn us to death. I asked God to help us, but He wasn't listening.

"I want Daddy," Rosa cried.

"I know, I know," I tried to comfort. The wind roared rain at us. In wet, thick globs, the drops hit my face. Then the thunder boomed, and the lightning crashed, and Rosa screamed. I did, too.

We ran back to the bus shelter. It wouldn't keep us dry, but I hoped—since it was lower than the trees—it would keep us safe from lightning. We slipped and splashed through puddles to get there and finally huddled together on the wet bench. Outside and inside, the rain fell and fell and fell.

"Peanut, I'm cold," Rosa cried.

Her lips were turning blue. Her whole body trembled. I moved closer, trying to keep her warm with my arms. I nudged her next to my belly. She shivered again and again. I unzipped my jacket and wrapped the opened ends around her hunched shoulders.

"It'll be okay, Rosa," I shouted over the wind. "It'll be okay."

I prayed a silent prayer. *Please, Blessed Mother, help us.* More lightning shot across the sky. I thought we were gonna die, but I didn't say that to Rosa. She'd get more scared, and then I wouldn't know what to do. I could barely think about how to get us out of this mess. Rosa cried against my belly. Her shoulders shook, and in between breaths, she sobbed, "Peanut, I wanna see Daddy. I wanna go home right now. Please, please, please."

With my whole heart, I wanted to take her there. I closed my eyes and saw the front porch of our old house in Pisa.

The slanted steps. The torn screen on the window frame. I knew if I could just open the porch door, we'd be all right. If I could just get us inside, into the living room, I could take off Rosa's wet coat, peel off her shoes and socks, and grab a blanket from Mama's old bedroom. I'd toss it around my sister's shoulders, and she'd stop shaking. We'd be home. We'd see Daddy again. And maybe Danny. And Zoomer. But not Joey. He was gone someplace where he didn't have to cry anymore. Someplace warm and dry and safe. But I didn't want that kind of safe. I wanted some hot soup in my belly and a bed to lie down on, so me and my sister could sleep for a while before I had to figure out a way to get us across Wisconsin and Illinois and Ohio, back to Pisa.

"What's this?"

A woman's voice came out of the wet, black night. The sound startled me. Through the dim light of the bus shelter, I saw two dark eyes set deep into an old white face. I couldn't see her mouth. Her neck and lips were covered with a scarf. Was she hiding war scars? I shuddered. She wore a big, floppy straw hat, like the kind my Aunt Stella wore in her garden to keep the sun off her neck. The woman leaned into the bus shelter and stared right at me. I froze.

"Are you girls lost?" The old woman's voice fought against the wind, but she didn't sound mean. "Come on off that soggy bench."

I don't know why, but we obeyed her. We hopped down, took a few deep breaths, and walked toward her. Lightning lit up the sky, and I could make out the edge of her cheekbones. They were soft, and her skin was wrinkled. But no scars. No war burns.

"Mean night to be huddling in a dirty bus shelter. Chill will kill you if you don't come in out of this rain." She reached out and cradled my shoulder. "Come on. Come home with Grace. I'll fix you up nice until we can find your mommy and daddy to take care of you proper."

The woman slid her hand down my arm and took hold of my fingers. Her skin was warm against my cold bones. I wrapped my other arm tightly around Rosa, letting her know it was okay to follow me. We walked a couple of blocks in the opposite direction from where we had searched for a church. In a few minutes, we were climbing the front steps and walking through the porch of the woman's house. She opened the door and nudged us into a small living room. She flipped on the light and warmed away the darkness. She faced us then and winced when her eyes landed on Rosa's shiner. In the back part of the house, from what I thought must be the kitchen, I smelled tomato soup. Rosa spoke before I could stop her from being rude.

"I'm hungry."

The woman chuckled. She smiled but didn't say anything about Rosa's bruised eye.

"Yes, darlin'. There's plenty of food for both of ya. Get you a hot bath, first. The soup can wait."

We climbed the stairs to the upper level of her small house. Rosa held Binkie close to her belly. The upstairs was as tiny as the downstairs. I spied a small room across the hall from the bathroom. I figured it was the woman's bedroom, but she ushered Rosa and me into the bathroom too fast for me to take a quick peek.

The bathroom was plain. Just a toilet and a sink and a tub, with feet like a wolf's. No shower even. Everything was neat and clean, though.

"Take your things off while I draw you a bath."

Rosa searched my face, asking if it was okay. I signalled the go-ahead. My sister set Binkie on the tile floor and stripped naked. Soon the bathroom was foggy with steam. My body ached for the bathwater.

The woman eyed the bumps and bruises on Rosa's legs and arms. She shook her head like her heart was muttering something to her brain, but her face stayed kind and open. "How 'bout some bath bubbles?" she asked. She smiled as we nodded our agreement, together.

"Get in there, now. That'll cut the chill. I'll get ya some clean clothes to wear for after."

Rosa and I soaked in the bubbly water until our toes and fingertips were as wrinkled as the old woman's face. We didn't talk the whole time. The woman came back just once and set towels and some dry clothes on the radiator. Then she left us alone in the bathroom, but her soft, sweet humming floated up the stairs to keep us company.

The warm water and the honey-sweet sound of the woman's melody made us both sleepy. Rosa yawned as she toweled herself off, careful not to pat too hard on her bruises.

"Don't forget to pee before you put those clean clothes on," I reminded her.

The clothes the woman gave us were too big. The shorts sort of fit us like pants, and the sweaters lay over us like wool dresses. But I didn't care. She gave us warm socks that hung too long over the ends of our toes. We both giggled as we tried to walk in them.

Rosa grabbed Binkie and kissed him. Dry, warm, tired, but still hungry, we stepped downstairs into the living room. The woman was sitting on the couch with a brush in her hands, waiting for us. She combed the wet out of our hair and took a good inspection of us with her serious brown eyes. She stood up, slow and stiff, and hobbled to the kitchen.

"Come on now, girls," she invited, "Time to tend to your tummies."

We followed her.

"Set yourselves down," she said, pointing to the kitchen chairs. She ladled hot tomato soup into two coffee mugs and placed one in front of each of us. She nudged a plate of saltines toward us without saying a word. Rosa and I ate like we'd never eaten before. We slurped the soup and shoved cracker after cracker into our mouths. All the while, the old woman busied herself at the counter. She hummed as she sliced a hunk of something off an old rootlike thing. She plopped the pinkish-orange stuff into cups of hot water and set them on the table in front of us. "It's ginger tea," she said. "It'll help warm ya." It tasted peppery, not sweet, like I thought something called ginger would. But she was right. It heated up my belly. I was full of soup and mashed-up crackers and ginger tea. I yawned.

"Time for bed," the woman announced.

She eased herself up from her chair and headed back to her living room. Rosa and I followed her again.

"Give me a hand with this," she said, nodding toward the couch.

We pulled sofa cushions onto the floor, and the woman lined them up to make a bed. "There's some afghans and a couple of extra bed pillows in there," she told me, pointing to the closet near the stairs. I hauled them out and helped her lay them over the couch cushions. When we were done, Rosa and I plopped ourselves onto our nest of green and gold and rose-colored blankets.

"Get some rest now, girls. Things will look better in the morning."

She turned off the light and climbed the stairs to her bedroom. Rosa fell asleep right away, with Binkie tucked between her chest and her arm. My sister's breathing was heavy and steady. Her poor little body was exhausted. I couldn't sleep, yet. I was tired, but something inside of me kept running fast and loud, thinking about Mama going crazy with worry over where we might be or what might have happened to us. I asked the Blessed Mother to send Mama some sign that we were safe. I listened to the creaking of the woman's footsteps above us in her bedroom and thought of Daddy getting ready for work at our house back in Pisa. The floors used to creak and moan there, too. Maybe this old woman could help us figure out a way to get back to him.

Before I fell asleep, I realized that the kind woman had never asked us our names.

Telling the Truth

A loud clang woke me up.

"Mama?" I shouted. "Mama."

I felt her looking down at me. Not Mama. The woman who'd found me and my sister last night in the rain. I opened my eyes and stared at the top button of her flower-printed dress, right where it met the edge of her blue-checkered apron. I raised my eyes to meet hers. In the morning light, her face looked older and kinder. She could have been somebody's grandma. She smiled at me, and for the first time, I noticed one of her front teeth was missing.

"Sorry to scare you, honey," the woman said. "It's just me, Grace. I was scrounging around in the cupboard looking for my fry pan. But my wrists aren't as strong as they used to be. That skillet slipped and crashed on the linoleum."

Rosa stirred next to me. She made little *mmmh, mmmh* noises and rubbed her good eye with the back of her hand. Her stuffed animal rolled off the cushion. She reached out, searching for where I might be.

I scooped her hand in mine. "Here I am."

"You girls sure are good sleepers," Grace said. "I've been up for hours, even done the laundry. Surprised I didn't wake you before this. 'Course, all that running around in the rain kind of tires a person out."

She winked and waddled toward the kitchen, calling back at us, "You girls hungry?" She didn't wait for us to answer. "Get yourselves washed up, then come eat some hotcakes. Your clothes are clean and dry. I left them on the radiator in the bathroom upstairs."

Rosa sat up slowly and cuddled Binkie. She seemed confused, like she couldn't remember where we were or how we got there. To tell you the truth, I could barely remember myself. All I knew is that the smell of those pancakes was making me hungry. I leaned over and whispered in my sister's ear so that woman, Grace, couldn't hear.

"Let's go pee."

Upstairs, without the old woman to stop me, I tiptoed to the bedroom door and swiped the look I'd wanted the night before. I saw a double bed, a small dresser, a lamp with a white shade decorated with pink polka dots, and a basket of yarn with two knitting needles sticking out of a ball of purple wool. Grace's furniture was old, but it wasn't scratched or broken, like the stuff we used to have back in Pisa or like the junky furniture at our apartment. I stepped into the room. It smelled sweet, like lilacs. A framed picture of a young woman, in a soldier's uniform, sat on the dresser. I picked it up. The soldier's smile was small, but her eyes were soft and happy. I wondered if it might be Grace, when she was younger. "Come on, Peanut," Rosa urged. "I don't want that lady to find us snooping."

I followed my sister into the bathroom. Our folded clothes waited on the radiator, just like Grace had said. They smelled like Tide, and I smiled, grateful for her kindness.

I washed my face while Rosa peed. Grace had put out more towels for both of us. They were frayed at the edges, but still thicker than the ones we had back home. I couldn't wait to rub my face in one. I scrubbed my cheeks and neck with creamy Ivory soap bubbles and rinsed off the sleep. I was stiff and sore from the couch-cushion bed, and the hot water felt good. Rosa got off the toilet and nudged me over so she could wash her hands.

"Do your face, too," I told her. "But careful with your eye."

"Peanut, I don't wanna stay with this lady."

"Her name's Grace, Rosa," I said. "And we aren't gonna stay. But we gotta eat, don't we? Let's just have some pancakes, then we'll say we got to go. We can tell her we're gonna meet our daddy downtown, at noon."

"How we gonna get there? We don't even know where we are now."

I shot Rosa an impatient look. "I need you to pretend in front of that lady that I know what's up. Or else, she'll probably figure it all out and call the cops, and they'll come get us and take us back to Mama and Patrick. You don't want that, do you?"

"No."

"Okay, then. Let's get dressed and go eat."

We both took extra long drying off with those soft towels. I folded the stuff Grace had let us wear last night and set it in neat piles on the radiator. Rosa rubbed Binkie with her towel. "I got to clean him up, too," she insisted. Afterward, we pulled on our own clean clothes and headed down to the kitchen.

Grace was standing at the stove, humming a sweet song again, like she had the night before when me and Rosa sat in our bubble bath. It made my heart twirl for a second, and I wished I could be this woman's daughter. But then I remembered, I had to be more careful. I didn't know anything about her. She could be one of those people who kidnaps little kids and sells 'em to evil men. I had to pay attention so nothing bad would happen to me and Rosa.

Grace had set the table with yellow plates and green plastic teacups. Knives and forks and spoons were bunched together in a big glass in the middle of her table. A stack of blue paper napkins waited in a pile at the end of the countertop. Her kitchen was small, but it had plenty of cupboard space. I didn't understand why she had to leave her stuff out in the open. I thought it was weird, but I didn't say nothing. I didn't want her to think I was rude.

"Set yourselves down, girls. Hotcakes will be ready in a jiffy."

Rosa and I slipped into our chairs. Grace flopped a huge, steaming pancake onto the center of each of our plates. She shuffled over to the cupboard and took out some Log Cabin syrup and set it next to me. Then, she grabbed some butter and a pitcher of orange juice from the fridge. Without saying a word, she poured the juice into our green teacups, grabbed herself a cup of coffee, and joined us at the table.

"Aren't you gonna eat?" I asked.

I started to worry. Maybe she had poisoned our pancakes so she could drug us or kill us. Or maybe she thought we were rich kids, and she was gonna lock us up and ask Mama for money to set us free. From what I'd seen so far, she sure could use it. I shoved my hand into my pocket, searching for the five dollars and spare change I'd left there. It was gone.

"I ate already," Grace said. "Had some toast before you girls were awake. Besides, I can't eat hotcakes. They bind me."

I didn't know what that meant. I just nodded as if I

understood. I was stalling. I was mad that my money was gone. I checked my other pocket to make sure. It wasn't in there, either. That lady must have stolen it. Nobody else, except Rosa, knew where I kept it stashed. I poked at my pancakes and searched the counter looking for a cookie jar or some other place she might have hid my cash.

"Oh," Grace said. "I knew there was somethin' I was forgettin'." She slowly pulled five one-dollar bills from her apron pocket plus my dimes and nickels and pennies. "Found this in your stuff last night. Thought you might be needing it."

She laid the money in a pile in front of my plate, acting like she'd just passed me a second helping of brownies instead of my life savings. I stared at the George Washington faces and at the other old presidents on the small stack of coins. My tight lips relaxed. For a second, I felt bad about thinking she'd robbed me. I took a deep breath and let it go before I looked straight into Grace's steady, brown eyes. I folded the dollars, scooped up the change, shoved the money back in my pocket. I shoveled a forkful of hotcakes into my mouth.

"So, how you girls doin' today?" she asked.

Grace cradled her coffee cup between her hands. She took slow sips and glanced at Rosa and then at me. It was clear she wasn't gonna let us eat and leave, so I decided to make the best of it. She wasn't a thief, and she sure made great pancakes. I didn't feel dizzy or sick, so I guessed they weren't poisoned. She had a cozy voice. I didn't mind visiting for a bit. I just hoped she liked to take afternoon naps. I figured when she fell asleep, Rosa and I could sneak out the back door and be on our way.

"I'm okay, thank you," I said.

"Me, too," Rosa added.

"How 'bout that cute puppy dog?" Grace asked, smiling at Binkie.

Rosa nodded back with a tiny grin. Grace rubbed her cheek with her wrinkled finger. She stared out the kitchen window, scrunching her nose up, thinking hard about something. After a minute or two, she turned and looked into my eyes.

"Do you girls have names?"

I panicked. Was she gonna turn us in?

"Girls?"

"Yes, Ma'am. I'm Peanut. And this here's my sister Rosa."

"And this is Binkie," Rosa mumbled, her mouth full of pancakes.

"Rosa and Binkie," Grace repeated, glancing first at my sister, then at her toy dog. "And Peanut." She squinted and wrinkled her lips into a funny pout.

"How'd a brave girl like you ever get a sissy name like that?"

I shrugged, afraid to answer. Mama named me that. She said when I was a baby I was tiny, no bigger than a peanut. I always hated it. Made me feel small. But the nickname stuck.

"Seems to me, anybody who could live through a thunder and lightning storm ought to have a warrior name like Athena. Or Medusa. Or at least Scout. Something strong."

"Regina," I said. "My real name's Regina."

"Regina!" Grace shouted. A big grin crept across her face. "Now that's more like it. That's regal. That's queenly. That suits you better."

I tried hard to hide a smile, but my heart danced—thinking she could see something like that in me.

"That Peanut stuff has got to go. You ain't no little scaredy-cat thing that could be crushed to death like a teeny-tiny peanut. You're a *warrior girl* as far as I can see. You're strong and sensible."

I changed my mind about her right then and there. I would have bet all the cash in my pocket that she wasn't gonna hurt us or turn us over to the cops.

"How 'bout if I call you Regina. Would you mind?"

"No, Ma'am," I said. "I'd like that just fine."

I glanced at Rosa, who was licking syrup off her fingertips. She turned to Grace and pronounced, "I like you."

Grace laughed. Her face burst into a million splinters of color and sun. Light rippled and shimmered through the space in her teeth where the front one had been. All that joy just made me and Rosa laugh, too. We laughed and laughed and laughed. Tears rolled down our faces, and I hugged my tummy from how sore and good it felt. When the last ha-ha-ha lifted off our tongues, Rosa and I wiped our eyes with clean paper napkins. Grace wiped her face with the corner of her blue checkered apron and leaned towards us with a friendly look.

"You girls want more hotcakes?" she asked.

"No, Ma'am," Rosa and I said at the same time.

"How 'bout Binkie?"

That made us giggle some more, and Grace chuckled to herself as she cleared our plates and set them in the sink. She poured another cup of coffee and settled herself back down, going slow like she was afraid she'd break something if she sat too fast.

"Well, Regina and Rosa, do you girls have a last name?"

Our mouths clamped shut. Neither one of us looked at Grace, and we dared not look at each other.

"Don't want to tell old Grace, do ya? Well how 'bout answering this question, then. What ya running from? Or should I ask *who* ya running from?"

My heart raced. I swallowed back tears. I tried to think of something to tell her that would get us off the hook. But my mind was flying around the kitchen way too fast. I couldn't catch it long enough to settle into an answer. I shrugged and opened my mouth, but nothing came out.

"Peanut," Rosa whined. It was clear my sister was real disappointed in me.

"Well now, girls," Grace said. "There's no need to get all worried. I'm on your side. Can't say why, really. Just feels like you're in some sort of situation that's bigger than the both of ya. Thought I might be able to help."

I studied her eyes. I wanted to open up and tell her everything, but I was scared, still. The only thing I knew for sure was that I didn't want us to go back to Patrick. I'd have given anything to disappear, right then and there, but I knew I had to tell Grace something. So I made up a story, hoping she'd fall for it and change the subject.

"Well, you see," I stammered. "Me and Rosa were just walking along and then it started raining real hard and Rosa tripped over a tree root and fell. That's how she got her shiner."

"Oh," Grace said. "Those trees can be mighty vicious."

"Rosa was crying real hard because it hurt real bad. When I saw Rosa's eyes, and the bruises on her legs and arms, I got worried that she might need a doctor. But I don't know any, so I got scared, and we started running as fast as we could. Then it started to thunder and lightning, so we hid in that bus shelter. That's when you found us."

"That's quite a story, Regina," Grace said. "I'd almost believe ya except I know those marks on Rosa's face and arms didn't come from no tree roots. Don't know of any tree with roots that leave marks like human knuckles. I'm sure you were scared. Can't say I'd blame ya, either. It sure would be nice if you told me what really happened. I can't help you unless you do."

I touched Rosa's hand before I blabbed the truth. I didn't want her to get upset or feel like I ratted on her. I wasn't gonna tell about Patrick hitting her if she wasn't ready for anybody else to know. "What do ya think, Rosa?"

My sister was quiet for a minute, then said, "You can tell her. Maybe she can help us get back to Daddy."

Rosa held my hand, and I felt my heart open, just a bit. I slowly began to tell Grace about Mama and Daddy and how they didn't love each other. I told her about the fighting and the yelling and the money worries. I told her about Mama—about how she gets all sad and goes away and how hard it is to make her smile. I told Grace about Mama falling in love with Patrick. How that broke Daddy's heart but made Mama's full and happy. I told her about Patrick being a priest and being sent to another parish when the bishop found out about him and Mama. And about how Mama would take us girls with her every Friday night to visit Patrick. I told her Mama brought us with her when she ran away because Winnie is Patrick's kid. I figured it out even though Mama never told me. When I said that part, Rosa dropped my hand. Her mouth fell open.

"Are you sure?" Rosa asked.

"Yep," I said. "Just think about it a second, Rosa. He's always kissing and hugging Winnie, giving her all kinds of attention. But not you. Not me."

"Wow," Rosa said.

"The worst of it, Grace," I continued, "is how we left Pisa without saying good-bye to Daddy and the boys. Mama wouldn't even let me take my dog, Zoomer. I miss him like crazy."

Once my heart started its confession, I couldn't stop. I kept no secrets from the old woman. It felt better than saying a hundred Hail Marys and two hundred Our Fathers. My soul shined brighter and lighter with every word. I even told her Joey had died, and how—after that—Daddy ran away to the monastery to be a monk and pray for us all. Because we need it.

"Joey dying made Mama go berserk," I said. "She got more depressed than ever. She couldn't take care of us at all. Patrick got mad. He only wanted to take care of Winnie. That's why Rosa swiped money outta Patrick's wallet. But he caught her and hit her. That's how she got her shiner and all those bruises."

"So, you girls ran away," Grace said.

"Rosa did," I said. "I mean we both wanted to, but I kept telling her we had to have more money. After Patrick beat her, Rosa couldn't wait anymore."

"I had to find my daddy," Rosa told Grace.

"That's when I decided to follow her and help her get there," I added. "I wanted to go back to Pisa, too, but I didn't know how to do it. Even if Daddy was studying to be a monk, maybe he'd change his mind if me and Rosa showed up. Then we could all live together again. Danny and Zoomer and him and us. Maybe Mama would come to her senses and leave Patrick. Come back home to us. We could be a family again."

I was done. I sat back in my chair and let my heart settle down. Grace sat quietly. She looked like one of the marble statues in church with stone eyes that can't blink or close. I wasn't sure if she was mad at us for running away or if she didn't believe my story. It made me nervous. I was used to being able to know what grown-ups thought. Their faces were like maps. I'd look at their eyes and mouths and know right away which way I had to go. But I couldn't figure out what Grace was thinking. I prayed she wouldn't make us go back to Mama and Patrick. What if she decided to rat on us?

"Well, Regina, that's quite a story for someone as young as you," Grace said. Her marble statue eyes softened. "You're welcome to stay as long as you need. 'Course, you'll have to help out. I expect you to make up your bed, help with the dishes and such. I'm an old woman, and all those chores tire me out faster than they used to—especially if I have to do them for three instead of one."

"Do you mean it, Grace? Can we really stay here with you?" Rosa asked. Her sore eye looked happy for a second.

"Yep. I don't have a lot, but whatever food I have, you can share with me. We'll see what happens. If I had any money, I'd put you on a Greyhound and send you back to your daddy. But all I got is my social security check. Anyway, maybe you'll figure out a way to quiet the aches in your hearts. I ain't got no medicine to cure that, but sometimes angels come along and fix it up without ya having to ask. It happened to me, once. Maybe it'll happen to you, too."

Rosa carefully set Binkie in Grace's lap, grabbed her hand, and held on tight. My stomach untangled.

"Thanks, Grace," I said. "We won't be any trouble. As soon as we can figure out a way to get to Daddy, we'll be out of your way."

"No need to hurry on my account, Regina. Time's the only thing I got left. Plus, I don't mind the company."

Grace's Story

We'd been at Grace's house nearly a week. She didn't have a TV, and she didn't read any newspapers, so I never did figure out if the police were looking for two lost girls. I wondered about it a lot, though. Every morning, I expected to wake up and find the cops pounding on Grace's front door. If Grace ever wondered if our mama might be heartsick over losing us, she never brought it up. I didn't, either. I was happy just to be someplace quiet for a change.

The first few days at Grace's house, Rosa and I slept a lot. We were tired from running away and getting caught in that thunderstorm. Tired, too, from all of Patrick's yelling and Mama's crying. Rosa was slowly getting better. Every day, her shiner got lighter and lighter, turning from deep purple to yellow green. You could hardly tell anymore what had happened to her, except when Rosa woke herself and me in the middle of the night, crying "Leave me alone, leave me alone!"

Grace said it would take Rosa's heart a while to get over

what Patrick had done. "Your bruised skin will clear a lot sooner than your bruised soul."

She said stuff like that all the time. She was dead sure about what she knew, and because she was, I was, too. Besides, I could see how it was true about Rosa, how her bruises were fading, but she still cried at night. The inside hurts took longer to get better. I couldn't just kiss them away. Maybe it was true about me, too. I didn't have any purple and yellow marks on my arms or legs or belly, at least on the outside. But deeper, in my bones and in between my muscles, I felt sore and achy, like somebody had slammed me into a wall.

More and more every day, I came to believe that Grace's house was the best place for me to be. She made us soup and biscuits, and she told us stories about her life. I loved how her words took us on a trip to visit long-ago scenery and people. When she talked, I could taste the wild strawberries she'd picked in the fields behind her daddy's dairy farm. How sweet and luscious they were.

One rainy afternoon when we were making chocolate-chip cookies, Grace told us that her mama died when she was ten. She and her two sisters, Clara and Ivy, had to take over running things around the house.

"My brothers rose before the sun every day to milk the cows," she told us. "We girls had to cook sausage and eggs, hotcakes and potatoes for them. Made them juice and strong coffee, too. It was our job to fill their bellies so they could get through the rest of their morning labor. In the spring, all of us children had to pick rocks in the fields. Stones rose from the winter ground, and Tommy and Bill and Jake and Ed and us girls would have to clear the fields so my brothers could help Daddy plant the crops. Afterward, we had to come home and tend to the cooking and cleaning."

"Did you miss your mama?" I asked.

"Missed her like the dickens," Grace said. "Still do." Her eyes got soft and wet.

"Were your daddy and brothers nice to you?" Rosa asked. She sat cross-legged on a kitchen chair, eyes wide, eager for the next story.

"My daddy was a stern man," Grace said. Her lips tightened a bit. "After Mama died, he fell into a well of sorrow that he never managed to get out of. He never touched us children. Not in a hard way. Or a soft way. To this day, I can't tell you what his skin felt like."

"My daddy's got a scratchy face and thick, yellow calluses on the inside of his hands," Rosa said.

"And his eyes are brown, and they get real quiet when he prays his rosary," I added.

"How 'bout your mama?" Grace asked. "What's she like?"

I spooned scoops of cookie dough onto the baking sheet with as much tenderness as I could muster. "She's got a sad heart," I said. "She worries all the time, and she tries not to yell at us, but we give her a headache. Especially lately, since Joey died."

I hadn't expected to talk about my dead brother. I sure didn't expect that saying his name would call him to Grace's kitchen. But there he was, as close as Grace and Rosa. He was smiling and wearing his Yankees cap, just as alive as can be. I shivered and dropped my spoon. Joey faded into the air.

"Dear child, you're as pale as a bedsheet," Grace said. "Sit down and rest yourself." She handed me a glass of water and patted my shoulder.

"I saw him, Rosa," I whispered.

"Who?" Rosa asked. Her voice was shaky.

"Joey."

"Don't scare me, Regina." The yellowed skin under her hurt eye darkened.

"I'm not trying to scare ya, Rosa. But I saw him. He was as real as you or Grace."

"Happens all the time, Regina," Grace reassured me. "I talk with Luisa nearly every night before I go to sleep."

"Who's Luisa?"

"She's my daughter."

"Is she dead?"

"Yep. Died a long time ago. In that war in Korea. She was a nurse. Her unit got bombed. She died trying to save young wounded fellas."

"And you see her, here in this house, every night before you go to sleep?" Rosa's face turned white now. Her hands shook. Grace wrapped her fingers around Rosa's until my sister's face turned natural again.

"There's plenty in life you can't explain," Grace told us. "But don't fret yourselves. Luisa won't hurt ya. She just stops by to say hi to me. That's probably all Joey wants, too. Maybe he just misses ya. Wants to tell you he loves you."

I wondered if that woman in the picture on Grace's bedroom dresser was her dead daughter. Thinking about how much she must miss her made me want to cry. I swallowed my tears. Maybe Grace was right, maybe Joey was just coming to visit. We never did say good-bye when we left Pisa. Maybe that's why he popped his dead face into Grace's kitchen.

"Do you have to be real good on earth before God makes you an angel?" I asked Grace.

"I guess it helps," she said. "But mostly I think angels are whoever helps you through. Alive or dead, it don't make a difference."

Her answer satisfied me. Grace scooped more cookie dough on the baking sheet and started singing. Her voice floated sweetly through the room. She was singing about love, telling me and Rosa that when you've got real love, nothing can hurt you. I thought about Mama. She had real love with Patrick. At least, she said she did. But does real love have to hurt your kids so much?

We baked cookies the rest of the afternoon. We never said another word about ghosts or angels or Joey or Luisa. The house smelled sweet like warm chocolate chips, and I was as happy as I could ever remember being. Joey never did come back. Later, when Grace took her nap, Rosa and I played Go Fish. I told my sister about how I thought Grace was right. Joey had come to say good-bye.

"Regina, maybe he came to help us figure out how to get back to Daddy."

"Why would he do that?"

"Maybe he's an angel, now. Grace said angels help people."

I had a hard time picturing Joey in a halo and angel's wings. "Well, I guess he didn't come to help us make cookies."

"Did he say anything?"

"No. He just sort of smiled, and then he disappeared. Besides, Joey probably doesn't even know how to get to Pisa from here."

"Regina, don't be stupid. God knows everything. God could tell Joey."

"Maybe Joey's not in heaven. Maybe God wouldn't let him in. Maybe He told Joey to wander around—kind of like a penance—until he could figure out how to be nicer to his sisters."

"If God kicked Joey out of heaven, he's got no place to go. Maybe he did come back to take us to Pisa. If he shows up again, I hope he brings a map and some money," Rosa said. "I miss Daddy."

I missed Mama, too, but I didn't tell Rosa. I didn't see how we could go back to the apartment after what Patrick had done. And I couldn't see Mama going home to Pisa with us, unless we went first, and she missed us too much to stay away. I just hoped Joey really was trying to help us, even though in real life he never would have acted that way. Maybe when you die, you get nicer.

※

Later that evening after supper, Grace washed the dishes, and Rosa and me dried them. We were quiet in the kitchen together, and Grace hummed softly to herself. I started thinking about her having a daughter, and I felt jealous.

"Is that Luisa in that picture up in your bedroom?"

"Yep."

"How come you have a daughter, but you don't have a husband?"

"Oh, I was married once," Grace said.

"Did your husband die?"

"Yes."

"In the war, same as Luisa?"

"No."

"How then?"

"Don't be poking in my business, Regina," Grace warned.

She'd never snipped at me before, and it hurt. "Sorry," I muttered. "I didn't mean to snoop. Just wondered, is all."

"Somebody shot him," Grace said. Her voice was sad and low.

"Why?"

"He was mean."

"To who?"

Grace set her dishrag on the counter and took a deep breath. "To me and Luisa."

"Did he hurt you?" I suddenly felt mad at a man I'd never met. "Is that why she went to war? To get away from him?"

"No, Regina." Grace turned away and walked to the kitchen door. She stared out the window at the rain that had begun to fall. "You sure do ask a lot of questions."

Outside, the clouds rumbled, and the rain poured harder and harder. Lightning cracked, and Rosa jumped, startled at the sudden flash. The side yard lit up as bright as noon.

Without saying a word, Grace grabbed her coat and the hat she'd worn the night she found us. She opened the door and stepped outside. Rosa and I watched her walk into the darkness.

"You should have shut up, Regina!" Rosa cried. "You got her all upset. Now she's gonna go call the cops."

"Maybe she just went to the 7-Eleven for some milk," I said, trying to reassure both of us. I threw my dish towel on the floor and ran into the living room. If she ratted to the police, I promised myself I'd never forgive her. If she came back with a milk bottle, I'd apologize and tell her I'd mind my own business and never ask about Luisa again.

Grace was gone for a long time. When she finally got home, the rain had stopped and Rosa was asleep on our couch-cushion bed. I waited in Grace's favorite chair, wrapped in one of her hand-knit afghans.

She opened the front door, wiped her shoes on the mat, and hung her sopping wet hat and coat on the peg beside the entryway. She turned to me and asked, "Do you really want to know who shot my husband?"

I nodded yes.

She walked into the kitchen, set the kettle on to boil,

and motioned with her head for me to take a seat. She sat beside me and stared at the tabletop.

"Who shot him?" I asked.

"I did . . ." She glanced at my open mouth.

"How come you aren't in jail?"

"I was. It's a long story, Regina. Too long and too messy for a youngster to hear."

"But I told you about me and Rosa," I insisted.

I was scared, but I wanted to know more. She didn't seem like she could kill someone. Her eyes were way too sweet, and her fingers were way too crooked.

"It was a long time ago," Grace said. Her voice got low and thin.

The kettle whistled. Grace fixed us both a cup of ginger tea, then sat back down. She folded her arms across her belly, took a deep breath, and continued.

"He beat me one night when he came home from playing poker with his drinking buddies. Took my tooth. He'd lost his entire paycheck. In his anger, he raged over every losing card. Flattened his fists against my sorry bones. We didn't have any money left to pay the mortgage or get groceries until he got paid again. But that wasn't gonna be for a whole week. We had some stuff in the cupboards, but it wasn't enough. If it had just been me, I could have made do, but I had my Luisa to think about."

Grace stared at the wall. A sad look came over her face. I took slow, deep breaths to steady my racing heart.

"He'd never hit me before. He'd been drunk plenty of times, but he'd never taken his fists to me. Or to my Luisa. After that night, seems like his fists found out they liked the feel of my bruised skin, and they couldn't get enough.

"He even bought a gun. A shotgun. Sometimes he'd pull his gun out of the hall closet, where he stored it, and prop the barrel up next to the bed before he thrashed me with his fists. 'Don't think I won't use it,' he threatened, full of whiskey and hate. 'Mind yourself.' He spat his ugly words at my face." Grace's mouth tightened. She rubbed her temples, then brushed her fingers across her cheekbone.

"For ten years, every Saturday night he beat me. 'Til I couldn't take it anymore. Luisa had been seeing me get smacked for too many years. A couple of times, she tried to stop her daddy, and he turned his fists against her. It broke my heart to see her pretty face all full of bruises. I wanted to leave—take my Luisa with me—but I didn't know how."

My eyes grew wider, fearful for Grace, fearful for Luisa. Grace just kept right on talking like I wasn't even in the room.

"One night, it was storming and raging outside, just like the night when I found you and your sister. That's why I was out there. That's why I had to go out there tonight. I always walk in the rain. It's kind of like a baptism to me."

I remembered Grace's face that night she'd taken us in, how soft it looked in the pouring rain. She'd seemed worried about us being all alone and soaking wet, but she had also seemed calm, almost peaceful.

"That night, my husband came home drunk and full of fury. He slapped Luisa upside the head 'cuz she forgot to put sugar in his coffee. 'Damn idiot!' he cussed. I scooped her into my arms, trying to kiss the stinging away, but that made him all the madder. 'She ain't a little girl no more! Don't coddle her.' He swung at us, but we stepped aside and missed his blow. I sent her off, then, knowin' his blood was about to boil over.

"'Go on, get to your room,' I whispered.

"'But Mama . . . ,' she started to refuse, wanting to make sure I would be okay.

"It was too late. He threw his coffee at me; the cup

nicked my face. The hot liquid singed my cheek. 'What's wrong with you, woman?' he scowled.

"Luisa screamed and ran upstairs. I heard her door slam shut. I stooped to pick up the cup shards, and he kicked me.

"'Answer me when I talk to you!' he roared.

"The pain in my side from where his foot had landed throbbed something terrible. I mumbled a cussword under my breath, mostly 'cuz of the pain, but also 'cuz of how much I hated him, how much I feared him.

"'Pick up that mess!' he shouted.

"I left the shattered pieces on the floor and hobbled upstairs to tend to my aches. He followed me.

"'Get back here, you bitch!'

"At the top of the stairs, I felt his heavy hand on my shoulder. It dug into my flesh like a terrible memory. He pulled me around and started slapping me, yelling, 'Don't you be smirking at me, woman. Don't you be disrespecting your husband.' He was all heated up from the liquor and his own self-importance, and the pummeling began. It went on for an hour."

My heart was pounding louder now. I kept picturing Patrick hitting Rosa. I stared at Grace, trying to see beyond her story to the kind woman who had cared for us. I kept telling myself I was safe. She wouldn't hurt me. Everything would be okay.

"Finally, he fell asleep, tired from all the hitting, I sneaked to the hallway and got down his gun. I cocked it and walked over to the bed where he slept. I aimed the thing right at his hateful face. And stood there for a second, asking the Lord above for forgiveness. Then I pulled the trigger, and a powerful roar burst from the barrel. And a powerful cry spilled from my chest.

"Luisa ran to the room, crying 'Mama! Mama!' thinking

her daddy had killed me. Her face was washed with sweet relief when she saw it was me who'd done the killing. Then she got fearful and ran to her room. Outside, the rain was crashing and splashing. I had to run into the wet night to wash my husband's brains from off my arms. The police found me racing through the streets, rain pouring every which way over my wailing head."

I cried then—soft, little tears. I wanted to burst open, but I held back, trying to be strong so Grace would finish her story.

"Of course, they sent me to jail. Spent ten years there. Would have spent the rest of my life if my sister hadn't arranged for that fancy lawyer from Chicago to help out. Her husband's cousin asked for the favor. Knew that lawyer fella from way back. He argued self-defense; told the jury I was a mistreated woman, just trying to keep myself and my daughter safe from a savage brute. Worst part of it was I never saw my Luisa again. They gave her to my sister, who thought it best not to let Luisa visit me in prison. While I was still there, Luisa joined the army. My sister wrote and told me. She sent me that picture that's up in my room. She knew I'd be proud. Said Luisa wanted to be a nurse, and the army would train her. They sent Luisa to Korea, and she died there. My sister passed on a year later. She was a sweet girl, that Luisa. My heart's treasure."

I felt sad and lonely, thinking about Grace losing her daughter. Never seeing her again. I wasn't scared of her. I kept thinking about how mean Grace's husband had been and how awful it must have been for her to go to jail. Even though Grace had killed a man, there was something about her that was just like me. I hated Patrick. Hated him enough to kill him. I'd felt that plenty of times—even before he hit Rosa. If my wishes were bullets, he'd be dead and gone by now. Sometimes, if the truth be known, I even dreamed of killing Mama. But that kind of thinking never stayed with me long. Usually it came around when I was way too angry for words, way too hurt to think straight. But I understood why Grace did it.

Grace wiped her eyes and blew her nose. A long sigh slipped out of her. I touched the edge of her elbow. She reached for my hand, suddenly remembering I was there. She looked at my crying face and said, "Oh, Regina, I didn't mean to upset ya. All that stuff about hitting and killing is a bit much for a young girl. I don't normally talk about it. I figured I done my time in jail and losing Luisa was a life sentence for me anyways. I don't owe nobody no explanation. But that's how I knew you and Rosa were running from something scary. I could see it in your eyes that night in the rain. It was like looking in a mirror."

"I'm sorry that happened to you, Grace."

"Life's a hell-of-a-thing, Regina. You just never know what's gonna come blowing around the corner."

The Scream

Everything about Grace's house was different from ours. It was quieter. Nobody shouted, nobody fought, nobody slammed the bedroom door, crying and crying. But most of all, what was different was the air. Not the way it smelled. But the way it was roomy and breezy. Only, it didn't blow like a breeze. It just floated around me and through me and over me. It didn't crowd me. It didn't rush in and steal away my stomach. It didn't wrap itself around my head in a tight band and squeeze my face. It just washed over everything, soft and sweet. And it sort of cradled me in a funny way. Like I could take a nap in its arms and not have to worry about anything.

Grace was like that, too. She didn't push me to talk, and she didn't expect me to listen to her or take her sadness away. Even after she told me about killing her husband and going to jail and losing her daughter, she didn't expect me to make it all better. She had her sorrow, but she cradled it close to her heart. It belonged to her. And we both knew it.

In Grace's house, I didn't have to be anything I wasn't. I could move any way I wanted to, twirl if I felt like twirling, hop if hopping was what I needed, sway if swaying felt right. It was okay to laugh, and best of all, it was okay to cry. But the funny thing was, I hadn't cried much since the night Grace found me and Rosa, clinging to each other in that bus shelter. There wasn't much of anything to cry about. For the first time in a long time, I felt peaceful. I don't understand how a woman who killed a man can have such kindness inside of her. But Grace did.

After supper, we used to hang out in Grace's living room. Me and Rosa would play cards, or I'd read old *Reader's Digests* to her. Grace would turn on the radio and play that station she liked so much, the one with violins and flutes—fancy music that was pretty, but hard to dance to. Sometimes hearing it made me lonesome for singing songs from *My Fair Lady* with Mama. Then, I would look at Rosa and see how her bruises were gone and her black eye was all better, and I'd remember that Mama was still with Patrick. And that was dangerous.

Some nights, Grace chatted with us. Some nights, she just pulled out her wool and worked on a sweater. The click, click, click of her knitting needles and the soft thump of her chair as it rocked against her wooden floor made me want to stay close to her forever.

One time, I asked Grace, "Did you ever hate your daddy for never hugging you?"

She glanced up from her yarn and laid her needles in her lap. She took a minute to answer, choosing the right words. That was one thing I could always count on: she was a careful woman.

"Hate's a powerful feeling, Regina," Grace said. "It can kill you worse than any bullet."

I felt bad for asking. Wrong for thinking that of her. "I didn't mean to upset you," I said.

"I ain't upset. Just wondering where your question came from. Are you asking me about my daddy, Regina? Or are you searching your own heart?"

I didn't want to think about her question, but I couldn't get around it. I slipped away from Rosa and sat up straight, pressing my shoulder blades into the back of the sofa. I needed room for all the feelings that were knocking against me.

"I hate my daddy for not trying harder to make Mama stay with him," I finally said. I kept going, in spite of my shaky voice. "And I hate Patrick for falling in love with my Mama and making her take us away from Daddy. And I hate him for hitting Rosa. I hate Mama, too, sometimes, because she looks right through me. Her eyes never stop. They just keep flying past, like I'm a useless thing. Or invisible."

"And yourself?" Grace asked.

Her tender eyes zeroed in on a soft spot deep inside me. I started to cry. "I hate being scared all the time. And I hate worrying. It makes me mad. But I can't stop it. I try and try. I want to scream. Sometimes, I want to scream so hard and so loud the whole world will shake."

"Go ahead," Grace invited.

"What?"

"Nobody here is gonna stop ya, right Rosa?"

Rosa agreed with a hesitant nod.

"What do you mean? Just scream? Just scream my head off? What if somebody hears me? What if they come rushing over, and we get busted?"

"Nonsense," Grace said. "Nobody's gonna come in here. I screamed and shouted all the time before you girls got here. When I needed to, that is. Nobody's gonna hear ya except me and Rosa, and we already gave you permission. So scream if that's what will free ya."

I stared at her. How could it be okay to just scream? I opened my mouth to try, and nothing came out except empty air. My lungs tightened.

"Take a deep breath first," Grace said. "That always helps me."

I grabbed a bellyful of air and let out a terrible noise.

"AHHHHHHHHHHHHHHHHHHHHHHHHHHHHHHHH!!!"

"Again, Regina, again," Grace encouraged.

"AHHHHHHHHHHHHHHHHHHHHHHHHHHHHHHHH!!"

"That's the girl," Grace applauded. "Again!"

"AHHHHHHHHHHHHHHHHHHHHHHHHHHHHHHHH!!"

Grace steadied herself against the arms of her rocker and stood to give me an ovation. Rosa joined her. "Brava! Brava, Regina!" they cheered.

My screaming trickled into a giggle, then grew into a laugh. I stood and bowed. I twirled around the rug and bowed again. I grabbed Rosa's hand and danced her around the room. We giggled and fell to the floor. Grace laughed, too. She crouched down beside us on the rug, until her knees gave out, and then she plopped next to us.

"A little screaming is a glorious thing, Regina," she proclaimed. "You too, Rosa, you should try it sometime. It'll clean out what ails ya."

I made my arms as wide as could be, and I hugged her. I planted kisses all over her wrinkled cheeks. She laughed and laughed.

"I love you, Grace," I said. "I wish you were my mother."

"Me, too," Rosa said. She grabbed Grace's hand and kissed her bony fingers.

"I love you girls, too." Grace said. Her smiling eyes turned serious for a second. "But you have a mother. You don't need another."

"But . . . ," I started to complain.

Grace put a finger to her lips.

"Let's sit up on the couch, girls. My bones are too tired for this hard floor."

We helped Grace to her feet. Her body was more flimsy than it looked. Her skin sagged under her arms, and her bony elbows stuck out. Her knees creaked when we finally pulled her to her feet. It was easy to forget that she was an old woman. Sometimes, she reminded me of Amelia, my best friend back in Pisa. Grace could be silly like Amelia, and she always listened to what I had to say, just like my friend. Grace wasn't like any grown-up I had ever known. I was afraid she would die before I got a chance to tell her all the things in my heart, my secrets and my dreams. I squeezed her hand and settled into the sofa, right beside her, getting as close as I could.

"Stuffing things inside is an ugly way of living," she said. "It's not a way I want to see either of you two girls choosing. I've seen way too much of it in my long life. Sorrow is waiting everywhere. Everyone has some hard pain they're nursing. Some folks steal, some lie, some cheat themselves or others, some even kill. Hate comes out every which way. Sorrow, too. But you don't have to be old to know that. I've seen it in your eyes. Both of you. That kind of sadness can eat you alive."

"But what if somebody is so mean that all you can do is hate them?" I asked.

"Hate's only a feeling, Regina. It can't do no harm unless you swallow it down or upchuck it on somebody else. My husband did that. And look where it got him. Dead and gone before his time. He'd had a hard life, even before I met him. His daddy beat him. His mama didn't do nothin' to stop it. It festered in him. All that loathing. 'Til it turned mean and nasty, and he had to take it somewhere. So, he took it to the bottle, and then he took it . . . well, you know the rest of that story."

"What story?" Rosa asked.

"I'll tell you when you get to be Regina's age, honey," Grace said.

"Just because your husband was bad doesn't mean everybody is bad if they hate someone who deserves it," I interrupted.

"There's a hitch to your way of thinking, Regina," Grace continued. "Having a hard life doesn't make you a bad person, neither does hating someone. It's what you do with all that hate and sadness that matters."

"What do you mean?"

"Having feelings is a natural, human thing. And hate's just one of many feelings. Everybody knows how to hate. My husband wasn't the only one. I hated him, too. Feared him, really. Hate's the stepchild of fear, girls. Remember that. But the thing is, hating my husband didn't make him stop being such a bully. It only dug me into an ugly hole, and I had a hard time climbing out."

"So, if we're not supposed to hate anybody, what do you do with all the boiling stuff inside that makes you want to kill 'cuz you're so mad?"

"You come to know it, Regina. You make friends with it."

"What?" I asked. That was the silliest thing I had ever heard. Love and joy, those could be my friends. But sadness and hate?

"Look here," Grace said. "Let me try to explain it in a different way. People love and people hate. People laugh and people cry. If you only laugh and never cry, you're gonna be just half a person. You're never going to really love—yourself or anybody else. When you stop thinking that hate and fear and sadness are trash, you stop feeling the need to toss them out the window. You respect yourself, and you quit trying to mess up other people's lives."

I was beginning to see her point. Mama and Daddy and Patrick were always spilling their sadness and their anger on everybody else. I didn't want to be like them. I wanted to find a different way. Maybe they had a good reason for doing what they did. But one thing was for sure, they didn't see how what they did made me and Rosa and the boys sad and mad, too.

"How do you make those feelings your friends?" I asked.

"Give yourself lots of room," Grace said. "Laugh and scream and cry and play. Don't let nobody take away what's rightfully yours. Stay true to your own nature—even when everybody around you wants you to be somebody else."

"If I screamed and cried every time I felt mad or sad at home, Mama would be real angry," I said.

"So, what do you do instead?"

"I try to be a good girl, so she'll have one less thing to worry about. So she'll be happy again."

Grace tapped her finger on my chest. "Good girls die young, Regina. This old red muscle in there shrivels up like a dried-out peach pit if you give your love away to people who don't treat you right. You grow up, and you have bigger bones and bigger ideas, but your heart's petrified—nothing but a stony, tiny, hard thing. Being good ain't the way to go. Being bad ain't, either. You just got to be yourself."

"But how do I know what being myself is? Maybe I was born to be a good girl."

"Nobody's always good or always bad, Regina. You'll know who you are by listening to your heart. It's kind of like a song, in its own way. You weren't put on this Earth to sing your mama's song, Regina. You got your own song to sing, your own way. You, too, Rosa. Once you figure that out, everything else takes care of itself."

"Sometimes at home, when things get real bad, I'm afraid I'm going to burst and gush blood and guts all over the place," I said. "That don't feel like a song to me."

"No," Grace agreed. "That kind of feeling is like a volcano. It stores itself up until it can't stand the pressure anymore. Then pow! Wouldn't happen that way if you could let it out a little bit at a time, when it first comes on. Every time your mama makes you sad or mad, let it out somehow. You got a right to it, Regina. Go to your room. Scream into your pillow. Go outside. Scream at the wind. Find someone or something to share your troubles with—a tree or a rock or the sky."

"Back in Pisa, me and Zoomer used to go to the woods. I'd tell him all my secrets. Sometimes, we'd hide in the closet in my bedroom and eat Vanilla Wafers together."

"I got a place like that, too, here in Madison," Rosa said. "Back behind the school playground."

"That's a beginning, girls. Hold tight to those places. Don't matter if your mama's sad or angry. Don't matter if Patrick's ranting and raving. They're both nursing some wild kind of pain. But that ain't your problem."

"When my mama yells about leaving the boys or cries about Joey dying or disappears into her room because she's too sad, it *is* my problem," I insisted. "I'm the one who gets stuck making supper or giving Winnie a bath or helping Rosa with her homework. I'm the one who has to take Mama some coffee, hold her hand until she feels better."

"It's harder when you're a kid," Grace agreed. "But even so, what I'm trying to tell you isn't about your mama or what she needs in this world. It's about *you* and how you can make yourself feel less crazy. When your mama or Patrick are mean or short with you, when you feel like all the love in the world has dried up and blown away, find a place to scream or dance it right out of your body. That's called cherishing yourself. And that's how you begin to know who you really are. That's what real love is, girls. And real respect. In the long run, that's all the comfort you really got to sleep with at night."

Rosa and I rested our heads on Grace's lap while she stroked our hair. I lay there, letting her comfort cradle me, the wonderful quiet of her house calm my mind. I thought about all the things she'd said. Maybe I did have something inside of me that was all mine, something joyful and angry. Something loud that Mama couldn't take away. I only wished I knew how to make it come out. Maybe someday I'd be able to fill my lungs and my throat with a wild song and give it to the wind. Then I'd be free. Then I'd be happy. No matter what Mama said.

The Reunion

I practiced Grace's suggestions the next morning. Every time I started to get mad at Mama or hate Patrick, I'd grab a pillow and scream into it, or I'd dance around the living room trying to twirl it out of me. Sometimes it worked. Sometimes it didn't.

I told Grace about my practicing and how hard it was to make it stick.

"Give it time, Regina," she said. "Nobody gets it right away. It's just a seed I planted in you. It'll take a while to blossom."

I wondered what kind of flower I'd be when that seed she tucked inside of me grew. Probably a chicory—kind of plain, but wild and free. I'd have purple-blue petals and grow along the back roads. And what about Rosa? She'd probably be a buttercup. All creamy yellow and pretty and shiny. No, Rosa deserved to be a flower in somebody's fancy garden. She'd blossom into a red, red rose—like her name. Or maybe not. I guess she'll have to decide if that fits for her.

When Grace went to the grocery store later, Rosa and I promised to clean the living room. Rosa grabbed a dust cloth and some Pledge and started dusting. I pulled the old Eureka out of the hall closet. It roared and sucked its way across the rug. I had to practically run to keep up with it. Rosa laughed. "It's gonna take off and fly you back to Pisa!"

It was good to see her smile. She was beginning to look happy again. She was sleeping all through the night now, not crying herself awake. And she didn't hold Binkie so tight. She let him breathe just a little, gave him room to stretch his legs and arms. The bruises on Rosa's arms and legs were gone. Her shiner was, too. You could see how sweet her face really was. How round and pink her cheeks could be, how chocolaty her eyes were, how pretty and thick her hair was. It made me glad to know that she could get some of her little girl look back.

Rosa finished her chores before me. "Should I do anything else?" she hollered over the roar of the vacuum cleaner. I shook my head, and she headed toward the kitchen. When I was finally done, I stuffed the Eureka back in the closet and joined her. I found my sister sitting by the window, staring outside. The sun lit up the yellow curtains and washed her round face in a light glow. I wished she could be this worry-free forever.

"I like not goin' to school," she said. "And I like that it's so quiet here. No yelling. No crying. But I miss Winnie. We missed her birthday, ya know."

"Yeah, I know. Are you homesick?"

"Sort of. Mostly, I just worry that Winnie is sad 'cuz we left her with Patrick and Mama. Even though you told me Patrick's her daddy, she doesn't know it, and maybe she doesn't like him, either."

"I think she likes him enough. He's always extra nice to her. I bet he had a big birthday bash for her, even though he doesn't know if we're dead or alive. Bet he bought her tons of presents, too."

"Maybe Mama wouldn't let him."

"Who knows? But one thing's for sure. Patrick wouldn't hit Winnie. I betcha he doesn't even care that you and me aren't there."

"Mama cares," Rosa said. "I bet she's crying all the time. We made her real sad."

"Yeah." I stared at the linoleum and tried to push Mama's face out of my mind.

Rosa was right. We had made Mama sad. And I felt bad about it. I always thought if I ever I had to choose between Mama and me, I'd choose Mama. I guess I was wrong. It was hard to leave her, to run away like we did, but something pushed my legs to keep going that day. Something inside of me said it was time to go, time to let Mama miss me as much as I've missed her. Maybe that's what Grace means about getting to know who you are. Maybe I already know how to do it, just a little.

"Rosa, do you still want to try to find Daddy?"

"Yeah, but . . ."

"But what?"

"I guess it's too hard. We don't have any money, and we'd probably just get lost again. And Grace wouldn't be there to rescue us, next time. Pisa's so far away. And Daddy's in that place. He can't have little girls with him. Besides, I wanna stay here with Grace."

"Are you mad at me 'cuz I didn't find a way to get us home?"

"Nope."

She faced me, eye-to-eye, so I knew she was telling the truth, not just saying "nope" so I'd feel better. It mattered a whole lot to me. I didn't want to disappoint her.

"Maybe it's time we thought about going home," I said.

I didn't mean it all the way, though. How Rosa answered was important. If she disagreed, I'd have to think it over. It wouldn't take much to convince me to stay with Grace. I wanted to learn more about screaming and laughing and dancing. But something tugged at me. I kept thinking about Zoomer and Danny all alone in Pisa now that Joey was dead. And Daddy. Even though what Rosa said was true about the monastery, Daddy loved us, I think. Maybe he just loved Jesus more. Maybe Jesus was like Grace to him, somebody who showed him what happiness feels like. And then there was Mama. I did love her, even though sometimes she made me so tired. Maybe if she could meet Grace, she'd feel a whole lot better, too. Patrick was the biggest reason I didn't want to go back. I couldn't stop wishing he'd die or just go home to Buffalo or move to Chicago or somewhere. But he had Winnie now, and he was staying put.

"I don't wanna go back to the apartment. I don't ever wanna see Patrick again," Rosa told me.

"But what about Mama?"

My sister hesitated before answering. "I . . . I miss Mama. But . . ."

"Are you scared of Patrick?"

Rosa started to cry. I hugged her close. "It'll be all right. I promise. I won't ever let him hit you again."

My sister cried harder then, and I decided to drop the question of going home for a while. We didn't have to decide, yet. We could stay with Grace a little longer. Someday, if we did go home and Patrick was mean to us again, maybe Grace would take us back. Or I could call Aunt Stella, and maybe she'd help us. I'd do my best for my sister. I knew I would. I just had to make her see that.

"Don't worry, Rosa, don't worry. I'll keep you safe."

"How?"

Before I could answer, the front door opened, and Grace

stepped inside carrying a Krogers grocery sack. "Regina, come here and give me a hand," she called, a little out of breath.

I rushed to help her. I took the bag from Grace's arms and followed her into the kitchen. Grace noticed Rosa's sloppy face and went to comfort her. "Why the tears, sweetie?"

"I don't wanna go home."

"Who says you have to?"

"Regina . . ."

"I was just thinking it might be time . . . not now . . . in a little while. That's all."

"I don't wanna live with Patrick." Rosa cried again, and Grace held her.

"Sweetie. You don't have to worry. You're safe now. You're safe."

"I told her I'd protect her if we did go home," I asserted. My face felt hot. I wished I'd kept my big mouth shut. Why'd I have to be such a jerk and get Rosa all upset? Now Grace was probably mad at me, too.

She must have read my mind. "Regina, you didn't do anything wrong. It's a natural thing to want to be with your Mama. Rosa's just upset. She'll be fine. Why don't you go unpack the grocery bags while I tend to your sister?"

I did as she asked, swallowing my own tears the whole time. I unpacked a dozen eggs, a sack of flour, a quart of buttermilk, and some baking chocolate. I set the food on the counter, then folded the bag and put it in Grace's bag drawer.

"Thank you, honeycake," Grace said. She rested her hand on my shoulder and kissed the top of my head. "Everything's all right now."

Rosa grabbed my hand and held it tight. "I'm not mad at you, Regina."

"I'm sorry, Rosa. I didn't mean to get you all sad."

"Feel better now?" Grace asked us. "Good. Let's have a party." She drummed her fingertips on the tabletop in a happy tap dance.

"A party? What for?" I asked.

"Today's my Luisa's birthday. Would have been thirty, bless her soul."

Grace's eyes got all teary. I grabbed a couple of Kleenexes from the box on the counter and tucked them in her hand. She thanked me with a smile and asked, "You girls like chocolate buttermilk cake?"

"Yum!" we squealed.

"I'll take that as a 'yes,'" Grace laughed.

"Chocolate's our favorite," I added. I couldn't keep from grinning.

"Let's get the table cleared and start makin' it then," Grace said. She almost skipped across the floor putting stuff away, taking out the bowls and the mixer and the cake pans. It's like she flew back to a time when Luisa was alive and still a little girl, and they made a chocolate birthday cake together in a different kitchen, in a different house. Grace's life had its hard stones, too. Maybe that's the way it is for everybody. But she found a way to smooth the boulders into small pebbles.

I started singing "Happy Birthday" and dancing around the kitchen. Rosa joined me. "Happy birthday, dear Luisa," we sang. "Happy birthday to you." We twirled on ballerina toes in the middle of Grace's kitchen. With each spin, my heart flew back to Pisa to play June Taylor Dancers with Amelia. We used to spend whole afternoons dancing and singing and laughing, not caring about anything. Grace twirled, too, on her skinny, wobbly legs, her housedress flapping in her own breeze. She stopped and clapped for us.

"Brava, brava," she said, with tears streaming down her kind face.

Seeing her that way made me think about the creek where Zoomer and I used to play. Grace would have liked that spot. She could have screamed as loud as she needed to there, and nobody would have bothered her. Grace's grown-up face was as wrinkled and wild as that creek bed. Her eyes were full of private sadness, but she didn't shut us out. I didn't know it then, but when she found us that rainy night in that bus shelter, Grace carried me and my sister to a place where nobody could hurt us ever again.

The morning after Luisa's birthday party, Grace pulled me aside and showed me a flyer she'd taken from the grocery store the day before. It had the words "Missing Girls" in big letters over the top and pictures of me and Rosa. "The police are looking for you," Grace said. "I didn't want to tell you yesterday, what with Rosa being all upset."

I panicked. "What should we do?"

"You can still stay here as long as you need to. Just thought you should know about the posting."

I stewed about that flyer. I didn't want Grace to get in trouble with the cops if they found out we were at her house. I didn't know what to do about Rosa not wanting to go back to the apartment. I knew she had a right to her fears. But we couldn't stay at Grace's too much longer.

That night, before we fell asleep, I talked to Rosa about our situation.

"I know you hate Patrick. I do, too. But the cops are looking for us. Grace showed me a flyer she got at the grocery store. I don't want to get her in trouble, Rosa. We gotta choose now. Either go back to Mama. Or really go back to Pisa."

"Pisa's too far away," Rosa whined. "We can't get there unless Grace helps."

"We could ask her tomorrow morning."

"Okay."

"Get some sleep now."

We grew quiet. I stared at the dark, thinking of the mess we were in, worrying about how to fix it. Maybe Grace could use the phone at the 7-Eleven to call Aunt Stella. If Grace told her about Patrick beating up Rosa, Stella would understand. She'd send money for us to get back to Daddy. There just had to be a way to keep Rosa safe. Even though I missed Mama and wanted to see her again, I couldn't fink out on my sister.

"Regina?" Rosa whispered. She touched my arm in the dark. "If we did go back home to Daddy, do you think we could still visit Grace sometimes?"

Her question sounded like a test. If I didn't answer yes, then she'd call the whole deal off.

"I don't know, Rosa. I hope so, but I don't know."

I choked back tears, missing Grace before we'd even left her. Why couldn't everybody have a mama like Grace? Why did some mamas have to carry rocks in their hearts? Why did *my* mama have to?

"Do you think Grace will be mad at us for leaving her?" Rosa whispered again.

"I don't think so. She'll be sad. But she won't hate us. She's not selfish like that. But, what if we can't get back to Daddy? We'll have to go home to Mama, then. Are you gonna be okay with that?"

"No!" Rosa gripped my arm.

"We got to go somewhere. We can't stay here, and we can't live on the corner."

"No."

"Rosa, I promise it'll be okay this time. I'll kill him if he hurts you."

"Honest?"

"Honest."

"Will you stay with me the whole time he's in the house?"

"Yep."

"Will you make sure he's not mean to Binkie?"

"Yep."

"Okay. I'll think about it."

The next morning, Rosa told me she was ready to go back to Mama.

"I had a dream last night. Mama was crying and crying. And then Daddy appeared and put his hand on her shoulder. He gave her a rosary and told her to pray for her daughters. Mama prayed and prayed. I've never seen Mama pray, ever. She promised the Blessed Virgin that she'd be a better mother if we came home. She promised she'd keep Patrick away from me and Binkie."

"What if the dream don't come true?"

"If you keep your promise about killing him, I'll give it a try. Besides, if Grace called Aunt Stella, she would probably just tell us to go back to Mama, anyway."

After breakfast, I told Grace that Rosa and I were ready to go back to Mama.

"Thought so," Grace said. She rubbed her hips, absentmindedly, like they were hurting.

Our timing was bad. Grace's hips were sore a lot these days, and she had trouble getting out of her chair. A couple of times, she even asked me to help her swing her legs onto her bed before she went to sleep at night. She'd been so good to us, I didn't want to leave her high and dry.

"Is your arthritis bothering you today, Grace?"

"Naw," she said. Her lips sagged into a small frown. "Just the change in weather. It's gonna be a humid June."

She stared out the window a while with her back to us. A couple of times, she brushed something from her face, but I couldn't tell if it was a wisp of hair or a fly until she let go a big sigh and pulled a Kleenex out of her apron pocket. I slipped my arms around her waist and held tight. Rosa joined me. Grace pulled us close and hugged us back.

"I know it's best for you to be with your mama, but I'm gonna miss you girls. You're like my own flesh and blood."

I wanted to take it back, tell her we'd changed our minds. We really did want to stay with her, be her daughters. But it was too late. Our time was up, and we all knew it. All we had to do was call, and we'd be back with Mama and Patrick and Winnie before lunch.

"Grace, will we be able to visit you sometimes?" My heart was hoping she'd say yes.

"Don't know, Regina. Depends on your mama. How mad she is at me for not telling her sooner where you two were."

"But you took good care of us," Rosa protested. "Mama won't be mad. We'll tell her she can't be."

Grace sighed softly. "It don't look so good for me to be harboring runaway children. They'll think I should've called. I believe they call it aiding and abetting."

I wondered if she was worried about getting into trouble with the cops because she had been in prison a long time ago. "We won't let them put you in jail, Grace," I promised. "We would have died in that thunderstorm if you hadn't saved us."

Grace laughed, full from her belly. "Died? I doubt it, Regina. You'd have been cold. You'd have been hungry. You'd have been wet. But you would have probably called your mama a whole lot sooner."

Rosa stated, "You took care of us. You fed us. Let us scream and laugh. Danced with us. You even made Binkie happy. Nobody's been able to do that for a long, long time. Not even me."

"Grace," I added. "I feel like I belong here . . . but I belong with Mama, too, in a different way. As much as I get mad at her for acting so crazy and tearing our family apart. It's just that her heart got broken a long time ago, and it never got better."

"No need to explain yourselves, girls," Grace said. She patted our heads and eased herself into a kitchen chair. "I know I touched your hearts. You touched mine, too. I've just never figured out how to take the sting away from leaving. I guess the only thing to do is to face it, bravelike, and get on with it."

Rosa nudged Binkie into Grace's lap. "Here, I wanna give you my dog, so you'll always remember me."

Grace kissed Rosa's cheek and searched her apron pocket. She pulled out a piece of purple yarn and tied a bow around Binkie's scrawny neck.

"Rosa, I'd never be able to accept a gift this precious. Take him home with this little bow tie, so we'll always have some comfort between us."

She tucked Binkie into Rosa's arms, then said, "Regina, go get me my knitting bag, honeycake."

I hurried to grab it, then hurried back to the kitchen. Every second away from Grace was too long. "Here ya go," I said.

Grace scrounged around in the bag for a few minutes before pulling out two pairs of purple mittens. "Kind of early for these," she said. "But I knew you wouldn't be here forever, so I made them for you. Sort of like a going-away present."

She placed the soft mittens into our open hands. I held them to my nose, inhaling the smell of her scent in the wool.

"Wow," Rosa squealed. "I never had my own pair of mittens, brand new."

It was true. Every pair of mittens or gloves Rosa had worn had passed over my hands first, and Joey's or Danny's before that, unless the boys tore 'em up having snowball fights and building winter forts in the woods.

"I'm honored," Grace laughed.

"But we don't have any present for you," I said.

"No need to fret, Regina. You've made me laugh. You've made me dance. Hell, you even got me to make chocolate cake again. I haven't celebrated Luisa's birthday since she died."

Still, it bugged me that I couldn't repay Grace for all she'd done. She was like the angel in that holy card with the two kids trying to cross that high, rickety bridge in the deep of night. "Angel of God, my guardian dear, to whom God's love commits me here; ever this night be at my side, to light and guard, to rule and guide. Amen." Grace didn't have big feathery wings, and her housedress wasn't a flowing robe, but her eyes were angel eyes. Her hands, even though they were crooked from too much worry and too much knitting, were soft as halo light.

"Well," she said. "I've got a phone call to make." She steadied herself against the kitchen table and stood.

"You don't have a phone," Rosa reminded her.

"I know that, child. I've got to take a walk to the 7-Eleven. They got a pay phone there I can use. What's your mama's number?"

I told her, and she jotted it down on a scrap of paper and tucked it into her pocket. Before she left, she reminded us to brush our teeth and comb our hair. "I don't want you going back to your mama looking like rag dolls," she pretended to scold. "Oh, and one more thing . . . if that Patrick gets out of hand again, you let me know. I'll help you any way I can." She handed me a piece of paper with her address written on it, then she walked out the front door. I tucked her note into my pants pocket as we watched her head down the road, still wearing her blue-checkered apron.

When Grace got back a while later, she looked tired and worried. "By the time I made it to the pay phone, I changed my mind about calling your mama. After all the things you girls have told me about her going off the deep end, I thought it best to go straight to the police. I figured they'd be a whole lot less hysterical."

"Are you worried about the cops coming here?" I asked.

"Well, there is that flyer. And you have been here just over a week . . . and I haven't notified the authorities. It might cause some trouble. But don't stew about it, Regina."

"Me and Rosa got a plan," I told her.

"Yeah," Rosa said. "While you were at the 7-Eleven, we made up a story you could tell Mama and the cops about finding us, so they won't throw you in jail for keeping us so long."

"Tell them you found us two days ago," I said. "When you were coming home from grocery shopping. Tell them we were standing in front of your house, tired and hungry, but we wouldn't tell you our names. So you couldn't call Mama or the cops. And you never saw a flyer. Tell them you gave us a bath and made us some supper and in a couple days, after we felt safe enough, we told you our names, and you called the police."

We promised to stick by that story 'til the day we died. She smiled and told us we were pretty smart kids and she was proud of us. "It might work. We'll just have to try it and see," she said.

Grace was right about the cops. She wasn't back home

from the 7-Eleven more than ten minutes before a police car pulled up to the front of her house. We sneaked one quick good-bye hug in before they came charging up to the porch, like they were rescuing us from some terrible thing.

They pounded on the door. "Mrs. Hartwell?" A tall cop with small blue eyes spoke first. "You called about the Giovanni girls?"

"Yes, yes, officer. Come right on in. They're here."

The shorter cop checked some papers he had in a folder. It looked like there were photos in there, too—the same ones I'd seen on the Krogers' flyer.

"Peanut Giovanni?" he said, looking first at the pictures, then at me.

"Regina," I said. "My name's Regina." Grace patted my shoulder. I could tell she was proud of my answer. "Used to be Peanut, but no more."

The cop smirked and turned to my sister. "You Rosa, or did you go and change your name, too?"

"I'm Rosa." My sister's voice sounded small and distant. She gripped Grace's hand.

The blue-eyed cop announced, "We'll need you to come down to the station with us, Mrs. Hartwell. To fill out some paperwork about how you found the girls and all."

"Certainly," Grace said. "But it's Grace Hartwell. No Mrs."

"Yes, Ma'am," he said. He was politer than the short cop, and he had kind hands. I expected them to be hard and rough from fighting crooks, but they were squishy and soft, like big sofa cushions.

All three of us piled into the back of the cop car and rode to the police station. When we got there, the cops called Mama.

"We have your daughters, Mrs. Shaughnessy," the short cop said into the phone. "They appear to be well and unharmed." His brown eyes were still investigating us. "A Mrs. Hartwell found them. They'll be safe here until you come pick them up."

A lady cop got me and Rosa some ice-cream bars while Grace talked to the blue-eyed cop about how we came to be in her care. She stuck to the story we'd come up with, and he seemed to believe her. He just kept writing it down, saying, "Yes, Ma'am. Okay, Ma'am." Grace's face and voice were calm the whole time. You couldn't tell she was lying. I was proud of her. I think our looking healthy and clean pulled the cops off track, too. I kept praying they wouldn't check their records and learn about Grace being in prison. And I hoped Mama didn't do anything weird like make the police lock Grace up. Rosa and I would have to try and talk her out of it, if she did.

By the time Rosa and I licked the last drop of chocolate from our ice-cream sticks, Mama had arrived at the station. Patrick was with her. Rosa grabbed my hand when she saw him. My heart froze.

Mama kissed and hugged us like we'd come back from the dead. And I guess, to her, we had. "Oh, my babies. I was so worried. You scared me half to death."

"Hi, Mama," I said as she squeezed me. It was good to see her, too, good even to feel her arms all tight around my shoulders.

Patrick's eyes said "I'm sorry." He pecked Rosa and me on the cheek. "Good to see you." He sounded like he meant it. Maybe things could turn out all right after all.

"Where have you been?" Mama asked.

"We got lost, then that lady found us, and took good care of us," I said, pointing to Grace.

"The important thing is you're safe with us now," Mama said.

Patrick nodded.

"Where's Winnie?" Rosa asked.

"Mrs. Anderson's watching her for us."

After Mama stopped hugging me, I showed her the purple mittens Grace had made for us. "Aren't they pretty?" I crowed.

"Yes, honey, they're very pretty." She grabbed the mittens and stuffed them in her pocketbook. "Let's look at them later," she said to my angry face. She kept touching my hair, squeezing my hand, crying, and blowing her nose, saying over and over again, "Thank God they found my babies. Thank God they found my babies."

My eyes searched the room for Grace. I was worried they'd locked her up when I wasn't paying attention. But during one of the times Mama stopped hugging me long enough to blow her nose, I caught a glimpse of Grace slowly walking toward the door. She turned just before she opened it and tossed me a smile. Her eyes were sloppy with tears. She blew me a kiss and sent one to Rosa, too. Then she covered her heart with her hand. I touched my heart and cried.

"Oh, baby," Mama said. "Don't cry, everything's gonna be all right. You're safe with us now."

Mama thought my tears were for her, for how happy I was to see her again. But they were Grace's tears. Only Grace's. A big hole in my chest opened and closed, opened and closed when Grace walked out of the police station.

Patrick settled stuff with the cops while Mama and me and Rosa were finishing our reunion. "All set," he said, finally.

They hurried me and Rosa to the car. We were quiet all the way home. By the time we walked through the door of our apartment, I'd made a sort of peace with it all. I'd give Patrick another chance as long as he didn't hurt Rosa or Binkie. I'd give Mama another chance, too. Maybe our taking off had scared them. Maybe now they realized we were just as important as Mama's broken heart. Patrick needed her, but we did, too. Maybe now that we were back with her, Mama could forget about losing Danny and Joey and start loving who she had right in front of her. We couldn't bring Danny here, or bring Joey back alive, but we still counted.

In a funny sort of way, it felt good to be back. I had missed Mama more than I realized. And Winnie, too. Mrs. Anderson brought my baby sister upstairs and gave Rosa and me a hug. She told us Mama and Patrick worried a lot when we were lost. She said everybody was glad we were safe. She told us if we ever needed anything to not be afraid to ask her or Mr. Anderson. They'd be glad to help.

I thanked her, and then she smiled and went home. Mama made spaghetti and meatballs for supper and chocolate cake for dessert. As good as it tasted, it wasn't like Luisa's birthday cake. I tried not to cry when I ate it. Mama didn't cry once the whole way through supper, and Patrick was nice, too. He kept saying how relieved he was that we girls were okay and that we were a family again, all together. I kept catching him staring at Rosa's face, like he wanted to make sure her shiner was gone.

Rosa and I slept in our own beds that night, but I missed our "make-do" couch cushions on Grace's living room floor. When I started to feel all worried and mad about leaving Grace, I imagined myself screaming in her living room. It worked for about fifteen minutes, but it made me miss her even more. I wondered if Grace was able to get her too-tired legs into bed on her own that night, without me and Rosa there to help swing her ankles onto the mattress. I wondered if her chest felt cold like a January night, so cold that not even her rose and green afghan could make her toasty again. I wondered if she turned one way and then the other in her bed all night long, like I did, trying to forget that in the morning we wouldn't be sitting at her table eating pancakes. I checked my pants pocket to make sure the piece of paper with her address was still in there. I'd have to keep it in a safe place so Mama wouldn't find it.

I fell asleep wishing I could slip between the gap in Grace's front teeth and hide. Then I could hear her stories and ride her laughter until I landed somewhere soft, always close to that woman I loved with all my heart.

The Ultimatum

I hid Grace's address under my mattress. I fetched it out every morning and shoved it in my pocket so it would be near me all day long, just in case I needed it.

I missed Grace like crazy, even though living with Mama wasn't as bad as before. She didn't spend her time holed up in her bedroom crying. She was up and at it, all dressed and combed when I got home from school every day. She even met me at the door with a huge smile. "Hey, honey. How was your day?" I'd tell her about a test I'd taken, or how Julie Farley got caught passing a note to Debbie Smith, or anything else that had happened at school. Mama didn't even yell when I told her I almost decked Jimmy Malone when he pushed me against the wall during recess.

"That boy isn't very nice, is he?" Mama comforted. "If you'd like, I'll talk to your teacher about his behavior. Maybe she can get him to shape up. Or I could call his mother. Talk to her. Straighten things out."

Mama was a different person from the woman I'd known

my whole entire life. The things I said and felt suddenly became important to her. And she stopped wanting to be someplace else. She didn't waste whole days staring out the window at the sky. She didn't cuss at the walls. She laughed more, at silly things, like Rosa saying when she grew up she was gonna marry Binkie and ask Grace to come to the wedding.

I still worried that Mama'd be able to read my heart and see how much I loved Grace. Every time Grace's face popped into my head, I expected Mama to cry, "You only got one mother. You'll be sorry when I'm dead and gone." But she never did say that.

Rosa and I didn't tell anybody the whole truth about us and Grace—how we'd lived with her for a little over a week, not two days like she told the cops. My sister and I also made up a second part to that story. After we got home, people kept telling us it was a miracle we survived.

"What'd you do about eating and staying warm before that woman found you?"

We told them we lived in the forest and ate wet twigs and worms. And that we built a fort of dead branches. I got that idea from the book *The Swiss Family Robinson.* I liked how those people built a big tree house and lived on coconuts and stuff they found. I was glad nobody ever asked me what earthworms tasted like. I prayed nobody dared me to eat one in front of them.

I was sort of famous at school. When the kids heard about my adventure, they hung around at recess asking questions. "Wow, didn't it get scary at night when it got dark? Weren't you afraid of wolves eating you? Or bears?"

Only Jimmy Malone and Timmy Johnson got smart alecky. Jimmy sassed, "Why didn't you just walk to a 7-Eleven and call your mother?"

166

Timmy shoved a fistful of squirmy worms in my face, "Here, Regina, have some lunch."

I spit at him. "You stupid jerk."

I was ready to haul off and punch his nose, but Mrs. Benson stepped in. "Now, now, children. There's no need to fight. Timmy, it's not nice to tease Regina about being lost. Apologize to her, then go put those worms back in the dirt."

We weren't back in school a week before it was summer vacation. Rosa's teacher passed her into the first grade without a hitch, even though she lost all those days while we were gone. I couldn't go on to the sixth grade until I did extra work to make up the stuff I'd missed. They got me a tutor from the college where Patrick worked. Her name was Helena, and she was studying to be an elementary school-teacher. She helped me as part of her schoolwork, and it didn't cost Mama and Patrick any money, which made me really glad. I didn't want to cause any fights.

Mama started taking us for walks in the afternoon that summer. Sometimes, we'd hop a bus and ride over to Lake Mendota to feed popcorn to the ducks. Once in a while, we'd go get ice-cream cones at the Memorial Union at the University. Mama called them our "little outings." I could hardly wait for my tutoring session to be over so we could go. It felt like we were a family again, Mama and Rosa and Winnie and me. I started to relax a little. I felt free—like those ducks on the lake, their feathery bodies bobbing and swaying whichever way the waves took them. That lasted until we got home and found Patrick waiting.

"Where have you been?" he scowled. "How come supper isn't ready? How much money did you throw away on ice-cream cones today?"

Then they'd go at it. I'd hurry Rosa and Winnie off to our

bedroom so we'd all be safe. But I could still hear them hollering through the closed door.

"What harm is there in taking the girls out?" Mama insisted. "It's summertime, for Christ's sake. We're supposed to have a little fun."

"Maybe you should get a part-time job if you want to spend money we don't have on field trips with your daughters," Patrick snipped. "We aren't going to make it to August, the way you're frittering it all away."

"What's a few bucks, every now and then?" Mama declared.

"It adds up fast!" Patrick hollered.

I'd swallow back tears and feel the watery bounce of the lake waves slipping away. I'd shove my face into my pillow and scream. Rosa escaped, too. She'd rush off to her secret place for a while. When she came back, she'd hide under her bed until she felt better. Her skin hadn't forgotten the feel of Patrick's heavy hands.

One afternoon in July, he really laid into us. We'd just gotten back from a trip to the library and found him on the steps with a bottle of wine in one hand and a Lucky Strike in the other. We girls slipped past him and went upstairs. Rosa tossed her stack of books on the coffee table and headed straight for our bedroom. Winnie followed her, but I stayed by the door so I could check on whether we needed to run back to Grace or not.

"How much did you spend this time?" Patrick seethed.

"Not a damn dime," Mama barked. "Books are free at the public library."

"I've had it with your disrespect, Marie. All I get from you is grief. You can't even make a decent home. I'm beginning to think Paulie was right about you. You're a lousy mother."

I held my breath. Mama's eyes steamed. She raised her hand to slug him but pulled it back to her side in a hurry.

"You son-of-a-bitch," she said. Her voice was low and hot. "Think you're holier than God. But you're a selfish pig. I thought Paulie was bad. At least he loved his kids. You don't give a damn about anybody but yourself."

"I care, Marie. You just don't notice. You got your head in the clouds, all fixated on those damn girls. Ever since they came back, they're all you think about. 'Peanut this and Rosa that.' You don't even know I'm alive. You're a cold woman, Marie. Paulie froze to death, that's for damn sure. I don't know why I never figured it out before."

"You're the icy bastard, not me," Mama accused.

Patrick kicked the door. I ducked into the kitchen to clear out of his way. He disappeared into their bedroom. Mama followed him. "Where you going?" she demanded.

"I can't take it anymore, Marie," Patrick shouted.

"You can't just pack up and leave."

"Watch me," Patrick yelled. He headed back toward the door with a suitcase in his hand.

Mama rushed after him, grabbing his arm. Patrick stopped and faced her. "I miss you, Marie. The way we used to be. We never bickered. I'm so tired of it. You haven't been the same since we got to Madison. I'm going to stay with Jack and Annie for a while. Give myself some time to think things over. You can reach me there if you need to. Or want to."

"Patrick, no," Mama begged. "Don't go. Things will work out, give it time. I don't want you to go. Please . . ."

He shook his head.

"Patrick," Mama called in a scared, little voice. "Can't we talk about this?"

"There's nothing more to say."

"How long are you going to stay at Jack's?" Mama cried, but Patrick didn't give in.

"I don't know. A week or two. I don't know."

He pulled out his wallet and set some cash on the kitchen table. "This should hold you until I figure out what I'm going to do next. If you run out, call me. I'll send more."

He left. The door closed softly behind him. I let out a little sigh of relief as the sound of his footsteps disappeared down the stairs. Mama stared at the closed door as if staring could will him back. Her face screamed his name. She grabbed the money and counted it, out loud.

"Twenty, thirty, forty, fifty, seventy, ninety. Goddamn son-of-a-bitch. How the hell does he expect me to take care of three kids on this?"

She covered her face and cried into the cash, still wadded in her hands. "It'll be okay, Mama. We don't need him. I got some money saved you can have."

After Patrick left, our summer outings stopped. Mama was too sad to go for a walk or get ice cream. She worried about money a lot. We ate Kraft Macaroni and Cheese dinners she bought at Krogers, four for a buck. One night, she splurged and tossed in some tuna fish and a can of green peas. Things were sliding back to the way they used to be. I was madder than ever. Screaming into my pillow didn't help at all.

Patrick called on my birthday, three days later. Mama was making me a chocolate cake with white frosting and colored sprinkles when the phone rang. I answered it quickly, hoping it might be Daddy calling from the monastery or Danny calling from Mrs. Marco's to wish me a happy birthday. When I heard Patrick's grouchy voice, I handed the phone to Mama.

"Patrick, listen to reason," Mama pleaded. "Give me a second chance. Don't I deserve a second chance?"

She leaned against the wall, working hard to conjure up reasons for him to come back. He wasn't buying any of it. Her hold on him was loosening. It made her desperate and bossy.

"Okay," she threatened. "Do what you want. But don't you think for one second I'm gonna let you get your hands on Winnie."

Mama slammed down the phone, tossed her spatula into the bowl of cake batter, and stormed around the apartment for half an hour. "Thinks he's so goddamn superior. He ain't gonna get Winnie. Even if she is his kid. I'll take him all the way to the Supreme Court if I have to."

Mama had never said it out loud like that before, never admitted that Winnie was Patrick's baby, not Daddy's. Rosa whispered, "You were right."

Mama called Aunt Stella, collect. She cried for another half hour. I don't think Stella had too much sympathy. Mama said, "I know you think I deserve this, Stel, but you got to listen to me. He wasn't crazy like this before we moved here."

Mama finally broke down and told Stella the real reason Rosa and I had run away. "He's been strange since the day he beat up Rosa. That's why the girls ran away. That other stuff I told you was a lie. I thought if I covered for him, he'd never do it again. Rosa ran off. Regina raced after her. Then they got lost."

Stella changed her mind and told Mama she'd do anything she could to help her out. Uncle Tony had a friend who had a cousin who was a lawyer in Minneapolis, and he'd see if he would help Mama if it got to the point where she was ready to divorce Patrick.

"Thing is, Stel, I don't think he's got a leg to stand on," Mama confessed. "We're not legally married."

That took some explaining. Mama told Stella that she and Daddy were just getting around to getting a divorce when Joey died. Things got off track after that, and Daddy ran off to that monastery in Cayuga. He never did follow through on the divorce stuff. "People around here know me as Mrs. Shaughnessy," Mama said. "But I'm really still Mrs. Giovanni."

Mama paced the kitchen floor. "Yeah, Stel. Okay. I understand. You're mad at me. Yes, I know it's a mortal sin. Give me a break. You ain't God. I don't need you pointing your finger at me. Are you gonna help me or not?"

In the end, Stella still agreed to get Uncle Tony to talk to that friend about his lawyer cousin. Before she hung up, Aunt Stella asked for me.

"Happy birthday, sweetie," she said. "Are you gonna have a party?"

"Nope. I'm too old for parties."

"Too old for parties? How the hell old are you, Peanut?"

"Eleven. And my name's Regina."

"Oh, yeah, I forgot. Well, honey, try to have some fun on your special day, okay?"

"Sure," I said, trying to sound happy. "Mama's making a cake, and I get to have zitis for supper."

"That's nice, sugar. Give Rosa and Winnie a kiss for me, okay? Bye-bye."

When I hung up, I found Mama plopped on the couch, blowing her nose and wiping her eyes. She called us girls to her.

"Regina, I know this has been a lousy birthday, but I'll make it up to you soon. Things are gonna be tough around here for a while, until I can figure out what to do. In the meantime, I need you to help me with Rosa and Winnie."

I nodded. "All right, Mama. I can do it." She smiled at me and kissed my forehead. "You're my sweet girl, aren't you?" She squeezed Rosa's hand. "I want you to mind Regina. What she says goes, understand?"

"Yes, Mama."

Mama kissed Rosa, then gave Winnie a smooch. "That goes for you, too, Winnie."

"'Kay."

"Nobody's gonna break us apart. Nobody," Mama said. "Now, let's go see if we can salvage that birthday cake. Regina, put *My Fair Lady* on the record player for me. I feel like singing."

Heart to Heart

Patrick didn't come back home. He stayed with Jack and Annie for a month. A couple of times, he asked Mama to bring Winnie over for a visit. She reminded him that we didn't have a car anymore. He told her he'd swing by and take them out to lunch.

"Breakfast is better," Mama told him.

Patrick never asked to see me and Rosa. We weren't too keen on seeing him, either. But it still made me mad to be left out on purpose like that. Mama read the hurt in our eyes and tried to make it better. She told us, "It's not about you girls. Patrick just can't handle *anyone* over three."

I bet how old you are won't matter when Winnie gets to be my age or Rosa's. He'll still want to see her. Mama never said anything about the real reason Patrick only wanted to see Winnie. She never admitted to our faces what I'd heard her say to Aunt Stella on the phone. I asked her straight out one night, "Is Winnie Patrick's daughter?"

All she said was, "Where'd you ever get a silly idea like that?"

Patrick drove up at half past eight on Saturday morning. He beeped the horn, and Mama called to us on the way out, "I'll be home for lunch." Rosa and I watched from the front window as they piled into Patrick's car.

"Wanna go visit Grace?" I pulled the address out of my pocket and waved it at my sister.

"We don't know how to get there," Rosa reminded me.

Grace's house was in a part of Madison we'd never been to before that day she found us in the bus shelter. And although I had her address, I didn't have a clue how to retrace our steps and find her. And she didn't have a phone, so we couldn't call her. If we needed her, we'd have to write a note, mail it to her, and wait for an answer.

I grabbed a box of Vanilla Wafers and joined Rosa on the steps. We sat there all morning telling Grace stories and drawing pictures. Rosa drew one of us in Grace's kitchen making a chocolate cake. I drew us dancing in her living room. I shoved a couple of cookies into my mouth and sucked the sweetness into mush while Rosa told me her favorite Grace story.

"I liked when Grace talked about growing up on a farm and picking stones out of the field."

"My favorite is the time Grace told me to scream my guts out."

"Sometimes I wish we still lived with her," Rosa said.

"Me, too."

At noon, a car pulled up. Rosa and I heard Mama saying, "Winnie, wave bye-bye to Patrick." A car door shut. Rosa and I rushed to collect our drawings and our crayons so Mama wouldn't see. We hauled our stuff into the house, hid the pictures in our bedroom, and got back to the living room in time to turn the TV on as Mama and Winnie came through the door.

"Hi, girls," Mama called. Rosa and I smiled guilty smiles, but she didn't notice. "I'm bushed," she sighed as she put Winnie down and sat on the couch.

"I got a new doll," Winnie bragged.

Rosa and I ignored her.

"Did he give you more money?" I asked Mama.

"Yeah. Enough for rent and two weeks' worth of groceries. But he told me he's moving into a place of his own in a couple of weeks. He won't be able to help us out much anymore. I made him promise he'd at least give me some for Winnie."

"Why just her?" I was trying to get her to admit Winnie was Patrick's kid.

"Oh, she's just a baby. She needs extra things."

"How we gonna pay for the rest of the stuff we need?" I worried out loud.

"I'm gonna have to find a job," Mama said. She bit her lip and looked scared.

Mama stewed about money for a few days until Aunt Stella finally convinced her that finding work was the way to go.

"It's for the best," Mama told me. "Besides, Stella said it'll look better to the judge if Patrick tries to take Winnie from me."

I stared at Mama but didn't say anything. I guess Stella was right. I never did quite understand grown-ups all the way. They were always trying to best each other. Always huffing and puffing to beat somebody at something so they could feel better. It seemed like a silly waste of time to me.

But I guess I was guilty of doing it, too, sometimes. Maybe that's just the way people are. Except Grace. She wasn't greedy like that. She just let things be the way they were and didn't make a fuss over it.

"Life sends you enough to fret and stew over," Grace had said when I asked her how come she didn't get all upset over stuff, like my mama did. "No need to go looking for trouble or making a boil out of a pimple. It'll just drive ya crazy."

In my heart, I preferred Grace's way of thinking. I guess I had too much of Mama in me to separate out the stuff I needed to stew about from the stuff I didn't. Mama's getting a job was one of those things. I worried about it a lot. I'd never seen her do nothing except be a mom, and there were plenty of times when that was too much for her to handle. Back in Pisa, Daddy used to get up every day and go to work—if he was sick or not. But Mama was different. She'd go lie down if that's what she needed. Didn't matter if it was time to cook supper or if Winnie needed a story or if Rosa wanted a cookie. If her heart wasn't feeling good, things didn't get done.

After supper one night, Mama said, "Regina, I'm gonna need you to take care of Rosa and Winnie when I get a job." She was washing dishes, thinking up a storm. She rubbed the plates with the washrag long after the crud was already gone. "I'll have to start work after you get home from school, so I can be here to take care of Winnie. Rosa starts first grade this fall, so both of you will be in school all day. After her class gets out, you pick her up and bring her home right away. Then I'll leave for work. Okay?"

"Yep, Mama."

I wanted her to put the clean plate in the dish drainer so I could dry it before she rubbed a hole in it. Helping her with the girls would be easy. I'd been doing it for years. When school started up again, I'd be in the sixth grade. I had turned eleven in July. Since Rosa and I'd run away, I knew I was brave, like Grace told me. I just didn't want Mama to wander back into that land of no-return she fell into when her worries piled up. That's the only thing I couldn't stop from happening, even though I was a warrior-girl.

"I'll fix supper and leave it in the fridge for you," Mama said.

She set the squeaky plate in the rack, then took it back again. She rinsed the plate over and over, under the hot water. "You'll have to reheat it on the stove, Regina. And make sure you and Rosa do your homework and get to bed by nine."

"Yes, Mama. I know what to do."

She finally set the plate in the dish rack. I snatched it up and dried it before she could shove it back into the soapy water. She was acting weird, talking out loud, getting things squared away before she even had a job. But at least she was thinking of all the stuff she had to do, instead of acting like she couldn't get up out of bed to save her soul. And she wasn't crying.

After the last plate was dried and put away, Mama pored over the want ads. She circled a few waitress jobs, picked up the phone, and called to find out more. "I've got the best qualifications," she boasted. "For seventeen years, I've waited hand and foot on my five kids."

That convinced them to talk with her in person. The next day, she took the bus downtown and interviewed at five different restaurants. When she got home, she rushed up the steps and burst through the door.

"I got a job!" she crowed.

She twirled a tiny circle of delight in the middle of the living room floor and handed me a white box. I popped the lid and took a whiff. Four chocolate cupcakes.

"I had to wait 'til the very last interview, but Mr.

Clancy—down at Clancy's Restaurant—hired me right on the spot. Said he liked my spunk," Mama boasted. "I'll be working the supper shift. Three-thirty to closing. I start tomorrow. The pay's lousy, but the tips are great. And they make all their desserts right at the restaurant. These cupcakes are from their kitchen."

Mama smiled the whole night. We ate toasted cheese sandwiches and tomato soup for supper and celebrated with Clancy's delicious cupcakes. We were on our way.

With her own money and Clancy's bakery treats, I didn't see how Mama could ever need Patrick again. That didn't stop him from calling, asking to see Winnie. Mama agreed a few times, but it was harder now that she had a job. When she wasn't working, he was. When he was free, she was at Clancy's. Even though his leaving made her have to get a job, Patrick didn't like it that Mama wasn't with Winnie every second of the day.

"You're a lousy mother, to leave your four-year-old," he told her.

"Shut up!" Mama had hollered. "We have to eat. And eating costs money."

Almost every day, Patrick called Mama just before she had to go to work. She'd be in a hurry, tying her apron, putting on her white waitress shoes, with the phone tucked between her shoulder and her ear. "If you're so concerned about Winnie, why the hell'd you leave us?" I watched the clock, afraid she'd be late. But she slammed the phone into the receiver, just in time, grabbed her purse and her bus money, kissed us a quick good-bye, and fumed all the way down the steps.

Mama's job made her tired. She never got home before

midnight. She had to stay late and help clean up Clancy's after the place closed. By the time she caught a bus and got back to our apartment, she was too wound up to sleep. I'd hear her sometimes, in the living room, at one or two in the morning, singing along with the *My Fair Lady* record, keeping the volume low so she wouldn't wake us up. Sometimes I'd hear her crying. I guess she missed Patrick and Danny and Joey. My heart broke, thinking of Mama working so hard and being so lonesome. I promised myself I'd work extra hard and make it so she didn't have to worry about me and my sisters.

When school started in September, we girls got up at six o'clock every weekday. I made us cereal and toast and put a pot of coffee on for Mama. Before Rosa and I left, I brought a cup to Mama and set it on the table next to her bed. "Mama, it's time to get up now. Me and Rosa have to go to school. Winnie's in the living room watching TV."

After school, I'd meet Rosa by her classroom door and rush home to take care of Winnie so Mama could make it to work on time. The afternoons were quiet without Mama around. Sometimes, it felt like we were back at Grace's house. I tried to find that radio station she used to listen to, but I never had any luck. Winnie played with her toys while Rosa and me did our homework. Mrs. Anderson usually stopped by just before supper to check on us, see if we needed anything. About five-thirty, I heated up whatever Mama had left us for supper, and we girls ate. Rosa helped me clean up afterwards, then we watched a little TV. Every other night, I made Rosa take a bath, whether she wanted to or not. I filled the tub, added some Mr. Bubble, and put her and Winnie in there together. Then, it was pajama time and one last TV show before we all went to bed.

One night after supper, I heard a car pull into our driveway. It was Patrick. I turned off all the lights and checked to make sure the door was locked. I prayed Mama had remembered to make him give back his key. I was afraid he'd come to hurt Rosa or take Winnie, and I didn't know if I'd be able to stop him. Or how I'd explain why I didn't, if I couldn't.

I heard footsteps on the stairs outside. "Go hide," I whispered to my sisters. We hurried, and I locked the bedroom door behind us.

"Hello," Patrick called. "Regina, Rosa, Winnie? Anybody here?" He was in our house! My heart raced. *Dear God,* I prayed, *don't let him find us.* Patrick knocked on our bedroom door.

"Regina. Open up."

He tried the knob. When it wouldn't turn, he knocked harder. "Regina. Unlock this door, now!"

"Go away," I shouted. "Leave us alone!" My legs shook, and I couldn't stop my heart from pounding. I kept seeing Mama's face, how awful she'd feel when she came home and found Rosa full of bruises again or Winnie gone. She'd be a wreck, and it would be all my fault. "Get under the bed," I whispered to Rosa. "Take Winnie, too."

"Nothing's gonna happen if you just open the door," Patrick said. His voice scared me. His words came out soft, but underneath there was something else—something mean and hard. "I just want to visit with you. It's all right. I talked with your mama. She knows I'm here."

I didn't believe him. Mama never said nothing about Patrick stopping by. But she had to leave in a hurry that afternoon because me and Rosa were five minutes late getting home. She could have just forgotten to tell me. If what he said was true, Mama'd be really mad if I disobeyed him.

"Regina!" His voice rose louder. Its fake, sweet tone fell away.

He rattled the doorknob harder and pounded the wall.

"I'm not going to tell you again. Open up, or I'll break the goddamn door down."

He was full of fury, now. Rosa screamed. I opened the door and prayed he wasn't gonna hit us.

"Jesus Christ, Regina," he yelled. "You drive me crazy. Everything's a big production with you."

I was glad Rosa was safe under her bed. Patrick pointed at my face, "Don't you ever disobey me again."

He pushed past me, nearly knocking me to the floor. He knelt down, reached under the bed. Rosa screamed and kicked his hand. "Ouch! You little son-of-a-bitch." My stomach twisted. He rubbed his sore knuckles then reached under the bed again. This time he pulled Winnie out. I panicked. "Come here, sweetie. How you doing?" He kissed her. "Wanna go get an ice-cream cone with me?"

"We had dessert already," I blurted out.

"I wasn't talking to you," Patrick snapped. "Come on, Winnie, let's go for a ride."

He cradled Winnie close to his heart. She wiggled to get away. "No," she said. "I want Peanut."

Patrick whispered, "We'll have fun, you'll see."

He held her arms, so she couldn't squirm, and carried her into the living room. I followed them. I had to beat him to the door, find a way to stop him from leaving. I'd bite his arm if I had to. I raced after Patrick. I grabbed his arms and tugged hard, trying to free Winnie. His strong hands didn't budge.

"Get the hell out of my way," he shouted.

I opened my mouth to bite him and a scream slipped out. "HELP! SOMEBODY HELP ME."

Two sets of feet raced up the steps. Patrick scowled, "You little bitch." He raised his hand to swat me as Mr. and Mrs. Anderson rushed through our door.

"Regina! Are you all right?" Mr. Anderson asked.

Mrs. Anderson stayed by the door, waiting.

"Oh, hello, Patrick," Mr. Anderson said. "We thought someone had broken in. We've been kind of keeping an eye out for the girls since their mother started working nights."

"That's very kind of you, Frank, but Regina's fine," Patrick said. He switched his voice from mean to kind and lied to our neighbors. "I just stopped by to visit the girls. I missed them. Regina got out of hand. She got a little miffed at me for disciplining her. You know how hysterical she can be. Eleven-year-olds are quite the drama queens. Especially Regina."

Patrick laughed and so did Mr. Anderson, but Mr. Anderson's laugh sounded nervous, like he didn't quite believe Patrick. Mrs. Anderson didn't laugh at all. She studied me for a second, then gently tugged on her husband's sweater. "Frank," she urged.

Her husband read her voice. "Well, perhaps if you're through visiting, you ought to leave," Mr. Anderson said.

"I was just gonna take the girls for an ice-cream cone. I'll bring them back in about an hour."

"Don't let him," I blurted out. "He just wants to take Winnie. He ain't gonna bring her back."

"Regina's such a liar, Frank. It's a big problem. Marie and I are trying to break her of it, but we're not getting very far."

"I think you should leave now," Mr. Anderson insisted. He locked eyes with Patrick.

"You've got no right to keep me from my kids," Patrick threatened.

"This is my property. If you don't leave immediately, I'm calling the cops." Mr. Anderson's eyes never left Patrick's.

Patrick set Winnie on the couch. "I'll stop by and take you out for ice cream some other time." He bent over and kissed her. "Good-bye, sweetie." He shoved his fists into his pants pockets and walked out the door.

The Andersons stayed with us until Patrick drove away.

"I guess you kids will be all right now," Mr. Anderson said, watching Patrick's taillights turn the corner away from our apartment.

"If you need anything, just give a holler," Mrs. Anderson added.

"Thanks," I said. "Thanks, a lot."

"Be sure to let your mother know about this," Mr. Anderson insisted. "We'll probably have to have the locks changed."

The next day, I told Mama the whole story. "Goddamn son-of-a-bitch," she muttered. "Thank God for the Andersons. I'll talk to them about getting a locksmith in here, today."

When Mama told my aunt what Patrick had done, Stella said, "That S.O.B will stop at nothing. Well, let him have his stupid antics. Damn fool. Every crazy thing he does just tightens his noose."

I felt better after we had new locks. Even if the Andersons weren't around, the next time Patrick showed up and tried to kidnap Winnie, he wouldn't be able to get in. Rosa felt better, too. Plenty of nights after Patrick was here, she woke up screaming, "Mama, Mama! Save me from the monsters." I knew she was having a bad dream about Patrick. It's how she'd been when we first got to Grace's house, before she'd had time to heal.

Mama phoned Patrick. "Don't you EVER pull a stunt like that again." She told him his key wasn't good anymore and that if he ever showed his sorry face around here, uninvited, she'd call the cops. "You ain't ever gonna see Winnie alone again, EVER."

Slowly, a new Mama was being born. One that was tougher, softer—less grouchy. She still got cranky and tired. She still cried and yelled at us. But not as often and not in the same way. I don't know how to explain it except that she looked taller, like somebody had stretched her legs. Her eyes were clear and bright. The broken pieces inside of her were starting to fit together, as if they'd been glued back into place. That was even better than having new locks.

I could tell she missed Patrick, but it wasn't like before when we still lived in Pisa and she had to wait until Friday to see him. Back then, she'd be antsy all week; crab at us for no good reason. Her attention could never settle on anything until she talked to him on the phone. In Madison, she didn't fuss about him being gone. She went about her business, cleaning and cooking and watching TV. Every once in a while, she'd stop and sigh, and I'd know she'd be thinking about him. She'd mutter to herself, "Not unless he gets his act together and treats *all* my girls better."

Mama had made a new friend at Clancy's. Her name was Doris. Mama'd come home from work and tell us Doris stories. "Her kids are all grown up. She's had three husbands. Said she had to teach each one how to respect her. She said there isn't a man alive who deserves a woman's love if he's gonna be mean to her children."

One Sunday morning in October, Mama invited Doris over for coffee. She had silvery blond hair and watery blue eyes. She wore five bracelets on her right arm and three rings on her left hand. She smelled like too much five-and-dime perfume. When she kissed me hello, she left pink lip marks on my cheek. I liked her a whole lot. After she came along, Mama spent less time talking to Aunt Stella and more time yakking on the phone with Doris. She was always trying to get Mama to stick up for herself. She wanted Mama to go to something she called Consciousness Raising meetings with her at the local women's center. But Mama said the only thing she wanted raised was her salary.

It was Doris's idea for Mama to write to Danny. "What harm could it do?" she asked. "Tell him Patrick isn't living with you anymore. Maybe that'll help him change his mind."

Mama took her friend's advice. She spent a whole week working on that letter. "I got to say it just right," she said. When it was all done, she read it to Doris and got her seal of approval.

"That's a fine letter, Marie. Even if he doesn't agree to move here, at least you cleared your heart, and that's gotta be good." Doris hugged Mama, and they both cried.

The next day, Mama mailed it. All three of us girls and Doris walked to the corner with Mama. We stood in a circle around the mailbox. Mama flipped the slot back and slid her letter into its dark, metal belly. We held hands, and Mama hummed. She sounded so sweet.

After Mama finished, Doris left for her shift at Clancy's. The rest of us walked through the park. The oak leaves were changing to gold, and the maples were fiery orange. Rosa and Winnie ran ahead to chase leaves. The sad, pretty afternoon reminded me of Joey. He always loved autumn, loved the World Series, and loved jumping in the leaves.

"I miss Joey," I said out loud. It was an accident. I was talking to the oak tree inside my head, telling it how pretty its leaves looked shining in the sunlight. They reminded me of how shiny Joey's eyes could be when he talked about the Yankees.

"I miss him, too," Mama said. "And Danny." She got quiet then. I waited for her to burst into tears or fall to the ground and roll around in the leaves, moaning. But she just kept walking. Her face stayed soft and open.

We strolled along in the quiet, me thinking about my brothers and how I'd grown used to not having them around. If Joey were still alive, I wasn't sure if I'd want him or Danny to move to Madison. Even though Mama did. I got to thinking about all those boys who went to war and got killed. How their mamas must miss them. How their sisters must have cried when they heard the news. Death was a weird thing to me. Sometimes, it felt as if Danny were as dead as Joey because I couldn't see him or touch him. Sometimes, Joey felt as alive as Danny, for the same reasons. It was no different with Daddy. He was at that monastery. He may as well be dead. I never talked to him. And he didn't know if we were alive or not. I was starting to wonder if he even cared. I didn't feel that way about Grace, though. Even if I *never* saw her again, she'd always be alive to me.

Mama reached for my hand. "Let's sit for a while."

We shared a bench under a huge maple tree.

"You know, Regina, I've made a lot of mistakes in my life. Everything I've ever wanted or hoped for came flying back at me."

I held my breath, waiting for her voice to tighten.

"I never loved your father, you know that. I couldn't squelch my loneliness, no matter how hard I tried. It just roared and roared and roared."

She let my hand go and leaned back into the park bench.

"After I lost that baby, I thought God had ripped my soul out. I didn't want to go on. But then you came along, and God gave me a second chance. It just wasn't enough. The fights started real bad then, between me and your father. Oh, how I hated the bickering. I'd see the life drain out of you kids' faces, and I couldn't bear it. After a while, I stopped looking. I couldn't make it better, so I had to pretend it wasn't there."

Mama had never talked like this before. It made me nervous.

"When Patrick came along, I thought I'd found my answer. For a while, I guess I had. He made me happier than I'd ever been. Things were complicated. I was married, for God's sake. And I had all you kids. But I just couldn't say no. I gave in to him. Gave in to myself, really. What I thought I needed and wanted. I couldn't have been more wrong. Guess it took a lot for me to see it."

I concentrated on Rosa and Winnie laughing and playing in the leaves. I guess I always knew that underneath it all, Mama loved us with her whole heart. Plenty of times, I had to just hang on and believe that, even when it didn't seem true. Things were better now, but it took a long time to get this way.

"Writing that letter to Danny got me thinking that I had some things I needed to say. To him. And to you. What I'm trying to get at is . . . well . . . I'm trying real hard now to be a better mother. I'm sorry for all the heartaches. I know I don't deserve your forgiveness. I was hoping my telling you all this could help you understand better. So you'd know none of it was your fault."

I closed my eyes. I couldn't look at her. The wind slapped my face, and I felt like crying, but I didn't. Grace popped into my head, and I heard her tell me, "Your mama's trying to mend things, give her a chance." That's when I knew I had to try. Mama and me were tied together by invisible strings. Sometimes they choked me, sometimes they kept me from falling off the edge into an even lonelier place. I loved her as much as I hated her. Most of the time, the love part won out. That's why I didn't stay with Grace. I'm Mama's daughter in body and in heart. And those strings will hold us to each other forever. But I didn't say any of this out loud. I searched my mama's face, looking for a way to explain it. Her wide eyes were waiting for a simpler answer.

"Mama, I know bad things have happened. You've been real sad. Me, too. But I love you. I think things are gonna get better. They feel better already."

She slipped her arm around my shoulder and gave me a sweet hug. The chilly air swirled around my head, and the leaves danced in front of us. For the first time since I'd left Grace's house, my bones were filled with hope.

Christmas Eve

Mama didn't hear from Danny until a week before Christmas. She walked back from the mailbox one morning clutching an envelope. She tossed the rest of the mail onto the table, closed her eyes, like she was praying, and then tore into the greeting card. "It's from Danny," she said, eyes wide now. She raced across the words inside. I stared at the picture on the front. It was fancy, with the Baby Jesus and Mary and Joseph, the manger and the Magi and a bunch of smiling angels keeping them all company. I couldn't imagine Danny taking the time to pick out something that special.

"He's coming, Regina," Mama sang out. Her eyes shined. "He's decided to visit us, over Christmas vacation. Aunt Stella, Uncle Tony, and Mrs. Marco chipped in and bought him a plane ticket. He'll be here next week. On Christmas Eve."

I smiled, but I wasn't as excited about it. For Mama, it was a good sign that Danny was even thinking about visiting us. But having him here didn't thrill me. It wouldn't be bad if he had changed and wasn't a big snot anymore. But I doubted that could have happened. Back in Pisa, Danny and I were always on opposite sides. He hated the things I liked, on purpose. I loved Broadway musicals—especially *My Fair Lady* and *The Sound of Music.* He loved rock & roll—the Rolling Stones and the Beatles. My favorite cake was devil's food with chocolate frosting. His was white with butter cream. He was a troublemaker. I liked peace and quiet—like those peaceniks on TV. About the only thing we agreed on was that we both hated Patrick. But for different reasons. Danny blamed Patrick for breaking up our family. I hated Patrick because he beat up Rosa, because he loved Winnie more than me and Rosa put together, and because he was mean and ugly when he got mad.

"Where's he gonna sleep when he gets here?" I asked.

"Oh, we'll make do. He can stay on the couch. Or, if we can figure out a way to put a little heater on the porch, he could sleep out there."

"How long is he gonna stay?" I tried not to sound too huffy, but I had to get the facts.

"About a week. He has to fly back before New Year's. He has to work."

We'd been in Madison nine months, and I'd gotten used to just living with Mama and my sisters. Since Patrick left, we'd been getting along fine without boys. I could put up with Danny for a week, for Mama's sake. I just hoped when he finally went back home, Mama didn't get upset and fall into one of her sad spells.

"We'll have to have Doris over for supper one night so she can meet Danny. Oh! We'll have to get a bigger turkey. Danny'll eat us out of house and home."

I was jealous. She was making all her plans, thinking out loud about him coming. It was her chance to show him how she'd changed, to prove to him that she wasn't the same mother who'd left him high and dry one windy day last March. I excused myself from the table and slipped away to my bedroom. I wanted to tell Rosa the bad news and get some sympathy.

"Danny's coming for Christmas."

"Is Patrick?" she asked.

"No. Just Danny. Isn't that bad enough?"

"Is he gonna bring us presents?"

"Who cares? I just don't want him to be a bossy butt. Things are finally starting to settle down. We don't need him blowing in here and ruining it all."

"Is he gonna stay?"

"I hope not."

Two days before Danny arrived, Doris took us shopping for a Christmas tree. She and Mama had the day off, so we piled into Doris's station wagon and headed to Bill's Tree Lot. Mama took hours to find the perfect Scotch pine. "It's Danny's favorite," she insisted. I tried to hurry her by complaining about how cold my toes and fingers were, but there was no budging her.

She finally picked one, and the tree man tied it to the top of the car. I was really cold by then. And grouchy. I pushed Rosa into a snowbank for no good reason. She got even with me by throwing snowballs at my head. Her aim was lousy, and she hit Winnie instead.

"Mama," Winnie cried. "Rosa's being mean."

"Girls, it's Christmas. Be nice," Mama half scolded. She dusted snow off of Winnie's coat and added, "It's so fluffy. Perfect for making snow angels."

It looked like Mama was gonna flop herself down on the ground and flap her arms into snow angel wings, but Doris noticed my blue lips and put a stop to that.

"How 'bout some hot chocolate?" she said.

"Perfect," Mama agreed. "Let's go to Clancy's."

On the drive to the restaurant, Mama turned the radio on, and we sang along to "Silent Night" and "Joy to the World." "It's gonna be a great Christmas," she said, waving out the car window to folks on the sidewalks.

At Clancy's, we slipped into a corner booth. Mama ordered us all steaming cups of hot cocoa. "Don't forget the whipping cream," she reminded the waitress. "Cocoa's not cocoa without it, right Regina?" Mama winked at me and touched the tip of my cold nose. "Sweetie-pie, you look like Rudolph."

Rosa and Winnie giggled. Doris laughed.

I folded my arms over my chest, still wearing the purple mittens Grace had made me. Grace would never embarrass me. I covered my nose with my mittened fingers and glared at Mama.

Mr. Clancy brought cupcakes, sprinkled with bits of green and red candy canes, to the table. "On the house," he said. "Merry Christmas, girls."

I gave in, in spite of my grouchy mood, and smiled a little. I "oohed" right along with Rosa and Winnie and reached for a cupcake as soon as Mr. Clancy walked away.

"Regina," Doris cautioned. "Your mittens!"

Winnie giggled, and then I did, too. I tucked my gloves into my coat pocket. The waitress strolled over with our hot chocolates, and we were set. I licked the whipped cream, then licked the sparkly cupcake frosting. I swallowed the sweetness down with a sip of hot cocoa and finally relaxed.

"Do you know where we can find some inexpensive ornaments?" Mama asked Doris.

"I have extras you can have," Doris offered. "Or try Kresge's. They usually have a pre-Christmas sale."

"Do they have that stuff that looks like angel hair and shines pretty when the lights blink?" Rosa asked.

"Tinsel?" Doris asked. "Yeah, they have plenty of stuff like that. But don't buy any. I got some left over from last Christmas."

Rosa hummed "We Wish You A Merry Christmas" as she licked whipped cream off her lips. Last Christmas back in Pisa, Joey threw tinsel into Rosa's hair, and she hollered. She looked like a crazy ice monster. He chased her around the living room until she finally tripped over a string of lights Danny had left in the middle of the rug.

"Will you kids stop it!" Mama had yelled. "You're giving me a headache."

"Marie, have you heard from Patrick?" Doris interrupted my memories.

"Yep. He wants to see Winnie on Christmas Day. Wants to come over for supper and bring presents."

"Does he know Danny's coming?"

"No, I haven't told him. I'm waiting for the right moment. Danny won't want Patrick around. But still, I want Patrick to see the girls, too. And I hate the thought of him being all alone on Christmas. Nobody should be alone then."

Mama's eyes got soft and sad.

"Isn't he going to Jack and Annie's house?" Doris asked.

"I suppose he might, but I don't know if they've invited him. He never said."

"Well, if need be, Winnie can come over to my house, and Patrick can visit with her there. I'll keep an eye out, make sure he doesn't run off with her."

"Thanks, Doris."

Mama reached across the booth and held her hand for a second. "You're such a good friend." I shoved my own hands into my coat pockets, searching for Grace's homemade mittens. I wondered what Grace was doing for Christmas. I wished I was back in her living room, reading *Reader's Digest* stories to Rosa, listening to the soft thump of her rocking chair against the floor.

Christmas Eve morning, Doris drove us to the airport to pick up my brother. Everywhere, people rushed around, arms and hands full of suitcases and boxes of presents. People smiled and hugged one another. "Merry Christmas," they called, whether you knew them or not. With strangers being so nice, it changed my mood. I even smiled when I saw Danny walking down the jet way. He'd gotten real tall since we'd seen him last. He was seventeen now. His shoulders were wider, and his hair longer and bushier. His voice was low and deep.

"Hey, Ma," he said as he squeezed her tight.

"Oh, Danny," Mama cried. She held him for the longest time, rubbing his back like she was afraid he'd disappear if she stopped.

When at last her hands got quiet, Danny took a deep breath and said hello to us girls. "Hey, Peanut. Rosa. Winnie, you little squirt!"

It was weird kissing my brother hello with all those strangers watching. Weirder still, that there was only one brother to kiss. It made Joey's dying more real to see just Danny standing there, tall and nervous and handsome. I worried that all those airport strangers could see into my sad bones, know what had happened, know what took us so far away from each other for so long. But those smiling strangers just kept saying "Merry Christmas." They didn't pay attention to my broken heart. Maybe they wouldn't have cared, that day. Christmas wasn't a time for tears. In spite of myself, I grabbed Danny's hand.

"Danny, this is Doris," Mama said, introducing her

friend. "She works at Clancy's with me. Remember? I told you about her in one of my letters."

"Yeah. I remember. Pleased to meet you, Doris." He was more polite and grown-up than I remembered. He shook Doris's hand and smiled. Mrs. Marco must have taught him some manners.

"Where's your grocery bags?" Rosa asked.

"Grocery bags?"

"Yeah," Rosa explained. "Didn't you bring any clothes with you?"

"Oh," Mama said, nervously. "You mean luggage, Rosa. Danny, did you check your bags?"

"Ya," Danny answered. "Uncle Tony loaned me his suitcase. I got a box, too, with some Christmas presents from him and Aunt Stella. And me."

"Did you bring one for me?" Rosa asked. She'd attached herself to Danny's hand and wouldn't let go.

"Yep. I got presents for everybody. Even you, Peanut." He said it kind of snotty. A little bit of the old Danny slipped through. He winked. "I'm just kidding."

"My name's Regina now."

"Regina? Since when?" He laughed. "That's a mouthful for a wimp like you."

"I ain't no wimp," I sassed.

"That's enough, you two." Mama clipped our fight short. "It's Christmas Eve, and we're together. Let's try to get along."

"Didn't mean nothing by it, Ma, honest," Danny assured. "Just a little tease, so she remembers I'm still her big brother." He rubbed the top of my head, gently. "Don't take it so personal, Ree-gii-naa."

On the way home from the airport, Mama asked Danny a million questions. Did he have a girlfriend? How was his job going? Was he applying for college? Was Mrs. Marco nice to him? Mama never did ask anything about Daddy. Or my dog.

"Is Zoomer okay? Does he miss me?"

"He's doing good. He misses you, all right. I took one of the sweaters you left and made a little bed out of it for him. He sleeps on it every night." I looked out the car window, blinking back tears.

"Who's taking care of him now?" Rosa asked.

"Mrs. Marco. Zoomer and her get along great."

I'd never met Mrs. Marco, but I guessed she wouldn't let Zoomer starve to death. I didn't want my dog to love her more than he loved me. But I liked the idea of him sleeping on my old sweater, even if it had to be in Danny's room in Mrs. Marco's house, instead of here.

We dropped Danny's suitcase and the box of presents at our apartment, introduced him to Mr. and Mrs. Anderson, and then gave him a driving tour of Madison. We showed him the capitol and the University. We drove past Memorial Union, where we sometimes got ice-cream cones, Lake Mendota, and State Street with all its shops. We even stopped at Clancy's. Mama's waitress friends visited our table to say hello. When Mama introduced Danny, they asked, "Where you been keeping this handsome young man, Marie?" Mama picked at her fingers as she told them he lived in Pisa, New York. "How come he doesn't live here with you and your daughters?"

"That's a long story," Mama said, to the tabletop. Danny stared at his folded hands. I chewed the side of my lip, waiting for those waitresses to yell at us.

Doris said, "That's nobody's business but Marie's. Her son's come to visit for Christmas, and that's all the news you need to know."

After Doris dropped us at home, Danny set his wrapped packages under the tree. When he joined Mama in the kitchen, Rosa and I sneaked a peek, shaking them, trying to guess what was inside.

"This one's gotta be clothes," Rosa pouted. "I hope it ain't for me."

"This one rattles," I said, shaking it so she could hear.

"Gimme one," Winnie insisted.

I slid a package toward her. She held it to her nose, took a quick smell, then shook it hard. "Cookies."

She was probably right. We always ate homemade Italian-cream cookies on Christmas Eve. Aunt Stella must have sent a batch with Danny.

"Don't be messin' with those presents, girls," Mama called. "We can't open them until after supper."

"Aw, Mama," Rosa complained.

I glanced up to see if Mama was gonna holler at Rosa for sassing, but she was busy wrapping her arms around Danny. She hugged him. "I've missed you so much."

"Sure is nice seeing you." His voice was soft and quiet. I hardly recognized it.

"Supper's ready," Mama announced to us girls. She kissed Danny's forehead and said, "Come on. I've made your favorite. Macaroni and cheese."

"Thanks, Ma," Danny said. He wiped the corner of his eyes fast, then tossed a dare at me. "Last one to the table has to wash all the dishes."

He beat me there, same as always. This Christmas wouldn't be any different from any of the others. We'd have to wait until after all the dishes were washed and put away before we could open presents. Even though I was hungry, I hardly ate anything. Eating would take too long, and the sooner we were finished, the quicker we could begin Christmas Eve. Danny ate three helpings of macaroni and cheese and talked to Mama about politics and the war in Vietnam. I shot him a "hurry up" look every now and then to rush him a little, but he didn't pay any attention.

"I turn eighteen next year, Ma. I gotta register for the draft."

"If you go to college, you'll get a deferment. By the time you get out, that damn war should be over."

"Not if Johnson runs again. *Hey, hey, LBJ, how many kids did you kill today?*"

"Hush now. It's Christmas Eve."

"Do you think those poor guys in 'Nam are celebrating?"

"If you go to college, are you gonna burn your draft card and protest like those other kids?" I asked.

"Hell, yeah. That war stinks. I ain't dying in no jungle."

Mama changed the subject. "It's supposed to snow tonight. Couple of inches. Maybe we can go sledding tomorrow."

"We don't have sleds," Rosa said.

"We can borrow some from the Andersons," Mama said. "Finish up now, so we can open presents."

I hurried through the dishes, excited to see what we all got. I dried the last plate and announced, "Mama, we're ready."

"Get your pj's on and brush your teeth first," Mama insisted.

"Aw, Mama."

"Don't give me any lip, Regina. The faster you get going, the faster you'll get to your gifts."

That's all the nudging I needed. Rosa, too. We had our pajamas on in no time, whipped a toothbrush over our teeth, and hurried to the living room, staking out our places in front of the Christmas tree.

"All set, girls?" Mama asked. She handed presents to each of us, reading the tags and calling our names as she went.

"To Rosa from Santa. Merry Christmas."

"To Regina from Aunt Stella. Merry Christmas."

"To Danny from Mom. Merry Christmas."

"To Marie from Uncle Tony."

"To Winnie from Danny."

"To Mama from Regina."

On and on it went until the very last present was set in front of the very last person. That's when it hit me. There were no presents for Joey or Daddy. I stared at my pile of unopened gifts. My stomach ached. Joey and Daddy were two ghosts hiding in the corner, crying "What about us? Don't we get any?" Mama noticed them, too. So did Danny. They smiled, pretending that all the presents and the tree lights made them happy, but their eyes didn't sparkle. When I couldn't wish the ghosts away, I ripped open my gifts and oohed and aahed over each one. The whole time, I swallowed back a cry. There wasn't any brand-new mitt for Joey, no black beaded rosary with a shiny silver crucifix for Daddy.

Danny finished opening his stack. He sat in a pile of crumpled wrapping paper and held out a small box he'd saved for last. Mama opened it and pulled out a porcelain Christmas ornament—a baseball bat and mitt with edges trimmed in gold. On the bat in green letters were the words "Peace on Earth." On the mitt, "Joey Giovanni." Mama's hand flew to her mouth. Tears rolled down her cheeks. Danny gently took the ornament from Mama and walked toward the tree. He placed it on a high branch, near the angel. When he turned around, his eyes were wet, too.

"Merry Christmas," he said.

Oh, Holy Night

On Christmas afternoon, Doris came to take Mama and Winnie over to her house so they could visit with Patrick. Mama asked Danny if he wanted to go, but he said, "No. I'll stay here with Regina and Rosa. We got some catching up to do." He still hates Patrick for taking Mama away. He didn't say that, but I could tell how his lips tightened when he refused Mama's offer.

"What about you, Regina?" Mama asked.

"Nope," I answered. It wouldn't be any fun seeing Patrick hugging and kissing Winnie, giving her presents, and treating her like a princess. Mama didn't even ask Rosa. I guess she knew that wasn't a good idea.

"Suit yourselves," Mama said. She pulled apple pies out of the oven and shoved in the turkey. "Don't forget to baste it while I'm gone, Regina."

After Mama left, Danny and me and Rosa played Monopoly. My brother managed to buy both Boardwalk and Park Place—with hotels. "I'm a rich son-of-a-bitch tycoon!" he bragged each time one of us landed on his spot and had to shell out rent money. It wasn't much fun for me or Rosa. A couple of times, I felt like kicking the game board clear across the floor, but I didn't. It was Christmas, after all, and I didn't want God to think I was a hateful girl. I just didn't understand boys and how selfish they could be sometimes. It wouldn't have hurt him to close his eyes once or twice and pretend he didn't see us land on his million-dollar empire. Instead, he rubbed his hands like a greedy jerk and took our money until it all ran out and we had to quit.

"I hate Monopoly," Rosa whined. "I wanna play Candy Land."

"Quit being such a baby," Danny snipped at her.

"Quit picking on her," I snipped back. "Why do you got to be such a pig on Christmas?"

"Shut up, smart-ass."

"You shut up. You think you know everything. But you don't."

"Yeah? Like what?"

"Like how come me and Rosa ran away." I wanted him to know we weren't the sissy turds he thought we were. I figured Mama never told him about Patrick beating on Rosa. That was back when she was still shoving the truth into tight little boxes and hiding it behind her eyes.

"Don't tell him." Rosa slapped my arm.

"Give it up, brat, or I'll make life hell for you," Danny threatened.

Rosa shook her head. Her eyes pleaded for me to keep quiet. Danny stared at me without flinching. I refused to look away. I was the oldest in this household now. He was just a visitor. I blurted out, "Winnie's Patrick's kid."

"Geez. I already knew about that."

"How?"

"Aunt Stella told me and Joey back in March, after you

guys took off. She said that's why Ma left. She said Patrick was tired of not being able to live with his daughter. Stella thought it would help us feel better about Ma going. It only pissed me off more. Why was it so much easier for us to live without Ma than for Patrick to live without Winnie?"

"What did Joey think?"

"Joey. Hell," Danny said, softly. He stared into his hands for the longest time, then rubbed his face, like it needed some comfort. "I can't hardly talk about it, Regina."

His eyes teared up. He reminded me of Rosa when I found her in the woods the day she ran off. His face looked like one long sigh.

"You don't have to say nothing, Danny." I reached for his hand. He pulled away, shoved his fingers under his sweater.

It was weird, seeing him soft like that. In a way, it made me love him. I could see his heart was breaking, and I knew what that felt like.

"Why'd she do it?" His question hit the air. He swallowed it back and struggled to keep the tears from falling.

I didn't know what to say. I used to blame Patrick for the whole thing. After I met Grace and she told me people do crazy things sometimes, I got to seeing how Mama had a part in it, too. She did it for love, I know that for sure. But it don't seem to matter somehow, now. Since Patrick was gone. All I knew was that Grace told me I shouldn't let it get to me. I'd been trying. But it wasn't easy. Too many days, I'd wind up with a stomach as tight as Danny's face.

"Why'd Ma have to fall in love with that son-of-a-bitch? Why'd she have to dump us?"

Danny stood up fast. He walked to the window and stared out. He didn't move or talk for a few minutes, then he took a couple of deep breaths and forced his feelings out.

"If I ever see him again, I'll kill him. I'll wring his neck and kick his balls all the way to Vietnam. That son-of-a-bitch killed Joey just as sure as if he'd taken a gun to his head."

Danny cried, wiping the tears away as fast as they came. He was mad at letting us see him that way. I thought about Grace taking a gun to her mean husband's head and how it sent her out into the rain, so she could feel clean again. Hate's ugly, Grace always said. But hate's real, too. And people got a reason to feel it, sometimes. Watching Danny cry made me and Rosa cry, too. We weren't loud about it, but our tears were coming from the same mucky mess. We were up to our necks in it. It snatched our voices, too. Nobody talked for the longest time.

Finally I asked, "Danny? What happened after we left?"

He pressed his palm hard against the window. I was afraid he was gonna break the glass, but he turned instead and faced me and Rosa. His mad eyes found mine. "You don't have to tell us if you don't want," I said. I didn't want him exploding all over the living room, like he used to in Pisa when he got pissed. It was a side of Danny I never wanted to see again.

"What if I did tell ya?" he boomed. "What difference would it make now?"

"Don't get so mad at us, Danny," Rosa said. "We didn't do nothing."

"Yeah, you did," Danny scowled. "You got away."

"It wasn't our fault. Mama took us," I asserted.

"It doesn't matter, anyhow," Danny said. "Can't go back and make it better. Nothing will bring Joey back. Nothing."

His eyes slammed shut, and he slouched onto the couch. "Hate will kill you if you let it," Rosa said to him.

"What the fuck does that mean?" Danny snarled.

"It's just something somebody told us once," I said. "A lady we met after we ran away. She was cool. Never yelled at us. Never told us we were stupid for running away. She said hate hurts you more than the other person. She said it eats you alive. If you're hurting or mad, it's all right to scream. Let it out. It doesn't make the hard stuff go away. But it makes you feel bigger or stronger or something."

"Bullshit," Danny scoffed. But I could tell something in him liked the idea of it. His eyes cleared just the tiniest bit.

"That's just like you, Regina. Some crazy old lady feeds you a line of crap, and you fall for it. When are you ever gonna learn? Nobody cares about nobody."

I didn't believe him. And I didn't like him saying mean things about Grace. He was just lying to make himself feel better. He never did tell us what it was like after we left, but it didn't take a big brain to figure it out. With Joey dying and Daddy running off to the monastery, it must have been real hard. Harder even than us being here with Patrick. At least we had Mama. Maybe if Joey had had Mama, he'd still be alive. And Danny wouldn't be as grouchy and mean. I guess Mrs. Marco didn't love him as much as Grace loved us, or else Danny wouldn't be acting like razors were ripping his insides to shreds.

"Why did Daddy run off to that monastery?" I asked.

"Hell, who knows?" Danny said. He folded his arms across his chest.

"Is Daddy gonna come take us home?" Rosa asked.

"Nope," Danny told her. "He's happy with those monks. He don't have to do anything there except pray and study. He thinks if he talks to God long enough, he'll get an answer about this whole mess. Maybe then he'll come back and tell us, Rosa. But he ain't gonna come back and be your daddy no more."

Rosa'd been holding on to that wish so long. Hearing Danny say it wasn't ever gonna happen made her face sink. She squeezed Binkie hard. Tears rolled down her cheeks.

"You don't know that one hundred percent for sure,

Danny," I insisted. I didn't want Rosa's heart to break on Christmas Day.

"No. But it sure don't look too hopeful. I visited him a few times. Uncle Tony took me. Dad barely recognized me. He stared at me like he couldn't quite place where he'd seen me before. Then he looked away. Uncle Tony shook his head like Dad was a lost cause, and we left. On the way home, Tony told me to forget about Dad. Take care of my own life now."

How could he take care of his own life when he was only seventeen? Maybe when you get to be that old, you don't need a daddy anymore. Daddy and Danny used to fight a lot anyway. Maybe it didn't really matter to my brother that Daddy wasn't around anymore. Maybe Uncle Tony felt more like a father to him. Maybe not. But Rosa had just turned seven. She still needed her daddy. So did I.

"Maybe he'll change his mind. Does he know that Patrick moved out? Maybe he and Mama will get married again. Maybe he just needs to know that we still love him."

"Yeah, and maybe you'll walk on the moon, too. Regina, you got rocks in your head. When you gonna grow up and face facts? You ain't a kid anymore."

I'd had it with his sassy mouth. Even if he was feeling sad and left out, he didn't have to take it out on us. I stabbed a look his way and tapped Rosa with my foot.

"You wanna play Candy Land?" I asked.

"Okay." Rosa grabbed the game from the closet.

I got up to check the turkey. A blast of heat hit my face as I pulled the oven door open. I shut my eyes against it, basted the bird, and shoved it back in. I slammed the oven door, thinking about my brother's way of seeing things. He was such a bossy butt. But he was right. I didn't want to stop wishing that Mama and Daddy could work things out. If Danny ever did decide to stay here in Madison, I'd have to set him straight on being nicer to me and Rosa. But, he would be leaving soon. I didn't have to take his crap much longer.

"You girls are too stupid to figure it out," Danny called from the other room.

"Figure what out?" I marched back in to the living room, ready for a fight.

"Joey. How he died . . ."

Rosa set the game board on the rug. "How did he die?"

Danny stared at her without speaking. His eyes deepened, and his mouth twisted down. Something horrible was running through his mind.

"Forget about it," I cautioned. "Let's just play Candy Land."

"Think it was an accident?" Danny spat out. "A car hit him? Or maybe some crazy drunk pulled a knife on him?"

I wanted to slap my hand over his mouth, keep him from spilling his secret.

"Dad found him . . . hanging in the church. He'd gone in for one of his daily rosary sessions, and there was Joey. Swaying over the altar. Joey'd climbed up high, wrapped a rope around his neck, slung it over the beam, and jumped. Father DiSante cut him down. Told Dad to leave. But he didn't. Watched everything from the front pew. Didn't cry. Didn't shout. Didn't swear. Just kept praying those Hail Marys, moving his fingers over the rosary beads as if it would bring his son back. Father DiSante found a note in Joey's pocket. 'Ma, I'm sorry. Love, Joey.' That's all it said. They gave him a Catholic funeral. Even though he'd killed himself. Whole town came. Old ladies with prayer books, nosy neighbors, teachers, relatives, total strangers. Everybody cried. Except me and Dad. Two days later, Dad took off for the monastery. Aunt Stella took me and Zoomer to her place."

My knees buckled. I slumped to the floor next to Rosa. The truth bit my heart, tore it wide open. I sobbed and reached for Rosa's hand. She sobbed, too. Long and hard we cried. Danny just sat on the couch, staring at nothing.

When Mama and Winnie got home, we ate Christmas dinner.

"Did you kids have fun this afternoon?" Mama asked.

We nodded, without a word. I didn't dare look at Mama or Rosa or my brother.

"We played Monopoly," Danny told her. He loaded up his plate and shoveled food into his mouth as fast as he could.

Mama smiled. "That's my boy. There's plenty more for seconds."

For dessert, we ate homemade apple pies. "They're Haralsons," she bragged to Danny. "We got them at the apple orchard, last weekend. I wanted Cortlands, just like from back home, but they didn't have any. I hope you still like it."

Her postcard smile was too much for me. All along, she had known the truth about Joey. Now, I hated the way she talked up Madison. In spite of all that had happened, she was advertising all over the place, trying to get Danny to change his mind and come live with us. She refused to see how mad he was at her. How mad we all were.

After supper, Mama put on Perry Como's Christmas album, and we sat in the living room, admiring the lighted tree.

"This is the best Christmas, ever," Mama sighed.

Nobody said a word. Danny stared at the tree, and Rosa stared at me, so I stared back. Winnie played with the baby doll Patrick had given her at Doris's house. Mama brought home a new dress and a new winter coat for Winnie, too. Both from Patrick.

"Oh," Mama said, like she'd forgotten something important. "Patrick sent along presents for you guys."

She rushed to her bedroom and came back with three
wrapped packages.

"Here you go," she said, handing one to each of us.
"Patrick said to say 'Merry Christmas.' He hopes you like
what he got you."

Rosa and Danny and I held the gifts in our laps.

"Well, aren't you gonna open them?"

Mama looked so disappointed, we couldn't stall any
longer. Danny went first. He ripped the paper to find a
Timex watchcase. He stared at it, but he didn't crack open
the plastic container to try the watch on.

"Isn't that great?" Mama asked. "What'd you get, Rosa?"

Rosa stared at the red and green bow. "I don't wanna
open it." She pushed the package away and looked at me. It
was my turn now. I glanced at the box tag. It read: "To
Regina, From Patrick. Happy Holidays." The writing was
Mama's.

"Hurry, Regina," she urged. "I'm dying to see what he got
you."

I pulled off the ribbon. I took my time, slowly peeling
tape off the creased edges of the wrapping paper, trying to
work up the courage to be like Rosa and shove the thing
away.

"Come on, honey," Mama urged. I finally opened the
small box. It was a tiny July garnet birthstone ring.

"It's 14 carat, gold-plated," Mama boasted.

"How can you tell from over there?"

"Oh," Mama caught herself. "I helped him pick it out,
last week, after work."

I swallowed her lie and smiled back at her. "It's real
pretty, Mama, thanks a lot."

"Oh, don't thank me. Thank Patrick," she insisted.

I knew Patrick never laid eyes on that ring or Danny's watch or Rosa's unopened gift. Mama had bought all of them. I wished she hadn't bothered. I slipped the ring on my finger, and Mama smiled. Rosa glared at me. If I explained later that the presents weren't really from Patrick, maybe I could convince Rosa to open hers.

"Anybody for seconds on pie?" Mama asked.

"I'll have another piece," Danny said.

"No, thanks," I said.

"I'll be right back," Mama said. "Regina, get Winnie into her pj's for me, will ya? It's almost her bedtime."

"Come on, Winnie." I tugged at her arm. "You heard what Mama said."

"I don't wanna," Winnie whined. She held on to that baby doll Patrick had given her like it was Santa himself. "I wanna play."

"You still can, we just got to get your pj's on in case you fall asleep," I told her.

That convinced her, and we were back in the living room with the rest of them in no time. Winnie wrapped her new doll in her tattered yellow blanket and held her close.

"You still got that scuzzy old thing?" Danny teased her.

She stuck out her tongue and crawled up on the couch. Mama brought in three slices of apple pie and coffee, a cup for Danny and one for herself.

"Here we go," she said, setting the tray on the coffee table.

She handed plates to me and Danny. I set mine on the floor, next to the ring box. I didn't want the pie, but she hadn't listened.

Mama handed a fork to Danny. "Here's a clean one," she said as she sat beside him on the couch.

"Don't have to lick 'em here in Madison, I guess," he teased.

"Nope," Mama laughed. "It's not like Pisa. Here, we have plenty of forks to go around. We even have special ones just for dessert. Thanks to Doris and garage sales. She's helped me learn how to live on a tight budget."

"I guess things are pretty hard, all in all, now that Patrick's out of the picture," Danny said, swallowing a big bite of pie. He reached for his coffee and took a swig.

I changed my mind about the pie. I needed something to pick at while Mama continued her Madison sales pitch.

"We get by. Right, girls? The Andersons are a big help. I didn't like them much when we first got here. I thought they were nosy. But they were so good to me when Regina and Rosa were lost and when Patrick left us." She set her cup on the coffee table and picked at her fingers.

"But that might change. We might work it out."

I dropped my fork. Apple pie splattered all over my pants. Mama was so caught up in the thought of Patrick coming back that she didn't even notice. I grabbed my paper napkin and wiped up the mess.

"Oh, and Doris," Mama went on bragging. "She's been such a good friend to me. We're doing great. Can't complain. Except it sure would be wonderful to have you come live with us."

Danny's swallow of coffee got caught in his throat. He coughed, straining for air.

"You okay, honey?"

He nodded. "Went down the wrong pipe, I guess."

Danny took a deep breath and cleared his throat.

"So, what do you think?" Mama asked, when he stopped choking.

"About what?"

"About living with us? Moving to Madison?"

My brother curled his hands. "I don't know, Ma. I don't think it would be such a good idea."

"Why not?" Mama pleaded. "You've been here. You've seen what a nice place we have. Lots better than Pisa. Quieter. Prettier. More forks. We got plenty. Don't we, girls? You'd love it here if you'd just give it a chance. Why won't you just give it a chance?"

"Ma, it ain't that simple," Danny insisted. He inched away from her. She didn't give up. She crept closer until he inched himself to the end of the couch. There was no place left to go, except the floor. He stood up. Bolted, really. And escaped to the other side of the room.

"You gotta understand, Ma," he continued, putting on his most convincing voice. "I got ties to Pisa. There's the pharmacy. I gotta work so I can go to college."

"We got drugstores in Madison," Mama argued. "Mr. Clancy's brother-in-law owns a Snyders. He could put in a good word for you."

Danny ignored her. "And I wanna finish high school with my friends."

"You're such a handsome young man, you'll make plenty of friends at the high school here. It's not more than five blocks from our house. Good school. And they got a great baseball program. You could be their star pitcher."

"Ma, I ain't playing baseball no more," he stammered. "Will ya just lay off me!"

"What's the real reason, Daniel? It's Patrick, isn't it? Well, he's out of the picture, for now. We might work it out. Too soon to tell. But even if he does come back, maybe you could learn to like him. He's a good man. Really, he is. He has his bad moods, like the rest of us, but underneath it all, he's loving and kind. You'll see."

"I ain't living with that son-of-a-bitch," Danny seethed.

He took the words right off my tongue, the words I would never let myself say out loud.

"Daniel, there's no need for talk like that," Mama scolded. "Especially on Christmas."

"I don't care what day it is," Danny insisted. "That's how I feel. If you want to know the truth. It's me or him, Ma. You can't have both. Not now. Not ever."

Mama fought back tears. "Always the hothead, aren't you, Daniel? Always pushing things to the line. Testing me. Why can't you just let it be?"

"Let what be, Ma?" Danny hollered. His fists were tight, and he clenched them to his side. I was afraid he'd let them loose, afraid of where they'd go, and who they'd hurt. "Joey's dead," he yelled. "Can I let that be? Dad's off in some fuckin' monastery praying like a goddamn zombie 'cuz he can't deal with real life. And you guys are hundreds of miles away. What do you want from me? To forget and forgive? It don't work like that, Ma."

"I thought my letter would help," Mama sobbed. Her chest heaved, and tears poured down her cheeks. "I tried to tell you I was sorry. All I got left is my kids. Can't you understand that? You and the girls are all that matter to me now."

"Well, you fuckin' should have thought about that before you took off with that jerk. Why didn't you just let Aunt Stella and Uncle Tony help you out? Why'd you have to leave us, Ma?"

Mama cried. "I couldn't stop myself. I wanted out so badly. You said you'd come. Then Paulie put his foot down. What was I supposed to do?"

"I don't know, Ma, I don't know." Danny hung his head, tired from fighting. He reached for Mama and held her close.

"I can't make it better," she moaned into his shoulder. "I can't go back and do it over. But I love you. How can I make you believe that?"

"I believe it, Ma," Danny comforted. "I know you love me. But it's a mess, and I don't know what to do about it. I love you. I just can't be here if he's gonna be here. Can't you understand that, just a little bit?"

Mama nodded and cried. Danny held her until her tears were done. All the while, Rosa and Winnie cuddled close to me, burying their heads in my lap. The Christmas tree bulbs blinked on and off, throwing light onto the walls. They looked like tiny wings, beating and beating. I wanted to melt into the blues and pinks and yellows, follow them to wherever it was they lived. I wanted to take my sisters and never come back. I thought of Joey, swinging by his neck in St. Joan of Arc's Church, and I wanted to throw up.

Danny could have Mama all to himself. I didn't want any of it anymore. Something happened to me that Christmas night. The silvery strings that held me to Mama untangled. Some of them even snapped off. I wandered away from her reach. She'd always be my mama, I knew. And I'd always love her, but I couldn't stay next to her broken heart one minute longer. There had to be another way to live. I had to find it.

Happy New Year

Danny flew back to Pisa the day before New Year's Eve. Doris drove us to the airport so Danny wouldn't have to take a bus or a cab. Before my brother got on the plane, he hugged each of us.

"Pick up a pen and write once in a while," Mama told him. "And think about coming back to live with us."

Danny's face tightened as he kissed her. "See ya," he said before he turned and walked down the jetway.

Mama cried the whole way back to our apartment. "I miss him already."

Doris patted her hand. "Give it time, Marie. He'll come around."

I stared out the window, watching the snow hit the highway. Rosa leaned against my shoulder and fell asleep. Winnie curled up next to Rosa and sucked the edges of her yellow blanket. I listened to Doris and Mama talking.

Doris's voice calmed me. It was steady and soft, and I always trusted what she said. Best of all, she knew it was important not to give up just 'cuz things got hard. She tried to make Mama see the good side of things. She was like Grace that way. Her heart was roomy enough for love and for sorrow.

"I'm all ready for my New Year's Eve party," Doris told Mama. "Shopping's done, the house is cleaned. After we get back to your place, I can stay and visit for a while. Keep you company."

"Thanks," Mama said. "But I've got a headache. I need to rest before I go to work."

"Call me if you change your mind," Doris said as she pulled in to our driveway.

"Come on, girls, we're home," Mama said.

I nudged Rosa to wake her, then helped Winnie button her coat. We stood in the driveway as Doris backed her car onto the street. "See you girls later," she called as she drove away.

We waved until she turned the corner. "Come on, girls. Let's go inside," Mama said. "It's too cold out here."

Mama nursed a sour mood the rest of the day. She lay down for a while, but it didn't help much. She got up, drank a cup of coffee, smoked a few Chesterfields, then peeled potatoes for supper.

"What you making?" I asked.

"Mashed potatoes and hamburgers."

"Can I put on *My Fair Lady?*"

"Sure."

I played "Wouldn't It Be Loverly" four times in a row until Mama barked, "Can't you play something else, for Christ's sake?"

She dialed the phone as I turned off the record player.

"Hi," she cooed. "Want to come over tomorrow for New Year's Eve?"

She had called Patrick. I turned the TV on loud so I wouldn't have to hear her acting gushy. More pictures of the war. Gunfire and helicopter sounds filled the room.

"Turn that damn thing down," Mama yelled at me.

No matter what I did, I was gonna catch hell, so I flipped the TV off and left Mama to her phone call. Winnie and Rosa were playing Candy Land in our bedroom. They'd be better company.

"Is Mama still grouchy?" Rosa asked.

"Yep."

I didn't tell her Mama was talking to Patrick, inviting him over for New Year's Eve supper. I plopped, belly-first, onto my bed and shoved my face into my pillow. I wanted to scream, to feel the hot air rush out of my mouth like a wild thing. Something punched my stomach, and it wouldn't stop. I kicked the mattress and squeezed my pillow as tight as I could. Then I threw it across the room, skimming my sisters' heads. It hit the wall and slid to the floor.

"What ya do that for, Regina?" Rosa complained.

"Shut up, stupid brat."

"You shut up, pig face," Rosa hollered back.

"Pig face, brat," Winnie added.

I was down on the floor in two seconds, shoving the tiny white cards and the red, yellow, blue, and green game pieces all over the place.

"Quit it, Regina!" Rosa screamed.

I kicked the game board across the room, picked the pillow up, and swung it across Rosa's back. She cried and slapped my arm. I slapped her back.

Rosa yelled, "Mama!" but she didn't wait to be rescued. She jumped at me, catching me off guard. I fell to the floor. She pushed her knees into my chest and pinned me down. I couldn't get her off me. She grabbed my pillow and slammed it against my head. Winnie grabbed my hand and bit me. I reached for Winnie's hair with my free hand and yanked as hard as I could. She wailed. Rosa screeched, "Leave her alone, you big bully!" before she punched me in the stomach. My insides collapsed into a tight, achy wad. By the time Mama rushed in to pull Rosa off, there wasn't any fighting left in me.

"What the hell's gotten in to you girls?" Mama hollered.

"It's Peanut's fault," Rosa shouted. "She threw a pillow at us and then wrecked our game. And she pulled Winnie's hair."

"Regina," Mama scolded. "I don't need this grief from you. I've got to go to work in an hour. Apologize to your sisters."

I tried to feel bad about what I'd done, but I was glad I'd done it. It didn't seem fair, my sisters sitting there happy and carefree while I felt as if somebody had set my legs on fire. I knew I couldn't explain it. Nobody would understand. They'd just think I was a jerk, like Danny or Joey, picking on little kids for no good reason. Maybe they'd be right. But it sure felt like I had a reason. A really good reason.

I stared at the floor and said, "Sorry, Rosa. Sorry, Winnie."

※

On New Year's Eve, Mama was in a good mood. She hummed all morning, getting things ready for later, when Patrick would come for supper. Mama was scheduled to work that morning, but she traded with another waitress so she could stay home and make homemade ravioli. She asked me and Rosa if we wanted to help. Rosa said "No."

"Then keep an eye on Winnie," Mama told her.

I helped Mama roll the dough and stuff the ravioli. We patted the edges shut and pinched them tight with forks. We laid them on floured pillowcases on the dining room table to dry.

When we were done, Mama started the sauce. She chopped tomatoes and scraped them into a big kettle. She stirred in basil, oregano, garlic, and rosemary. She set the pot to simmer and took a bath. "Stir it every once in a while, will ya, Regina? I've got to get ready."

"How long is Patrick gonna stay?" Rosa asked me after Mama disappeared into the bathroom.

"Just for dinner. Then him and Mama are going dancing. I'm watching you and Winnie. Mama said we could have popcorn and stay up late for Guy Lombardo. She promised to call us from the nightclub and wish us a Happy New Year."

Mama waltzed out of the bathroom, filling the air with Lily of the Valley scent. She hummed as she combed her hair in front of her mirror. I sat on the edge of her bed and watched. "Grab me my black pumps, honey." I found the right pair and brought them to her.

"Are you and Patrick gonna get back together?"

"I don't know, honey." She smoothed red lipstick over her lips. "We're just going on a date, tonight. See how it goes. Why?"

I looked away. "I wonder what Daddy's doing tonight?"

Mama laughed. "Probably praying the rosary with a hundred other monks."

I hated how her eyes shrunk to mean slits when she talked about Daddy being in that monastery. Her poison spoiled everything.

"Maybe he'll call us tonight, wish us Happy New Year." I knew it wouldn't happen, but I wished hard for it anyway. Daddy hadn't even sent us a Christmas card. And he forgot my birthday and Rosa's, too. I guess he was too busy praying for all the poor and starving people in the world.

"Your father isn't going to call you tonight. Or ever, Regina. You better get used to it."

She sprayed the Chanel No. 5 that Patrick had given her for Christmas on her wrists and dabbed some behind her ears. "I wish you'd give Patrick a second chance. He wants to be your daddy."

Mama had more practice believing things that weren't true. If she'd opened those pretty brown eyes of hers, she'd have seen the real truth. Me and Rosa were second-hand daughters to Patrick.

"He don't love us," I said. "Just Winnie."

"Nonsense, sweetie," Mama replied. "He loves you all the same."

I wanted to argue with her but decided not to get her or me all riled up. Instead, I fetched Mama's sparkly earrings from her jewelry box and pulled her black skirt from the closet. I hung her fancy white blouse on the doorknob so she could put it on when she was done spraying her hair. "I better go check on the girls. We got to get ready, too."

"Be sure Winnie wears that cute red and white dress Patrick gave her. And you and Rosa pick out something nice. I want you to look extra-pretty tonight. Wear those rings Patrick gave you for Christmas."

Four days after Christmas, I had finally convinced Rosa to open that present. I told her Mama had picked it out and had put Patrick's name on the tag so we'd think it was from him. It would be hard to convince her to wear it to supper.

"Let's go, girls," I ordered. "Get your fancy clothes on."

"I don't wanna," Rosa insisted.

"Don't lollygag. Patrick will be here soon."

"Why do we have to get all dressed up?"

"Because that's how Mama wants it. Quit asking so many questions, and don't forget to wear that birthstone ring you got for Christmas."

"I'm not gonna."

"Just do it without griping, for once."

"No."

"Come on, Rosa. Do you want Mama to get mad at both of us?"

Rosa scowled the whole time I was dressing Winnie. I shot her a couple of you-better-listen-to-me-or-else looks. Finally, she pushed the tiny ring on.

"Thanks."

"I ain't gonna wear it ever again," Rosa insisted.

"You look beautiful," I told my sisters.

To Rosa I added, "Don't worry. He's only gonna be here for a tiny bit."

She frowned again. "I won't kiss him hello. And you better sit by me at supper, Regina."

"Okay. Now go and watch some TV while I get myself ready."

I lay on my bed for a tiny rest, staring at the ceiling, wishing it would open up and suck me into the sky, take me far away. I was beginning to think Danny had the right idea about telling Mama she had to choose between Patrick and him. But Danny was back in Pisa with Mrs. Marco. If Mama wanted to let Patrick come back, there wasn't anything we could do about it.

Maybe me and Rosa made a mistake telling Grace it was time for us to go home. Maybe we'd thrown away our one chance. I needed Grace. I needed her brown eyes to nudge me, her stories and her laughter, and the click, click, click of her knitting needles to remind me that there could be a different way. Sometimes, I imagined her showing up at our apartment to take me back to her small house. We'd make chocolate cake and sing and dance. She'd let me shout and scream, if I needed to. She'd tell me anger ain't worth the trouble it causes. "It'll only kill you in the end," she'd say.

But I think she was wrong about that. I think, sometimes, anger keeps you alive.

On New Year's morning, I woke to the smell of cinnamon rolls baking in the oven and the sound of Patrick laughing in the kitchen. He and Mama were chatting. I couldn't make out what they were saying, but I could tell it was lovey-dovey. Every once in a while, Mama giggled, and then their voices would go quiet. I figured they were standing next to the sink, kissing. I peeked over at Rosa's bed. She was still sleeping. I pulled the covers over my face and prayed *Holy Mother of God, make this be just a bad dream.*

I couldn't pretend for long. I had to pee. I tiptoed to the bathroom as quietly as I could, so Mama and Patrick wouldn't see. It didn't work. Mama was watching for me. She called out, "Regina, look who's home." I nodded a quick hello and slipped into the bathroom. I locked the door and sat on the toilet for a few minutes, trying to think of some way to sneak back to my bedroom so I wouldn't have to join them.

Rosa knocked on the door. "Let me in," she urged.

I flipped open the lock, and my sister stepped in. Her eyes were wide and impatient. "What's he doing here?" she whispered. Her voice was hot.

I shrugged. "Maybe he just came back for breakfast."

"They're both in their pajamas." Rosa grabbed my hand. "Regina, what are we gonna do?"

"If he really is back, and things get bad again, we'll have to write a note to Grace. She'll help us. I know she will."

"Promise?"

"Promise. But first we got to pretend we're glad he's here. So Mama doesn't wig out. Maybe he'll be nicer this time. But, if he starts hitting you again, I'll haul off and kick him. Maybe I'll even kill him."

I didn't have a gun. Didn't even know how to use one or where to get one, but I'd figure out some way to keep Rosa safe. Even if it meant pushing myself between his fists and her face. I was bigger. I could take it.

"Let's go before Mama figures out we're stalling," I said.

I opened the bathroom door, and Rosa and me sucked in a bellyful of air. Mine hit something hard halfway down and knotted up. Winnie was awake now, too, and sitting on Patrick's lap. Mama rushed toward Rosa and me with open arms.

"Good morning, girls!" she gushed. "Happy New Year!"

She slobbered our faces with kisses.

"I've made a special breakfast," Mama cooed. "Let's eat before it gets cold."

She ushered us to the table and set juice and hot cocoa in front of us. She'd topped our cups with real whipped cream and chocolate shavings. She served hot cinnamon rolls and a platter of scrambled eggs and bacon. "Eat up, girls! Can't start 1968 on an empty tummy!"

I wasn't hungry. Patrick loaded his plate and grabbed the biggest sweet roll for himself and the second biggest for Winnie. "Here you go, honey," he said. He cut it into smaller pieces for my little sister.

"Did you girls have fun last night?" he asked.

"Ya," Winnie said with a mouth full of sweet roll.

Mama told me with a look that I better answer him. "We watched Guy Lombardo, then we went to sleep, after Mama called us from the nightclub."

"Sounds like a helluva New Year's Eve," Patrick joked.

Mama giggled and blushed. "Well, we had a great time," Patrick bragged. "We drank champagne and danced and laughed, just like old times. Right, Marie?"

"It was wonderful," Mama agreed. "And we've got some great news."

I wrapped my fingers around my cocoa cup, hoping her idea of good news matched mine.

"I've asked Patrick to move back in. Isn't that great? You girls deserve a good family, and we want to give that to you."

I pressed the cup to my mouth, held it against my lips until it burned. I didn't look at Rosa. I would have blurted out what I was really feeling. Mama looked at me, waiting. I couldn't give her what she wanted.

"When are you moving back?" I asked Patrick. I didn't smile. I didn't frown, either. I kept my face blank so he couldn't see the fire behind my eyes.

"Today," he announced. He took a sip of coffee and set his cup down slowly without taking his eyes off mine. "After breakfast, your mother's coming back to my place to help me get a few things. I'll bring the rest over during the week."

I matched his stare and didn't back down. I wanted him to know I was a different kid from the one he used to live with. I might have to obey him and pretend he was my daddy to keep Mama happy, but I wasn't gonna love him.

I nodded but kept quiet. I bit into a sweet roll and let the sugary frosting melt on my tongue. It was my reward for not being a wimp. I tapped Rosa's foot under the table so she'd know I hadn't gone back on what I'd promised her in the bathroom.

"It's gonna be perfect," Mama gushed. She kissed Patrick. He kissed her back. He reached for her fingers, then held Winnie's hand, too.

"We're a family again," he said. "That's all that matters."

Easter Sunday

Mama quit her job the week Patrick moved back. "The kids need you at home, Marie," he convinced her. "And so do I. If you work nights, you won't be able to go to faculty functions with me. How's it going to look if my wife isn't beside me?"

I wanted to blurt out—how's it gonna look if they find out you guys aren't really married? Mama never did get around to divorcing Daddy. And besides, Patrick was still a priest according to the Pope. He hadn't filled out the stack of papers the diocese had sent him. When Mama worked at the restaurant, she called herself Marie Giovanni. As soon as Patrick was home, Mama switched back to Shaughnessy.

Two weeks after quitting Clancy's, Mama got cranky. "I've got too much time on my hands," she told Patrick one night after supper. "I sit around all day and stew about Danny and Joey."

"Take Winnie to the playground."

"It's twenty below zero. I can't take her out in that."

"You know what I mean, Marie. Just get out of the house and do something, for Christ's sake. Give Annie a call."

Mama wrinkled her nose at that suggestion. She hadn't seen Annie since the day we first arrived in Madison—last March. Instead, Mama started taking Winnie with her to see Doris. When Patrick found out, he fussed about how much time she spent with her friend. "Doris is too crass," Patrick insisted. "You can do better than that."

So, Mama started calling Aunt Stella a lot again, which made Patrick even madder. "That phone bill's too high this month, Marie," he scolded. "Write her a letter once in a while. It's cheaper."

Despite Patrick's objections, Mama still invited Doris over for coffee sometimes, when she had an afternoon off. I'd come home from school and find them chatting and laughing, playing 500 Rummy. It made me happy to see Mama having fun. One day, Patrick came home from work early and told Doris she had to leave.

"We're not done with our game," Mama insisted.

"It's okay, Marie," Doris said. "I've got supper to fix. My sons are stopping over tonight."

After Doris left, Mama told Patrick he'd embarrassed her. "She's my friend. What's wrong with spending an afternoon with her every now and then?"

"I don't like her," he told Mama. "She puts crazy ideas into your head."

"What crazy ideas? All we do is play cards. What's so crazy about that?"

"You know what I mean," Patrick insisted. "All that Women's Lib crap. She's a goddamn dyke."

"She is not. She's got two grown sons."

"You are *so* naive, Marie. Besides, she's the one who told you to go to college after Winnie starts school."

"What's wrong with that?"

"Who the hell is she to tell you how to run your life?"

"She's just being a good friend. Trying to help me better myself. Don't you want that for me, too?"

"One college degree is enough for this family," he insisted.

Mama started making up excuses when Doris would call or stop by for a short visit. "I've got too much laundry to do," she'd say. Or, "The kids have bad colds."

Doris got the hint quick enough. She stopped calling and dropping by. Mama got more and more sad. She started slipping back to how she'd been before. She'd shut herself up in her room. And forget to start dinner. Patrick would come home, and there'd be nothing to eat. Then they'd start fighting.

"You've got all day to sit on your ass," Patrick hollered. "How hard could it be to have supper ready when I come home?"

"Don't talk to me like that," Mama yelled. "You don't understand how hard it is. You have people to talk to all day long. I got nobody."

"Know what your problem is, Marie?" Patrick shouted back. "You're never satisfied."

He stomped off to the living room. He flipped on the evening news and watched Walter Cronkite talk about a group of protest organizers who held a sit-in in front of an armed forces examining station in California. "Those ungrateful, commie pigs," Patrick shouted at the TV screen. "I hope the judge locks them up and throws away the key." I stared at the priests and college kids, nuns and mothers— even that folk singer Joan Baez—protesting against the draft, until Mama called me to help her get supper ready.

On Valentine's Day, Danny sent a frilly card with a short note telling Mama he was thinking about coming to live with us. Maybe he'd move in this summer, he said, if things worked out. Mama twirled around the living room, shouting "Yes, yes, yes!" When Patrick came home and heard the news, he crabbed. "One more mouth to feed, Marie. I don't know if we can swing it."

"I'll get my old job back. That should help."

"I don't want you working," he said.

"Part-time can't hurt, if it would make things easier."

"No," he ordered.

That didn't sit well with Mama. She refused to give up. I was proud of her. "He's my son. The only one I have left. I want him to be with us."

For the longest time, Patrick kept insisting it was a money thing. I knew it was something else. He just couldn't stand to share Mama with anyone except Winnie. That's what he really hated about me and Rosa. Mama loved us. That meant there was less of Mama for him. Patrick never got mad when she fussed over Winnie. But every time she'd take a second or two to hug me or kiss Rosa, he'd complain about something. "The food's too cold" or "It's too hot." "The coffee's too strong" or "It's too weak."

He even started to mess with Binkie again. Rosa had been telling us about how her classmate Scotty had fallen off the jungle gym and hurt his eye. "He's got a big shiner," Rosa announced. "I wanna bring Binkie to school tomorrow so Scotty can feel better."

"You're way too old to be dragging that stupid dog around," Patrick scoffed. He dropped Binkie into the waste-basket.

"Mama! Regina!" Rosa shrieked. She ran to bail Binkie from the mess.

"Leave that be, Rosa," Patrick ordered. "Or you'll get a spanking."

My sister froze. My heart raced. Mama used her sweet, sugary voice to try to change Patrick's mind without him thinking she was trying to go against him. She wrapped her arms around his neck and kissed him. "Honey, what's so bad about her wanting to share her favorite stuffed animal? I think it's kind of sweet, myself."

"She's your daughter," he said. "If you want her to hang on to infantile habits and embarrass herself in front of the other first graders, so be it."

Mama and I rescued Binkie. I dusted coffee grounds off his nose and wiped bread crumbs from his head. "We'll take him to the laundromat tomorrow and give him a bath in the washing machine, sweetie," Mama told Rosa. "He'll be good as new."

Later that evening, Mama wrote to Danny. She read it to me before she sealed the envelope. She told him we were excited about him wanting to come live with us. She said we'd probably have to find a bigger apartment so he could have his own room, but that would be fine. She was getting tired of the one we had anyway.

"What do you think?" Mama asked me.

"Aren't you gonna tell him that Patrick's living with us, too?"

"I thought I'd wait until he wrote back."

"He'll be real mad, Mama. Remember what he said when he was here for Christmas."

"Oh, he probably didn't really mean that. He was still mad at Patrick and me. He's probably over that by now. Don't you think?"

I shrugged. Inside, I knew Mama was wrong. Patrick was one thing Danny wouldn't budge on. I'd bet Zoomer on it.

A week later, my brother called to tell Mama he'd decided to move to Madison. Mama shouted, "Hooray!" When Danny heard Patrick's voice in the background, he got mad. "Yes, Patrick's back," Mama confessed. "No, Danny, don't hang up . . ."

After that, Mama got another letter from my brother telling her he was gonna stay in Pisa with Mrs. Marco after all. He was pissed at Mama for lying.

Mama and Patrick fought for a week.

"Who cares what he thinks?" Patrick yelled. "Let him stay in Pisa where he belongs."

"I want him here," Mama insisted.

"You can't have it both ways, Marie. It's me or him. You choose."

Mama stormed out of the kitchen. She escaped to her bedroom, ranting and raving, "Goddamn son-of-a-bitch. I didn't raise him to have a heart of stone. Why the hell can't he just let the past go?"

By April, things were bad again. Mama couldn't decide between Danny and Patrick, and she was making everybody miserable. Patrick got more short-tempered with me and Rosa. Every day, I thought about writing to Grace, telling her to come get us quick. Winnie cried a lot 'cuz she was scared by all the fighting. Patrick blamed me and Rosa. He said we were picking on her, calling her names, and refusing to play with her. That was a lie. When I wasn't in school or doing my homework or helping Mama, I spent all my time with my sisters. We holed ourselves up in our bedroom, playing Candy Land and Chutes and Ladders and cards and Barbie dolls. We did everything we could think of to drown out their shouting and Mama's tears. The air got tighter, and the rooms began to shrink. Little by little, the walls pressed against my shoulders and the ceiling bumped against my head. I expected to come home from school one day and find the roof blown off—pieces of wall and ceiling hanging from tree branches all messy and loose and free. Finally free.

Mama called Doris and invited her over for Easter Sunday dessert. "I know it's been a long time," Mama said into the phone. "But I miss you. I made a coconut cake. Will you come?"

Patrick pressed his finger against the receiver, clicking the phone off. "I don't want that woman in my house."

"It's my house, too," Mama argued back.

"Not as long as I'm paying the bills."

"Who the hell died and made you God?" Mama yelled.

Later, while Patrick was in the bathroom, Mama grabbed her purse and the coconut cake. "Regina, get your coat and help your sisters with theirs." I did as she said, and then she rushed us outside. We headed for Patrick's car.

"Where the hell do you think you're going?" Patrick threatened. He chased after us and yanked the car keys out of Mama's hand.

"If you won't let Doris come here, we'll go to Doris."

Patrick slapped Mama's face. The cake flew from her hands and fell, bottom side up, on the driveway. Mama rubbed the red mark where his fingers had landed, then spit at him. "You son-of-a-bitch."

Rosa squeezed my arm and held on tight. Patrick's hands went flying. His mean eyes searched for something to hit. He swung his palm at Rosa. I yanked her away before his hand could land on her and shoved myself between my sister and Patrick to take the second swing. Rosa scrambled for a hiding place. Patrick's next blow hit my shoulder. I landed on the gravel driveway a few feet from Mama's smashed homemade Easter cake. I grabbed a stone and threw it at Patrick's head. It nicked the side of his cheek.

"You little bitch," he raged as he lunged at me.

"Mama!" I screamed.

She pushed herself between his fist and my face. "You lay a hand on her, and I'll call the cops."

Somebody had beat her to it. A police car screeched to a

stop at our curb. Two officers hopped out. They were the same guys who'd picked me and Rosa up at Grace's house almost a year before.

"What's the problem here, folks?"

"Nothing, officer," Patrick stated. He stood between Mama and the cops with his arms open wide and innocent-like. "Just a little disagreement about who's gonna drive to Grandma's house."

The shorter cop studied Patrick's face. The older cop walked over to Mama. "You okay, Ma'am?"

"Yes, sir," Mama answered. Her cheek was reddish purple where Patrick had hit her. "We'll settle this without your help. Thank you."

Mr. and Mrs. Anderson watched us from their front porch. The shorter cop wrote a few notes in his notebook and chatted with Patrick.

"Look, I'm a married man. I know how hot things get sometimes. Do you think you could settle this matter without further provocation and get on with it? You're disturbing your neighbors."

"Absolutely, Officer," Patrick insisted.

"Good," the cop said. "I'm sure the kids' grandma is anxious to give them their Easter treats."

"Yes," Patrick smiled. "She sure is."

"Let's go, Charlie," the short cop called to the other one.

The older cop nodded. Before he left, he tipped his hat to Mama and said, "If you need anything, Ma'am, don't hesitate to call."

"Thank you," Mama said.

When the cops drove away, Patrick scooped the car keys off the ground and shoved them into his pocket. "Let's go inside now."

Patrick took Winnie's hand, and Mama followed him back into the duplex. They nodded to the Andersons as they passed. Mrs. Anderson waited until Mama, Patrick, and Winnie were inside before she called to me. "Regina, are you and Rosa all right?"

I nodded a quick yes and searched for Rosa. It took me fifteen minutes to coax my sister out from under the car. She shivered and stuttered the whole time. "N-n-no, Peanut! N-n-n-no!"

"Look, I know it's bad, but I promise, we don't have to stay here long. I hate him, too. I'll write a letter to Grace and mail it today. I promise."

Rosa finally crawled out, her face full of tears and snot. I cleaned her up with a couple of Kleenexes I found in my pocket. Then I hugged her until she stopped shaking. "You can sleep with me in my bed tonight," I told her. "And every night, if it helps."

She grabbed my hand. Her fingers were cold and stiff. Mr. Anderson met us as we headed back toward our house. "You girls try to have a nice Easter, now." He shoved three chocolate bunnies into my arms.

"There's one for each of you," he said.

"Thanks."

I wanted to jump into his quiet eyes. He patted my head and winked at Rosa. We climbed the steps to our apartment slowly. When we got to the door, we stopped. Without looking at Rosa, I dropped the candy bunnies. We turned around and tore back down the stairs and across the yard on our way to Rosa's secret hiding spot. Halfway across the lawn, we heard Mama call out.

"Rosa. Regina. Time to come in."

We never looked back. We kept running. At the edge of our yard, Rosa's foot got caught in a hole, and she tumbled onto the grass. I stooped to help her up, but by then it was too late. Mama grabbed our coat collars and held on tight.

"Don't even think about it," she stammered, then she burst into tears.

Rosa cried, too. I bit my lip until I tasted blood.

"It won't be like this for long," Mama promised. She pulled us to her and held us tight. "I won't let him hurt you anymore. When he goes to work tomorrow, I'll call Doris and Aunt Stella. We'll figure a way to leave, don't worry."

The wet from her tears smudged my face, and her fingers dug into my ribs. In the cave of my heart, something shouted with relief. I loved Mama then, more than I've ever loved her. I wanted to trust her, wanted to believe what she said was true. I wanted her to love us more than Patrick, more than her own sadness. I wanted her to love us like Grace loved us. And I wanted it to last for more than one hour or one day. I needed her to not back down. To not escape into the dark sadness of lost eyes and tight lips. I needed her to be all grown up, not afraid of anybody or anything. I wanted so hard to believe that she could be.

Mama's Decision

The next morning, Mama got up and fixed coffee, toast, and juice for Patrick, same as always. Before he left for work, she hugged him and gave him a kiss good-bye. She watched from the window as he drove away, waiting until he was out of sight before she tied her bathrobe tight around her waist and hurried down the steps to the Andersons' kitchen door. Me and Rosa watched her from our door stoop. We had to be sure she was really gonna do it.

Mama's fist landed hard on the Andersons' kitchen door. The door swung open, and Mrs. Anderson stood there in a flowered bathrobe and curlers, her hand clenched to her chest. When she saw it was Mama, she relaxed. Before Mrs. Anderson could even invite her in, Mama blurted out her reason for interrupting their breakfast.

"I need you to change the locks again." The words charged out of Mama's mouth. She had to talk fast before she changed her mind.

She shoved her shaking hands into her bathrobe pockets. "I know you've done it once already, but I'll pay you for your trouble this time. It may take a while, but I'm good for it. I just can't let him back in. I know it's short notice, and it might take a few days to get a locksmith, but please, you've got to help me."

Mrs. Anderson touched Mama's shoulder and winced at the bruise Patrick had left on Mama's face. Mr. Anderson was sitting at the table in his own bathrobe. He had the morning newspaper in front of him, but his eyes were busy reading Mama's worries.

"You just come on in here, Marie, have a cup of coffee," Mrs. Anderson said. She talked all soft and careful, like Mama was going to break all over her kitchen floor. "We'll get this thing figured out."

The last thing I saw before the door closed was Mr. Anderson offering a cup of coffee to Mama.

"Think they'll do it?" Rosa asked.

I nodded, hoping I was right.

I stared at the Andersons' kitchen door, wishing I could hear through the wood. I flicked paint chips off our stair railing. Rosa plopped herself down on the top step. She wiggled her jittery feet at the air, even though I asked her three times to stop. Winnie wandered out, dragging her yellow blanket. "Where's Mama?" she asked.

"She's visiting the Andersons. Just sit next to Rosa and shush."

She obeyed. We waited in our pj's for a while, but still, no sign of Mama. Winnie fussed a few times but settled down after I ran back into our apartment to fetch a Barbie doll. I could hardly breathe from the watching and the waiting.

"I'm cold," Rosa said.

"Me, too," Winnie whined. She tossed her doll on the step.

"Okay, let's go in. I'll make us some hot cocoa."

We weren't inside two seconds before the phone rang. It was Patrick.

"Where's your mother?"

"Taking a shower."

"Have her call me when she gets out."

"Sure."

I hung up, and the phone rang again. This time it was Doris.

"Hey, Regina, can I talk to your Mama?"

"She's visiting the Andersons."

"Is everything all right?" she asked. "Your Mama hung up suddenly before we finished talking yesterday. When I tried to call back, the phone just rang and rang all night."

I didn't know what to say. Me being quiet must have got Doris's brain going. She started asking me questions. "Is your mother hurt? Is Rosa? Where's Patrick? How come you aren't saying anything?"

I tried to talk, but nothing came out. I wanted her to know about Patrick flipping out, and me and Rosa trying to run away again, and Mama catching us and promising to make things all better. I leaned against the stove, took a deep breath, and tried again.

"We're fine." The words stumbled from my mouth.

"Regina, is Patrick there right now?"

"No."

"I'm coming right over."

Mama wasn't back home more than five minutes before Doris was at our door. The knock startled us. Mama let out a tiny squeak of a scream.

"Marie, open up. It's me." Doris was panting from running up the stairs. Mama opened the door and Doris pushed past us, headed right for a kitchen chair, and plopped herself down.

Mama knelt beside her friend. "Regina, get her some water."

I filled a glass and set it in front of Doris. She swallowed it down in two gulps.

"Marie, what the hell's going on?"

"What do you mean? You're the one huffing and puffing like an old wheeze bag."

"Don't lie to me, Marie." Doris grabbed Mama's hand and looked her square in the eyes. "I see that bruise on your face. You didn't answer your phone last night. I called a dozen times. Are you gonna tell me what's going on so I can help? Or are you gonna be a stubborn old fool?"

"Grab us some coffee, Regina," Mama said, without taking her eyes off Doris. I poured two cups and set them on the table. Then I grabbed a chair and sat across from Doris.

Mama said, "I thought this time he'd changed. He said he loved us, said he wanted to make it work. I wanted to believe him, I guess, more than I wanted to believe my own eyes."

Mama told Doris everything that had happened.

"He hit me. And Regina. Then, Winnie started wailing, and I couldn't think straight. All I knew is I couldn't take it anymore. I was gonna explode all over the place if I didn't do something. The Andersons saw everything. I was so embarrassed. I told them we were fine, but I knew it was such a mess. I had to do something to make it right. But I didn't know what or how."

"Sounds like he lost it," Doris sympathized.

"The whole thing made my blood ice over. Made me hate him worse than I ever hated Paulie, worse than I hated God for all those years of making me have to put up with that rotten marriage."

Doris nodded.

"I talked with the Andersons this morning. They called the locksmith for me. He'll be here tomorrow at ten."

Mama eased back into her chair. She sighed. Something heavy had finally slid off her chest. She took a sip of coffee, lit a Chesterfield, closed her eyes, and took a deep drag off of her cigarette.

"You did the right thing, Marie," Doris said. She leaned toward Mama. "I don't know if changing the locks will do the trick. You might need a backup plan. I think you and the girls should stay at my house until things blow over."

"No, we can't put you out like that."

I prayed, *Dear Blessed Virgin, make Mama say yes, please, make Mama say yes.*

"I wouldn't offer if I didn't want to do it, Marie. There's no telling what kind of nonsense he'll try to pull when he finds you're serious about ditching him."

Mama's eyes closed to tiny slits of worry. She rubbed her temples and cried. "How'd I ever get myself in this mess?"

"Don't much matter," Doris told her. "It's time to concentrate on getting out of it. You got to do it for your girls, Marie. If nothing else, think of them."

Doris pulled a few Kleenexes from her pocket and tucked them into Mama's hand. Mama wiped her eyes and whispered, "Okay, Doris. Okay."

"Regina? Can you get yourself and your sisters out of your pj's? Then pack up a few things, so we can head on over to my place?"

I nodded a confident yes.

"Why don't you get started?" Doris said. "We'll help, too, in a few minutes."

I felt hopeful, even though Mama's face was a blotchy mess. I hurried to the broom closet, grabbed a handful of Kroger grocery bags, and hauled them to my bedroom.

"What's going on?" Rosa asked.

"We're gonna go stay with Doris."

"For how long?"

"Just until they change the locks and Patrick simmers down. Change outta your pj's, then put your stuff in this bag."

"Why can't we use the suitcase?"

"Just do it, Rosa!"

My sister filled the paper bag with underwear and pants, socks and shirts. I thought about leaving Pisa and how we had stuffed clothes into A&P bags and hurried so we could be out of the house before Joey and Danny and Daddy came home. Running from Patrick felt a whole lot better. This time, I even remembered to grab a couple of books for Winnie.

"Now go brush your teeth and comb your hair," I ordered Rosa. "And don't forget Binkie."

I packed some clothes for Winnie, changed her out of her pj's, brought her to the bathroom, and cleaned her up. I raced back to the bedroom to get myself ready. When we girls were all set to go, we lined up by the dining room table, looking shiny and clean like the von Trapp kids from *The Sound of Music.*

"My, that was fast," Doris remarked.

Rosa said, "Can we go now?"

"As soon as your Mama gets dressed, honey."

Mama wasn't moving very fast. She was scrounging through her pocketbook, looking for something, muttering to herself when the phone rang. I jumped to get it, but she beat me to it.

"Hello?" She sounded distracted, like her mouth was talking, but her mind was a million miles away.

"Oh. Patrick." Her voice dropped. "No, Regina didn't tell me you called."

She glared at me.

"I forgot . . . ," I whispered.

"Oh, yes, I was in the shower. No, no, there's nothing wrong. I'm just a bit distracted. It's been a busy morning. You know how that goes. I've had to break up two fights already between Regina and Rosa." She bit her fingernails as she lied. Doris gave her a "don't-give-in" look. Mama found her confidence.

"I don't think he suspects anything," she said, after she hung up. "I better go get dressed quick, in case I'm wrong, and he decides to come home for lunch."

While Mama was changing, Doris gave each of us girls a big hug.

"You deserve better than this," she said. Her eyes were red and wet. Her strong hands felt warm where she touched my back. "Your mama's a good woman. She's just scared, that's all. But she loves you. We'll do everything we can to get you out of this jam."

I stared at her mouth the whole time. Her lips were chapped and sad, and her teeth peeped out every now and then through her smile. "I know your mama's let you down in the past. But I got a good feeling this time, girls."

"What if he follows us to your house?" I finally asked.

"Don't you worry, honey," Doris said. "I'll ask my Larry and George to come stay with us for a while. They're grown men, but they're still my good boys. They'll help their mama out when she needs it."

"Where's everybody gonna fit?" Rosa asked, rubbing her nose with Binkie's ear.

"I've got plenty of room, sweetie," Doris chuckled. "You girls can stay with your Mama in my second bedroom. Larry and George will bunk in the den."

Rosa laid her head in Doris's lap.

"There, there," Doris said. She patted Rosa's hair and reached for Winnie's hand.

"Can you take us to see Grace?" I asked.

"Who's that, Regina?"

"The lady who took care of me and Rosa that time we ran away. She doesn't have a phone. All we have is her address." I pulled the slip of paper from my pants pocket.

"Oh. Does your mama know you want to go see her?"

"No."

Doris nodded slowly. Maybe she was trying to figure out why I'd ask her instead of Mama. But she was pretty smart. It didn't take her too long to put it all together.

"This Grace is pretty special to you?"

"Yep. But don't tell Mama."

Doris studied my eyes. I tried to make them clear and open so she could see I didn't mean any harm. I just missed Grace. I knew I had better make some plans, in case Mama chickened out again. If Mama went back to Patrick, I wasn't gonna stick around. Rosa, neither. I'd made up my mind. Mama was gonna have to choose, just like Danny said.

"I'll see what I can do," Doris agreed, finally.

"All set," Mama announced as she came around the corner with her paper-bag suitcase in one hand and her purse in the other.

"Good," Doris said. She took my Kroger bag from me. "On the way out, we can let the Andersons know where you'll be. They can call you after the locksmith comes tomorrow."

"Doris, what if he goes berserk and comes after us?" Mama asked.

"Marie, do you want to do this or not?" Doris asked. She set my paper sack on the floor and waited. "You got to know before we leave, 'cuz if you ain't ready, it ain't worth it. If you come to my house and he gets all pissed off and you go back to him, it's gonna get harder and harder to cut the strings. So, you take a few minutes to decide."

I held my breath. I counted to thirty before the air inside

pushed its way out and I had to take another swallow. I counted to thirty again and again and again, waiting for the darkness to lift from Mama's eyes, waiting for her mouth to relax, and her face to agree with her heart. *Please, Holy Mother, tell God to wake up, it's real important this time. Tell Him that Mama needs a shove. Tell Him if He doesn't hurry it will be too late and Doris will drive away in her car and Patrick will come home for lunch and my stomach will explode from fistfuls of air I had to swallow to keep from screaming my head off. Please, Holy Mother, don't let God goof up this time. Make Him tell Mama to shake a leg.*

"What's it gonna be, Marie?" Doris moved closer to Mama. "I know it's hard. Believe me. I've been in your shoes. Remember that time I told you about my ex-husband Ronny? Well, there's a part I left out. He didn't leave me, like I said. Me and Larry and George left him. Ronny had a problem with the bottle, just like Patrick. He loved it more than he loved his family. He got mean and ugly one night and lit into my Georgie, nearly killed him. I had to take the poor child to the emergency room. He was in a coma for a long while. I thought I'd lost him. I never prayed so hard in my whole life. God brought him back to me. That's when I promised we'd all seen the last of Ronny. My sister took us in until I could figure out a way to get back on my feet. Saved our lives, she did. Do you hear what I'm saying, Marie?"

Mama glanced at me and Rosa and Winnie. Then she fixed her hair, even though it wasn't messy, and reached for her grocery-bag suitcase. "Let's go, before I change my mind."

Free at Last

It didn't take Patrick long to find us at Doris's. He was plenty mad. "I know you're in there, Marie," he shouted, pounding on the door. I was glad that Doris's son Larry was there, eating lunch with us. As soon as Patrick's fists hit the wood, Larry sprang up, opened the door, and looked Patrick square in the eyes. "You aren't welcome here, mister." Larry sounded mean and nasty. "You come round here acting disrespectful to my mother and her guests one more time, and you'll have to contend with this." He pushed his fist at Patrick's face. "Get the hell off my mother's property!"

Patrick shouted over Larry's strong arms, "Don't think I won't come back for Winnie, Marie."

He backed away from Larry's reach, hurried to his car, slammed the door, and peeled away.

"I wasn't really gonna hit him," Larry said to Rosa's wide, scared eyes. He sat down to finish his soup. "Just wanted to scare him. Make him think twice about coming back here and being a big bully."

Later that afternoon, Mrs. Anderson called. "No. No need to apologize, Ruth," Mama said. "Yes, I know. He'd scare the crap out of anyone when he's in one of his ugly moods. Yes, I understand you feel bad about telling him where to find us. Don't worry, Ruth. We're safe. He's not going to hurt us here. Don't cry, now."

Mama called the cops to tell them that Patrick had come after us. She asked for their protection. They told her they couldn't do anything unless Patrick threatened to kill one of us. They told her to let them know when there was real danger.

I didn't know how it could get more real or more dangerous. Me and Rosa had a hard time sleeping at night. Mama kept us home from school for a week, thinking Patrick might do something crazy like hurt us on the playground or try to kidnap us. Winnie was safe at Doris's with Mama all day. I didn't worry about Patrick snatching me or Rosa from school. I worried that Mama would decide to go back to Patrick and take Winnie with her. I worried she'd be gone one day when Rosa and I got back to Doris's house. Or worse yet, that Patrick would really lose it, and Mama and Winnie and Doris would be dead on Doris's kitchen floor. Every afternoon, I rushed Rosa back to Doris's and raced up her front steps, praying the whole time. I couldn't relax until I heard Mama's voice.

Days and weeks passed with no signs of Mama backing down. Every day, I prayed a thank you to the Blessed Mother. Mama complained about money and making ends meet, but she never talked about taking Patrick back. We stayed with Doris longer than we'd first expected, even after the locksmith put in new locks. We were too scared to go back to the apartment.

Finally, one morning, Mama told us that we'd be leaving Doris's soon. She said there were a few things she had to settle before we could go home. One of those things was getting a job. Mama asked Mr. Clancy for her old job back. She said he hemmed and hawed at first and told her he needed someone he could depend on. She tried hard to convince him, but it took Doris's urging to get him to change his mind. After about a week, Mr. Clancy softened up to Mama again. I think he liked her. He called her "The Empress" because he said she didn't take crap from anybody. Even icky customers who laid their hands on her butt and called her darlin'. She'd give them a look, then turn and walk away, with her head high and proud. "Just like a goddamn empress," Mr. Clancy told her. "You're classy, Marie. Pure class."

During Mama's second week back at the restaurant, Mr. Clancy's bookkeeper quit 'cuz she was having a baby. He complained about it while Mama was filling sugar containers and refilling ketchup bottles at the end of her shift one night. She told him any fool could balance his books. "Yeah, Empress?" he teased. "Well, if you think it's so damn easy, you do it." So she did. Mama was pretty good at it, too. Mr. Clancy told her he'd even pay for her to go take some accounting classes at the junior college. That's when Mama started school. "Maybe I'll like it enough to stick with it," Mama told Doris.

"You could even become a CPA," Doris encouraged.

"Why not?" Mama chuckled.

When Patrick didn't have any luck trying to scare his way back into our lives, he went the sugary-sweet route. After we moved home, he sent Mama flowers, cards, and small presents. She gave the gifts to a nursing home in town. He called every Sunday morning for a whole month.

She hung up on him each time. "I'll call the cops if you keep bugging us," she warned.

I was beginning to see what Mr. Clancy meant about Mama being an empress.

By May, things were settling down. Even President Johnson was talking about trying to make peace. Some other guys were going to run for president in November, and Mama said she was gonna vote for Eugene McCarthy because he was against the war. "I don't want my Danny to die in Vietnam."

Things were better, but we still had to keep an eye on Winnie all the time and not let her go anywhere alone. Mama was afraid Patrick would sneak up and steal her. "Where's Winnie?" she shouted every time my baby sister slipped out of view. "Here," I'd say, or "She's with Rosa. Don't worry so much, Mama."

"You can't be too careful," Mama would tell me.

Before June, Mama wrote to tell Danny she had left Patrick for good. She let him know about her new job and about taking accounting classes. She said she was serious this time. She was going to make something of her life. She asked for a second chance. And she told him she wanted him to move in with us. Mama read the letter to me before she mailed it.

"What do you think, Regina?"

I couldn't keep my mouth from hanging open. For a second, I didn't recognize her. "That sounds great, Mama."

She licked the envelope flap, slapped a stamp on the front, and headed out to the corner mailbox. After she got back, she called Aunt Stella and asked her to talk to Danny, tell him things were different now. "He'll believe you, Stel," Mama pleaded.

It didn't take long for Danny to write back. When Mama got the letter, she plopped down on the couch and read it as fast as she could. Her tight lips relaxed as her eyes raced over the page.

"He's coming, Regina," Mama said.

She called me to her side. I settled in, getting as close as I could. She kissed my forehead and called, "Rosa, Winnie. Come here, we got great news."

The girls raced over. "What, Mama?"

"Danny's gonna move to Madison."

Winnie clapped her hands. Rosa hesitated, looking at me first, to be sure this was a good idea. I nodded, and she hugged Mama. "When's he coming?" she asked.

"In a few weeks. After he graduates from high school. Aunt Stella and Uncle Tony are driving him out. They're bringing all his stuff. He's gonna take six months off and find a job before he goes to college. Said he'd enroll at Madison, if they'd take him. He'll live here while he goes to school. I just hope he doesn't get drafted first."

"What about Zoomer?" I asked. My heart pounded hard.

"Zoomer?" Mama said, absentmindedly. "Oh, I suppose he'll have to come, too. But we'll have to ask the Andersons if we can have a dog. And we'll have to see if Stella and Tony will take him cross-country in their car."

I asked if we could call Aunt Stella right away, but Mama said we'd do it later. We had to get supper ready, and I had to finish my homework, and she still had to ask the Andersons. But I couldn't concentrate on peeling potatoes or setting the table. Trying to answer the questions in the back of my social studies chapter was nearly impossible. I smelled Zoomer everywhere, felt his cold nose against my shins, heard his soft whine as I cleared the table and wiped the dishes.

"Mama, can we go talk to the Andersons?" I pleaded after the dishes were put away. "Please."

"Later, Regina," Mama told me. "I've got to give Winnie a

bath and finish some accounting homework. You're not the only one around here who's got to get A's, you know."

"I'll take care of Winnie," I insisted. "Please, Mama, please go ask them."

"I'd have thought you'd forgotten about that damn dog a long time ago, Regina," Mama said, shaking her head. "I'll see what I can do."

She went downstairs. I filled the tub for Winnie's bath. "Come on, Winnie." I pulled her clothes off and set her in the water.

"I want bubbles," she complained.

I grabbed the Mr. Bubble box and poured a bunch under the faucet. "Here you go, bubbles all over the place."

The bathwater sparkled with pink suds. Winnie squealed.

"I wanna play, too." Rosa poked her head into the room. She peeled off her clothes and jumped in.

I grabbed a washcloth and scrubbed them both—arms, legs, faces. When they were squeaky-clean, I ordered, "Time to get out, girls."

"We wanna stay longer," Rosa demanded.

"You'll get too cold," I insisted.

"No, we won't, Regina. Quit being such a pig face."

I splashed soapy water in her eyes, and she cried out. "You creep. I'm gonna tell Mama, and she won't let Zoomer come live here."

I grabbed a towel and wiped her face. "I'm sorry, Rosa. I didn't mean it. I wanna be done in here when Mama gets back. That's all. I'm sorry. Honest."

"Okay," Rosa said, forgiving me. "Just let us play for a little bit more."

I leaned against the wall and watched my sisters dress up their heads and chins with bubbles. I thought about those times back in Pisa when Rosa and me would take baths, and Zoomer would stretch out on the floor beside the tub and bark if we blew suds at him. The Andersons just had to say yes. They just *had* to.

"Regina," Mama called. She was back with an answer. She opened the bathroom door wearing a big smile.

"I told them Zoomer was a good dog. He wouldn't wreck anything. I told them you'd pick the yard up after he did his business and make sure he didn't dig any holes. They said okay."

"Yeah!" I twirled a tiny twirl on the cramped floor and threw my arms around Mama. "Thank you! Thank you!"

"It's not over yet, Regina," Mama reminded me. "I still got to talk to Stella."

I knew Uncle Tony would convince Aunt Stella to take Zoomer. He was the one who'd given Zoomer to me in the first place. More than anybody else, he knew how much I loved that dog.

"Sure, Mama," I grinned. I jumped into the tub with my clothes on, splashing water and suds all over the place.

"Regina!" Rosa and Winnie squealed.

"Regina!" Mama hollered. Then she laughed at the three of us all wet and full of suds.

I let out a whoop! Zoomer was coming! Zoomer.

The Box

The Saturday that Zoomer and Danny came to live with us, the sun was bright and hot. It poked the edges of my bedroom window shade and woke me. I'd been dreaming about the creek, back home. I was sitting on the bank with Zoomer, telling him everything that had happened to me since we'd left. My dog would like Wisconsin, I decided. There were plenty of places to run and play. I could hardly wait to show him. I pulled the shade up and peeked to see if Uncle Tony's car was in our driveway yet, even though I knew it was way too early.

Too antsy to fall back to sleep, I got dressed and headed for the living room. Mama was up, too, staring out the window on the front porch, sipping a cup of coffee. I stood beside her. "Special day," she said, slipping her arm around me. We stood for a few minutes in the quiet, just looking outside at the morning.

"Want some breakfast?" she asked.

She fixed me a bowl of Cap'n Crunch and let me eat it by

the window. I practically swallowed the whole thing without chewing. What if the car rolled up the driveway, and I got caught with a mouthful of cereal? I'd have to spit it back into the bowl, just so I could run down the steps and scoop Zoomer into my arms.

Mama busied herself in the kitchen. From time to time, she'd stroll out to the porch for an update.

"Any sign of them?"

"Not yet."

She checked her watch. "It's only eight-fifteen."

A short while later, she was back, asking the same question. "It's just eight-thirty now." She laughed at herself. "I guess obsessing isn't gonna make the time pass any faster. I've got to change the sheets in my room so Aunt Stella and Uncle Tony will have a clean bed when they go to sleep tonight. Wanna help me?"

"No," I said. Mama didn't holler. She kissed me instead and said, "Call if you see anything."

Aunt Stella and Uncle Tony were staying a whole week. They were gonna sleep in Mama's room. Mama was gonna sleep on the couch. She planned to put Danny in a sleeping bag on the floor. "We'll make do," Mama insisted.

After Stella and Tony went back to Pisa, we were gonna let Danny take my bed and sleep in the same room as the girls until we could figure out a way to make the three-season porch into a bedroom for him. I was supposed to sleep with Mama. I hoped she didn't mind having Zoomer on the bed. I hadn't told her about that part yet.

I was still waiting on our front porch, watching out the window, when Rosa and Winnie got up. Mama let them eat their cereal out there with me. Afterward, they played Chutes and Ladders, until they got bored and went in to watch cartoons. Just before lunch, I caught a glimpse of

Uncle Tony's shiny, black station wagon turning the corner onto our street.

"They're here!" I screamed. I tore through the living room and rushed out the door. I flew down the steps. I hopped around the sidewalk on wiggly legs as Uncle Tony pulled into our driveway. Aunt Stella waved. Uncle Tony leaned out the window and said, "Hey, Peanut, how ya doin'?"

I leaned in, gave him a kiss hello, and searched the car for Zoomer. There he was—in the backseat, squeezed between bunches of boxes and Danny's big head. My heart raced. I yelled, "Zooooomer, Zooooomer!"

My dog's tongue wagged as fast as his tail. He barked and jumped over Danny to get at the window. Danny yelled, "Settle down, you dumb fart." He opened the back door, and Zoomer leapt out. In a second, he was on me. I tumbled to the grass as he licked my face over and over again. I cried and laughed. I hugged his furry black neck and took a deep breath. He smelled good. I could have soared, sky-high over the rooftops. But I wasn't going anywhere without Zoomer. Ever again.

Mama and the girls had joined us in the front yard by then. Mama planted kisses on Aunt Stella, Uncle Tony, and Danny. Everybody cried. "Come here, cutie," Aunt Stella purred at Winnie and held her tight. Uncle Tony kissed Rosa's head and scooped her into his strong arms. "Oh, I missed you, kids," he sighed. I picked myself up off the ground and skipped over to steal a few hugs. Zoomer flicked his tail against the back of my legs. Madison could feel more like home, now.

All that hugging and kissing in the front yard brought the Andersons to their picture window. Mama waved and called, "Come, come meet my sister." They stepped outside, looking shy and polite. Aunt Stella and Uncle Tony shook their hands and said, "Pleased to meet you."

"Are you staying long?" Mrs. Anderson asked.

"Afraid we're taking over the place, aren't ya?" Uncle Tony kidded. He let loose one of his loud laughs, and Mrs. Anderson looked startled.

"Oh, that's Tony for ya," Mama said. She smiled to reassure Mrs. Anderson. "He's got to make a joke out of everything."

"Well," Mrs. Anderson said, trying to smile, "we'll let you get back to your company. Perhaps we'll see you all later."

Tony waved, and Stella ribbed him with her elbow. "Be nice," she pretended to scold. "You haven't been in this town more than fifteen minutes, and already you're getting in trouble. Go unpack the car and make yourself useful."

We all had a good laugh at that one. Stella was right. Uncle Tony loved to stir things up. But he had a big heart, too, and mostly his kind of play wasn't mean, just a way to make people have a good time.

"Can't the car wait 'til later?" Mama asked. "I'll make some sandwiches. You must be starving. Let's go eat first."

"I never turn down a meal," Uncle Tony chuckled.

We took them up to our apartment and showed them around. Our place in Madison wasn't as run down as our old house back in Pisa. Even though the furniture was old and ratty, the place had lots of windows, and the front porch was cool.

Aunt Stella oohed and aahed. "It's nice, Marie." She said it like she could hardly believe it. "Danny, how come you didn't tell me your mother's place was so nice?"

"I forgot," Danny shrugged and bit into a bologna sandwich.

"Women . . . ," Uncle Tony smirked, nudging Danny's arm.

The two nodded and chuckled and helped themselves to more potato chips and soda. Aunt Stella slapped the back of Uncle Tony's head. "Can't you wait 'til everybody's at the table before you start stuffing your face?"

"Oh, let them be, Stel," Mama said. "Tony's been driving all morning, and Danny's always hungry."

I figured if they got to eat, then I did, too. I grabbed some bread and fixed myself a sandwich. "Make one for me, too, Regina," Rosa whined.

"Me, too," Winnie chimed in.

"What's with the Regina crap?" Uncle Tony asked.

"That's her name now," Danny answered for me. "Ever since she ran away from home and came back, she don't go by Peanut no more."

"Why not?" Tony said. He stared me down until I answered.

"'Cuz Peanut's a name for sissies. I ain't no sissy. I'm a warrior."

Tony's whole body shook as he laughed. "Warrior?! You gonna go do battle with some bad guys?"

Danny snorted. My face got hot. I gripped my butter knife. I took a deep breath and laid some bologna on a slice of white bread. I dipped the knife into the mustard jar and spread it over the lunch meat. I laid the other piece of bread on top and sliced the sandwich down the middle, pretending the whole time that I was cutting Uncle Tony's laugh to bits. The only thing that kept me from hauling off and screaming at him was the cool, wet touch of Zoomer's nose against my leg.

"Lay off her, Tony." Aunt Stella came to my rescue. "It's her name, for Christ's sake. She can call herself whatever she damn well wants."

She smiled and blew me a little kiss. I felt my face cool.

Stella and Mama joined us at the table. They'd put an end to Uncle Tony's teasing if he got out of hand again.

"Sorry, sweet pea," Uncle Tony said. "I mean, Regina." He wrapped his apology up in a soft smile, but it was too late. I couldn't hold it in my heart. I was too busy by then, worrying that he had turned into a jerk, like Patrick. Tony had always been my favorite uncle, but now I wasn't so sure. Before, his teasing had always been funny. But I didn't like how it felt when he aimed at me. I suddenly understood why Mrs. Anderson had looked so startled. I reached under the table and slipped Zoomer a piece of bologna.

"So how you guys been?" Stella asked Mama.

"Not too bad. Especially now that Danny's here. Work's good. My accounting classes are going good, too. This war shit is a pain in the ass. You didn't register for the draft, did you, Danny?"

"Yep. I turned eighteen, Ma. I had to."

"God damned S-O-B's," Mama cussed. "Why are they so eager to ship our boys off to die?"

"Well, maybe it'll be over, soon."

"Soon, my ass, Stella. All LBJ does is escalate."

"But he ain't running again. Nixon or one of the Democrats will pull us out."

"Too bad about Bobby Kennedy," Mama said.

"I was gonna vote for the guy," Stella added. "Such a shame."

"And Martin Luther King, Jr., too," Tony added. "What's this world coming to?"

After lunch, Uncle Tony and Danny unpacked the station wagon and hauled everything up to our house. When they were done, Danny took a shower and got cleaned up. Uncle Tony sat beside me on the couch and gulped down a glass of lemonade. He wrapped his arm around my shoulder and whispered in my ear.

"I'm sorry, Regina. I didn't mean to hurt your feelings. It's just that you've always been my little Peanut. It's just gonna take some getting used to, this Regina thing. But if that's what you want, you got it. Okay?"

I nodded and kissed his cheek. "You're still my girl," he said. His eyes got all mushy. "Go see what I brought ya."

He nodded toward the boxes on the front porch. "Check the box from McCurdy's."

McCurdy's was a fancy department store back in Pisa. It was where rich people went to buy good clothes. We hardly ever shopped there. Once in a while, when we needed something special, Patrick used to give Mama money to take us there. He'd slip in an extra twenty so she could treat us to lunch, too. But that was a long time ago.

I hurried past the other boxes—the ones Stella and Tony had brought from home. They were marked "Girls' clothes," "Girls' toys," and "Marie's clothes." It was stuff we'd left behind, stuff that didn't fit into our A&P paper-bag suitcases. My eyes zoomed toward the McCurdy's box, my head full of crazy ideas about what could be inside. A new dress. A lacy blouse. Some bell-bottoms. Maybe a yellow swimsuit, like the one I'd been eyeing in the window at that shop across from Clancy's. I tore off the box top, tossed it on the floor, and rifled through the tissue paper, but I didn't find any fancy new clothes. Inside were old drawings of black-eyed Susans that I'd made for Mama when I was younger, to help make her happy. "Check underneath those," Tony said. I set the drawings aside and found my old tablets, crayons, and colored pencils. And a framed picture of me and my old best friend, Amelia, twirling on our tiptoes on her back patio. Uncle Tony had taken the photo one afternoon when he'd stopped by with his new Kodak.

I grabbed the frame and stared at Amelia, wishing I could make myself tiny enough to crawl under the glass and stand beside her. I wanted to hold her hand and laugh again. I wanted to twirl on my tiptoes and sing at the top of my lungs. I swallowed an urge to cry. Zoomer rubbed his soft head against my legs. I tugged gently at his ears.

"Whadaya think, Regina?" Uncle Tony called from across the room. "I thought you might be missing your old buddy. By the way, she said to say hi."

I swung around. "She did?"

"Yep," he said. "And she asked if you were ever gonna come back and visit."

"She did?"

"I told her I didn't know, but if you did, you'd be sure to drop by."

"Mama, can we?"

"Can we what?"

"Go visit?"

"Not for a long while, Regina."

"How come? Aunt Stella and Uncle Tony came here. Why can't we go to Pisa?"

"It's way too complicated, Regina."

"We could stay with Uncle Tony and Aunt Stella. You'd let us, wouldn't you, Uncle Tony?"

"Any time, sweetie. But only when your mama's ready."

"Please, Mama. Please."

"Don't start with me, Regina," Mama snipped. "See what you did, Tony?"

"Hey," Tony shrugged. "I was only trying to give the kid a present. I didn't know it would wind up like this."

"Marie, don't get all huffy," Aunt Stella said. "He didn't mean anything by it."

"Yeah, yeah. All right," Mama said.

I put the framed picture on the coffee table and suddenly thought of Julie Farley—that girl at school who'd given me her phone number last year. For a second, my heart raced, thinking ahead to September. Maybe now that stuff had settled down here, I could see if she still wanted to be friends with me. I could give her my phone number when I went back to school. She wasn't Amelia, but she sure was nice. It was worth a try.

I smiled to myself and peeked into some of the other boxes. Most of them were Danny's junk. His clothes. His record player and a bunch of Beatles albums. His baseball stuff—his cleats and his glove, his cap and a couple of baseballs. One big cardboard box had "Marie" written across the closed flaps. "There's one for you, Mama."

"Let's leave that for later," Stella insisted.

"What'd you bring me?" Mama asked. Her eyes opened wide.

"Oh, just some stuff we thought you might want," Stella said. She snuggled in close to Uncle Tony. "Nothing that can't wait for later."

"Now you got me wondering," Mama said. She set her coffee cup on the coffee table and stood up.

Aunt Stella grabbed Mama's arm. "Not now, Marie."

Mama laughed. "What the hell is in that box that's so secretive, Stel?" She yanked her arm free and strolled out to the porch. "It's sure a big one," Mama said as she bent to pick up the box. She carried it into the living room, set it on the floor in front of the couch, and plopped down beside it on the rug. Uncle Tony looked really nervous. Aunt Stella bit the corner of her lip. Danny joined us, fresh from his shower. "What's up?" he asked.

"I'm gonna open this box of stuff from Tony and Stella," Mama told him. "Come see what they brought me."

"Why don't you wait on that one, Ma," he warned.

"What for?" Her eyes danced from him to Stella to Tony. "What's going on?"

Mama pulled back the crisscrossed corners of the box

top. Danny knelt beside her. Mama peeked inside and cried, "Oh, my God." She closed her eyes, raised her hand to her mouth. "Oh, my God," she said again before she let out a long, sad howl of a cry.

Danny put his arms around Mama. "It's okay, Ma. Just let it out. It's okay," he comforted, over and over and over. Aunt Stella held Uncle Tony's hand. They both cried, too. Rosa and Winnie came running in to see what all the commotion was about. They stayed back by the wall, away from Mama's tears and her shaking shoulders. I crept over and looked in the box. My heart shuddered. Inside was Joey's mitt, baseball cap, and one of his old baseball jerseys. A faded number 10 stared back at me from his worn uniform. "Giovanni" was stitched in blue across the back.

I closed my eyes. All I could see was Joey standing at home plate with his bat cocked, waiting for the pitch. He swung and popped the ball to the outfield fence. He tore to first base, then to second. He slid into third as the ump called, "Safe!" Mama and the girls, Danny, Daddy, and me cheered. "Yea, Joey! Way to go, slugger!" He picked himself up from the dust and squinted through the sun to find us in the bleachers. He wore a proud, satisfied grin.

Mama stayed in her bedroom with Aunt Stella the rest of the afternoon. Uncle Tony and Danny offered to take me and the girls for ice cream, but none of us felt like it. Instead, we went outside and sat in the backyard. I tossed a Frisbee to Zoomer, and he jumped to catch it in midair. Rosa and Winnie liked that, so I kept doing it as long as Zoomer wanted, which was a long time. Danny took over when my arms got tired, and I sat next to Uncle Tony on the bottom step.

"She'll be all right, Regina," he told me. "She's just got to get it all out of her."

I nodded but didn't say anything. I thought of Mama

going back to being the sad, tired, worried woman I'd known most of my life. It made my bones ache. I was mad at Tony and Stella for bringing Joey's stuff, but I could understand why they did it. It was better to give it to Mama than leave it in a trash can in Pisa.

"Have you seen my Daddy?" I asked Uncle Tony.

"Yep," he said. He lowered his voice. "Saw him the day before we left to come here. I took Danny over so he could say good-bye. Told Paulie we were taking Danny and Zoomer to be with Marie. He seemed to think it was for the best. He looked good. Kind of skinny from all that praying. But he seemed happy. Even though they won't let him be a monk on account of him being married and having all you kids. But Father DiSante pulled some strings and landed him a job as the caretaker. He lives in a small cottage on the grounds, and he gets to go to the chapel anytime he wants. I tell ya one thing, his eyes sure looked peaceful. Like he'd found something he'd lost. He said to say hello to you and the girls. Said to tell you that he loved you. He gave me this to give to you."

Uncle Tony took my hand and dropped a coil of black beads into my palm. It was Daddy's rosary, the one he used to pray with at night in the green recliner at our house back in Pisa. I used to watch his lips move as he whispered Hail Marys to himself and the angels. His fingers would slide over the soft stones as he prayed for a way out of the mess we'd all fallen into.

"Can I visit him at that monastery?" I asked, staring at the beads.

"Maybe someday, Regina," Uncle Tony whispered. "Maybe someday." He patted my shoulder.

"If you see him again, would you tell him I miss him?"

"Sure."

"Tell him I love him, too."

"Okay."

I slid Daddy's rosary into my pants pocket and raced off to join my brother and sisters. And my dog.

Chocolate Cake & Ginger Tea

Uncle Tony and Aunt Stella stayed an extra week until Mama felt better. Doris helped out a lot, too. Mama invited her over to meet her sister and brother-in-law, and they hit it off real well. We did a lot of fun stuff together. One night, we went to Clancy's for hamburgers and French fries so Stella and Tony could see where Mama and Doris worked. Mr. Clancy pulled out all the stops. He gave us free chocolate sundaes and laughed at all of Uncle Tony's jokes. He even agreed to talk to his brother-in-law over at Snyders Drug Store about a job for Danny.

"Maybe he can pull some strings and get you in at the U in the fall so you won't get drafted," Mr. Clancy added.

"You got a great boss there, Marie," Tony said. "Not everybody would find your son a job, pay for you to go back to school to better yourself, and keep your son out of Vietnam."

Mama agreed. "I've been lucky, that's for sure." She smiled at Doris.

I wanted Doris and Tony and Stella to meet Grace. I thought they'd like her a lot. She knows how to laugh and have fun, like them. Ever since Zoomer had arrived, I'd been wanting to take him over to Grace's house. But, I still didn't want to ask Mama, especially after she got so upset about getting Joey's baseball stuff. It seemed pretty easy for her to fall back into her old ways. I decided to wait a while before I popped the Grace question.

One day, Mama and Stella went shopping, and Uncle Tony stayed home with us kids. I told him about Grace.

"She's real nice. And she's got a funny way of doing things, like how she calls pancakes 'hotcakes,' and how she listens to music that don't have any words, just violins and stuff. And she knits. She made me and Rosa homemade mittens." I ran to the closet and pulled them out. "See?" I showed them to him proudly. "Aren't they beautiful?"

"Oh, ya," Tony agreed.

"Grace let me scream in her living room when I was feeling like I was gonna explode. 'Just let it out,' she told me. I did, and she was right. I felt a whole lot better."

Tony leaned across the kitchen table and fixed his eyes on mine. "You feel like screaming now?"

"Nope. But some days I do. Stuff just stays all cramped up inside, and I think my brain is gonna burst, and my heart is gonna explode and shoot blood all over the place."

"Sounds pretty serious," Tony kidded.

I smiled, but I didn't like his teasing. I guess Uncle Tony just didn't understand stuff the way Grace did. Anyway, I told him I missed Grace and that I wanted to see her but was too afraid to ask Mama. "I got her address." I showed him the piece of paper Grace had given me the day we left her.

"Why don't you just ask your mama to take you for a visit?" Tony asked.

"We couldn't just barge in without being invited."

"Write her a letter first. Then, she could write you back and tell you when you could come see her."

It was the best idea. So good, I couldn't sit in my chair anymore. I jumped up, held the edge of Uncle Tony's shirtsleeve, afraid I'd fly away if I didn't.

"Do you think Mama would get upset?"

"Why should she mind if you want to go visit a friend? She visits Doris, don't she?"

"Yeah. But this is different."

"How?"

"Just 'cuz it is."

I couldn't rat on Mama. I couldn't tell Tony how Mama got all jealous and felt left out if I loved somebody more than her. Besides, that was the old Mama. Maybe it wasn't so true anymore. Now that she had Danny back and Doris and a good job and school, maybe she didn't need me to love her so hard anymore.

"Well, ask your mama," Uncle Tony insisted. "Couldn't hurt to try."

※

Uncle Tony and Aunt Stella left at the end of June. I felt sad they wouldn't be around for my birthday. "Can't you stay just a few more weeks?" I pleaded.

"Oh, honey, Tony's got to get back to work," Aunt Stella said. "But we'll call. I promise."

"How old you gonna be, Regina?" Tony asked.

"Twelve."

"Geez, you're growing up so fast," he said. "Pretty soon you'll be going off to college, just like your brother and your mama."

The day they left, Uncle Tony winked and whispered to me, "Don't forget to ask your mama about Grace."

They loaded a cooler with soda pop and sandwiches that Mama and Aunt Stella had made. They promised to call when they got home to let us know they'd arrived safely.

Before they drove away, Mama thanked them for bringing her Joey's stuff. She told them, "At least some tiny part of him is with me here, now."

We stood on the sidewalk and waved good-bye until their car disappeared. Then Mama took us to Lake Mendota for a picnic, so we could celebrate being together, just the five of us and Zoomer.

Mama packed our favorite picnic lunch—cold chicken, potato chips, brownies, and orange pop. We found a spot by the lake, and Rosa and Winnie tore off for the shore, clutching a sack of stale bread. Zoomer picked a spot in the shade under a big tree while I helped Mama lay a blanket on the grass. Danny stretched out and took a nap. While he was snoring, I grabbed Mama's hand. She gave me a soft squeeze back.

"Did you have fun with Uncle Tony and Aunt Stella?" she asked.

"Yeah. How 'bout you?"

Mama nodded and stared past the trees to the lake. She watched Rosa and Winnie tossing bread to the ducks. "It was good to see them. I miss having family around."

"You got family, here. Me and the girls and Danny. And Doris. She's kind of like family, ain't she?"

"Yes. But Stella's my sister. Nobody can take her place."

I thought about how sad I'd be if I couldn't see Rosa anymore. And Winnie, too. She was a nice kid, and I didn't feel so jealous now that Patrick was gone. I'd miss her, too, if he decided to get mean and take her away from us. And I thought about Grace. I'd die for sure if I never got to see her again.

"Mama, is Patrick gonna steal Winnie?"

"No, Regina," Mama said, still keeping her eye on my sisters. "You don't have to worry about him anymore. He's not gonna try anything funny. I think Doris's son Larry scared him out of it."

Larry could look pretty mean sometimes. He used to be a boxer when he was younger, and he had bulging arms and a crooked nose from being hit in the face too many times. Mama said that's what made him stop fighting. One too many punches in the head. His ears rang almost all the time, and sometimes he got a faraway look in his eyes, like Mama used to, only his didn't look sad, just confused, as if he were trying to remember something he couldn't quite catch hold of.

Mama lay on the blanket and leaned back against her propped elbows so she could watch my sisters. The sun fell across her face, and she looked like a soft black-eyed Susan, with warm skin and dark eyes. The air all around her smelled like Lily of the Valley. I felt calm. I closed my eyes and tried to picture Grace's living room—her couch, her rocker, the basket of yarn with her knitting needles. I inhaled Mama's perfume and felt Grace's soft fingers brushing chocolate cake crumbs off my cheek. I looked and looked behind my closed eyes for Grace's face. I searched for her kind eyes and soft wrinkles, the gap in her front teeth. I wanted to ask her to hold me, just one more time.

"I miss you, Grace," I said, to the wind. But I accidentally said it out loud, and Mama heard me.

"What's that, honey?"

I held my breath, hoping Mama wouldn't be upset.

"Who'd you say you missed?" Mama asked. She didn't snap at me. She just said it like she was asking me how many pieces of toast I wanted for breakfast.

"Nobody."

"Yes, you did, Regina. I heard you. You said something about that woman, Grace. The one who helped you and Rosa. Tony mentioned something about her, too. He said you wanted to visit her. Is that true?"

My heart screamed "yes!" but my lips stayed locked. I picked at the grass at the edge of the blanket and wondered if I could be brave enough to tell Mama the truth. Maybe she wouldn't have to know everything. Just enough so that she would agree to at least think about letting us visit Grace. I could tell her Grace was just a friend, like Doris. I wouldn't have to say how I loved her in the deepest parts of my heart, where I felt brave and calm. I didn't want Mama to cry.

"Grace is my friend, Mama. I miss her, like you miss Aunt Stella."

"Well, I doubt that, Regina. You hardly know her. But Tony said it might not be a bad idea to let you visit. Might make you not miss Amelia so much. Stella agreed, too. Tony said you had her address. Said you should send her a note. I don't see why we can't give it a try."

"Really? Do you mean it? Do you promise?"

"I promise."

I jumped to my feet, and Zoomer chased me around the blanket. I twirled and skipped, tripping over Danny's feet when I spun past his leg. I landed on his foot and woke him up.

"What the hell you doing, twerp?" he crabbed.

"Oh, she didn't mean anything, Danny," Mama said. "Wake up. It's time to eat anyway."

She called for my sisters. "Rosa, Winnie! Lunchtime."

"I'll get them, Mama," I yelled back over my shoulder as I tore off toward the shore.

That night, after the supper dishes were done, Rosa and I sat down with a piece of paper and a pen and wrote to Grace.

"Tell her we miss her," Rosa said. "A lot." She whispered the last part so Mama couldn't hear.

"I will, I will. Just give me a chance here."

I finished my letter, then read it to Rosa.

> *Dear Grace,*
>
> *This is Regina Giovanni. I hope you remember me. Last year, you took care of me and my sister Rosa for a while. We miss you a lot and want to come visit you. Please write back soon, and let us know if it's OK.*
>
> *Love, Regina and Rosa*

"How's that sound?" I asked Rosa.

"Good. But don't forget to tell her that Binkie says hello, too. And that he's still wearing the purple yarn bow tie she gave him."

"You can tell her yourself when we see her," I insisted.

Mama included a short note, too, telling Grace that it was fine with her if we visited, as long as Grace didn't mind. She said she could bring us by some Saturday afternoon for an hour or two, if that worked for Grace.

Every day, Rosa and I ran to the mailbox to check if Grace had written back. For days, there was nothing in there except bills for Mama and a letter from Aunt Stella. Then one day, a week before my birthday, we scooped the mail out of the box, and a small purple envelope fell to the grass. I picked it up.

"It's from Grace! It's from Grace!" I shouted.

Rosa grabbed the letter, but I snatched it back and sat on the grass, right in front of the mailbox, and tore it open. Rosa urged, "Read it out loud! Read it out loud!"

> *Dear Regina and Rosa,*
>
> *Of course I remember you. I've thought about you both a lot this past year, hoping everything was all right with you. Yes, come see me. I'll make a choco-*

late cake. Tell your mama to bring you by next Satur-
day at 2 p.m. If that day doesn't work, drop me
another note and tell me what does. I'm not goin'
nowhere. I'll be here any day you can come.

   Much love, Grace

I read the last part over and over again. *Much love, Grace. Much love.* She hadn't forgotten about us. And we were gonna see her, soon. Next Saturday. I prayed Mama didn't have to work, so she could take us. Rosa and I raced into the house.

"Mama, Mama!"

"Shush," Mama snipped. "Winnie's taking a nap. You'll wake her."

"Sorry," we said together.

"We got a letter. Grace said we could visit her next Saturday. Can we, Mama? Can we?!"

"I don't see why not. I'll check with Doris to see if she can give us a ride."

"Call her, please, Mama. Call her now," Rosa pleaded.

"I'm in the middle of fixin' lunch, Rosa," Mama said. "I'll call her later."

It took all afternoon before we had our answer. Rosa and I tried to relax and play cards, but we couldn't concentrate. We took Zoomer to Rosa's favorite hiding spot behind the school playground. Zoomer chased squirrels and barked up trees and zipped around bushes. Rosa and I lay on the grass and stared at the sky, wishing it would swallow up all the hours and minutes until we could know for sure if we were going to see Grace.

"Maybe she'll let us have a sleep-over," Rosa dreamed out loud.

"Maybe," I agreed. "But we got to be careful, Rosa, so we don't hurt Mama's feelings. If she gets jealous, she won't let us go visit anymore."

"Yeah, you're right."

"That don't mean we can't be excited. She is our friend. But we just can't get too excited. Not in front of Mama."

Rosa agreed. "But sometimes I still want to stay with her forever. Is that bad, Regina?"

"Naw. It isn't."

I felt that way about Grace, too. Even though things were a whole lot better at our house lately, even with Danny around. There was still something about Grace and her house that was different—better. It wasn't that the furniture was newer or the food was more delicious or the house was bigger. It wasn't anything like that at all. Being with Grace made me feel like I could dance all day, without ever having to worry about bumping into something. I smiled more when I was with her, but it wasn't to make somebody else happy. It was just a natural thing.

When Rosa and I got home, Mama told us, "Doris is gonna take you girls on Saturday." We got out a piece of paper right away and jotted a quick note to Grace. *We'll be there. Two p.m. sharp.* In the P.S., I told her that I was gonna bring my dog Zoomer and Rosa was bringing Binkie.

That Saturday, Rosa and I were up before the sun rose. We changed our clothes, ate breakfast, brushed our teeth and our hair all before seven-thirty. Mama and Danny and Winnie didn't get up until eight-thirty. Danny had to work at the drugstore that morning, and he had to be there by ten. Mama made them some coffee and toast, and they ate their breakfast with their noses lost in the newspaper.

Rosa and I watched cartoons for a bit with Winnie, but we could hardly stand how slow the morning was going. "You girls are so antsy, you're gonna drive me crazy if you stay inside one more minute." Mama handed me a couple of dollars. "Here, go down to the 7-Eleven and buy me a quart of milk. Get yourselves a candy bar, too."

We took Zoomer and headed out.

"Do you think Grace looks the same?" Rosa asked.

"Don't see why she wouldn't," I told her. "Except she's a little bit older. But so are we. You're seven already, and I'm almost twelve."

"Yeah." Rosa added, "And I don't have any bruises any more. Inside or out." We stretched out the minutes, picking out candy bars at the 7-Eleven. Rosa grabbed a Mars bar, and I got a 5th Avenue. I plopped them on the counter and pulled out the money Mama had given us. "Regina, the milk!" Rosa said.

"Oops!" I ran to get a quart from the refrigerated case.

At one-thirty that afternoon, Doris pulled into our drive-way.

"She's here!" I hollered. I tore down the steps, Rosa and Zoomer close behind me.

"Winnie and I will be down in a second," Mama called to us.

Rosa, Binkie, Zoomer, and me ran to Doris's car and hopped in the backseat.

"You girls in a big hurry, here?" Doris laughed. "You'd think we were going to visit Santa Claus."

I closed my eyes so Doris wouldn't see how excited I was. I didn't want her telling Mama later that she'd noticed something on my face, a kind of joy she'd never seen before. Mama and Winnie came soon and settled into the front seat.

"Let's go," Doris said. She put the car into reverse and backed up.

I stared out the window, looking at the houses and the trees as we passed. They whispered *Hurry, hurry!* as my heart sank deeper and deeper into a pool of minutes that never seemed to go fast enough. Mama had said it would take a half hour to get to Grace's house. I couldn't stand how slow Doris was driving. I wanted to scream at every stoplight. By the time we got to the freeway, my shirt was soaking wet from sweat.

At last, Doris pulled in front of Grace's house. I grabbed Rosa's hand, and she squeezed back. Everything was the way I remembered it. Zoomer sat on my lap and hung his head out the car window. "There it is," I whispered. "That's where Grace lives."

Grace peeked from behind her curtain. Then she opened the front door and stepped outside. She was still as wobbly as ever. She hobbled down her front steps, holding onto the railing with one hand and waving at us with the other. I opened the car door, and Zoomer barked, then tore off over Grace's front lawn. I scrambled out, too, and raced toward Grace. Rosa grabbed Binkie and followed me, running as fast as she could.

Grace wrapped her bony arms around my shoulder and hugged me. I slipped my arm around her and held on tight. Rosa did, too. Grace kissed the tops of our heads.

"It's so good to see you girls," she said.

I couldn't say anything. If I opened my mouth, a million tears would spill out.

Mama and Winnie and Doris strolled up to meet Grace.

"Hello," Mama said, offering her hand. "I'm Marie Giovanni, the girls' mother. I'm pleased to be able to finally meet you."

"Hello," Grace said, taking Mama's hand.

"This here's my other daughter, Winnie, and my friend Doris," Mama said.

"Pleased to meet ya," Grace said.

"This is Zoomer," I added.

"Oh, I figured that might be the famous dog you told me so much about," Grace said.

Everybody laughed.

"Can you come in for a cup of tea?" Grace asked Mama and Doris. "I've made chocolate cake, too."

"That'd be nice, thank you very much." Mama said. "We won't stay long. I know how much the girls want to visit with you."

Rosa shot me a glance, telling me with her eyes to do something about this, telling me this was supposed to be our time with Grace, but I didn't know how to get out of it. I only hoped Mama and Doris would drink their tea fast and go away.

All six of us crowded around Grace's small kitchen table. She placed teacups and saucers out on tiny place mats that I didn't recognize. She didn't have those when we lived with her. Grace cut slices of cake for everybody and poured tea for the grown-ups. She filled glasses with milk for me and my sisters.

Mama, Doris, and Grace chatted about stuff, but I didn't listen much. I was busy, soaking up the feeling of being in Grace's kitchen again. I stared at everything. The refrigerator, the cupboards, the sink where we did the dishes, the oven where we baked a cake, like the one we were eating, to celebrate Grace's dead daughter's birthday. I smiled, remembering how fun it was to dance around her table. This place was my place. Even though it belonged to Grace, part of it lived inside me still, and I shared it with her, without taking it from her. Somehow, there was enough air and light and space in all those rooms for each of us.

"Well, we better be going if we're ever going to get our shopping done," Doris said.

"I suppose you're right," Mama said. But she didn't seem like she was in any hurry to leave.

Doris stood up first.

"Thank you, Grace, for the delicious tea and cake. It was a pleasure to meet you."

"You're very welcome," Grace said. "Come back any time."

She turned to Mama. "You needn't worry about leaving the girls here with me, Marie. I'll be sure no harm comes to them."

"Oh, I know you'll take good care of them," Mama stammered. "You girls be good, now. Do what Grace tells you to do. Don't embarrass me."

Mama stood up finally and brushed cake crumbs into her cupped hand. She dumped them into her napkin and set it on the table by her empty plate.

"We'll see you in a couple of hours," Mama said to me and Rosa.

"Okay," I said.

Mama kissed us good-bye. She hugged us like she was never gonna see us again. We waited on the front steps as Mama and Winnie and Doris piled back into the car and drove off.

"Your mama's a nice lady," Grace said. "She loves you very much."

"Yeah," I said. "I hope she lets us visit you again."

"She will, Regina," Grace told me. "She just had to check me out, make sure I wasn't gonna steal you away from her."

"But I want you to," I said.

"No need to steal ya, darlin'," Grace said. "I got you free and clear. You're all wrapped up in my heart, tight as can be. You never left it. Been there the whole time. Both of you. Always have been. Always will be."

"You mean it?" I started to cry, and Grace wiped my tears with the edge of her sleeve. Zoomer whined and nudged the back of my legs.

"There, there, Regina. Ain't no need for sorrow. Love's a good thing. Caring for somebody like how we care for each other, that's even better."

I wiped my nose and looked into her kind eyes. Something stared back at me, something old and new at the same time, something I remembered deep in my bones. I grabbed her hand.

"Let's go inside now," I told her. "Me and Rosa got a lot to tell you."

We walked into the warm smell of chocolate cake and ginger tea. Some small hard place inside of me melted into the light of Grace's kitchen. The dark, ghostly parts of me slipped into the air and floated out the open window. I cut two more slices of cake for Rosa and for me. Grace turned on the radio. Flutes and violins filled the room. I laughed then and twirled around. Rosa danced, too. Zoomer barked and darted between us. Grace filled her cup with warmed-up tea and smiled at us from her chair.

"Welcome back, girls," she said. "Welcome back."

Other Novels Available from Spinsters Ink

Spinsters Ink

Spinsters Ink was founded in 1978 to produce vital books for diverse women's communities. In 1986, we merged with Aunt Lute Books to become Spinsters/Aunt Lute. In 1990, the Aunt Lute Foundation became an independent nonprofit publishing program. In 1992, Spinsters moved to Minnesota.

Spinsters Ink publishes novels and nonfiction works that deal with significant issues in women's lives from a feminist perspective: books that not only name these crucial issues, but—more important—encourage change and growth. We are committed to publishing works by women writing from the periphery: fat women, Jewish women, lesbians, old women, poor women, rural women, women examining classism, women of color, women with disabilities, women who are writing books that help make the best in our lives more possible.

Spinsters titles are available at your local booksellers or by mail order through Spinsters Ink. A free catalog is available upon request. Please include $2.00 for the first title ordered and 50¢ for every title thereafter. Visa and Mastercard are accepted.

Spinsters Ink
32 E. First St., #330
Duluth, MN 55802-2002
USA

218-727-3222 (phone)   **(fax) 218-727-3119**

(e-mail) spinster@spinsters-ink.com
(website) http://www.spinsters-ink.com

Photo by Ann Marsden

Mary Saracino's first novel, *No Matter What* (Spinsters Ink, 1993), was a 1994 Minnesota Book Award finalist in the fiction category. Ms. Saracino's work has appeared in a variety of literary magazines and anthologies. She lives in Denver, Colorado.